# LYNN MONTAGANO

A fresh, new voice in contemporary romance, I'm a former TV news writer who decided to take the plunge and write more than just the day's top stories. I grew up in a small town in Rhode Island before venturing out into the world and have lived everywhere from Los Angeles to Boston to Orlando. An avid traveler, I've been as far away as Australia and as close as Canada. My favorite place to visit is London. This small town girl is back on the east coast after a brief stint in Northern California. I currently reside in Massachusetts, comfortably close to my beloved football team.

www.facebook.com/AuthorLynnMontagano
@LynnMontagano

# *Effortless*

## LYNN MONTAGANO

Harper*Impulse* an imprint of
HarperCollins*Publishers* Ltd
77–85 Fulham Palace Road
Hammersmith, London W6 8JB

www.harpercollins.co.uk

A Paperback Original 2015

First published in Great Britain in ebook format by Harper*Impulse* 2015



A catalogue record for this book is
available from the British Library

ISBN: 978-0-00-812769-5



Automatically produced by Atomik ePublisher from Easypress

*For you, the reader.*

*Thank you for taking this journey with me. See you on the next adventure...*

# CHAPTER ONE

"Amelia Meyers."

Julian Archer always announced my name so the entire newsroom could hear it even though we were in the confines of my office. Part of me liked the way it sounded wrapped in his Scottish accent. The other part of me knew he wanted something big. He perched himself on the edge of my desk and fidgeted with a pen. The brash, allegedly difficult host of The Archer Hour bubbled with excited energy. I leaned back in my chair, ready for whatever insane request he'd no doubt throw at me.

"We have Brent Garrison on this week." His sharp blue eyes gleamed. I stifled an eye roll. I'd been dreading this week's show since my first day of work here.

"He's my biggest get all year and I expect nothing but perfection," he continued. "Your track record so far is impeccable. Since you started our ratings have soared. This week should be no exception."

Julian hopped off the desk and started pacing. Everything he did had a certain flourish to it. Tugging at his shirtsleeves, he spouted off another round of 'expectations' mostly to hear himself talk.

"It's a five minute segment," I interrupted. "Just stick to the talking points and you'll be fine."

"Be prepared to make changes if needed."

"Be prepared to follow the rundown exactly as I've laid it out." I lifted an eyebrow. "This isn't the Brent Garrison hour. He's part of one segment."

Exhaling in dramatic fashion, he placed his hands on his hips and looked at me. "I don't like being on a leash. Although I've grown quite fond of the way you tug at me." His smile was flirtatious and gross at the same time. "Alastair Holden is a lucky man."

Not a day goes by when Julian doesn't invoke the name of my fiancé. Not that I minded too much. Anytime Alastair filled my thoughts was like being in heaven. Julian's constant mentioning of his name was done out of pure determination. He wanted an interview with Alastair and he wanted it yesterday. I was the concrete wall he'd have to bust through in order for that to happen. Unfortunately for him, I wasn't about to budge.

"Tell that boyfriend of yours if he ever changes his mind about that exclusive—"

"—*to call me*," I said in unison with him. "Don't hold your breath waiting for the phone to ring."

"Feisty." He grinned.

After Julian finally left my office, I sighed and focused on the checklist of tasks I wanted to finish before noon. I had a standing lunch date with my best friend Stephanie Tempe and couldn't wait to get out of the office for a little while.

Before that could happen though, I had my morning meeting with my news director, Sam Dunning and producer, Robbie Watson. They'd both welcomed me into The Archer Hour family with open arms before summarily throwing me out of the frying pan and into the fire. This program was in shambles when I'd started. There'd been a revolving door of executive producers, a lack of direction and a general feeling of apathy among the staff. The past few weeks had seen a drastic improvement but we still had a long way to go.

"Excuse me, Miss Meyers?"

I looked up and was greeted by my intern smiling shyly, holding several files.

"Mr. Dunning asked me to drop these at your desk. It's for Friday's show."

"Thanks, Meredith."

Robbie waltzed in several minutes later and we chatted on our way to Sam's office. Unlike my old news director, Sam exuded an air of sophistication. Not one blond hair sat out of place on his head. He was younger than I'd expect someone in his position to be as well. My estimation put him at around thirty-four. Once he finished typing, he turned his attention towards us.

"Another brilliant show last Friday you two. The ratings are still at a steady climb. I think the program is finally getting the injection it needs."

Our meeting was mostly spent brainstorming and planning. Sam was a sharp guy. He had some definite ideas of how he wanted the show to be presented and I thought he was on the right track. In the past, the news magazine program had been a frenetic series of over-dramatic, packaged stories. My thoughts on making it more focused and more conversational with viewers dovetailed nicely with his ideas.

We both wanted the hour to be designed around providing in-depth coverage of the week's biggest headlines, but we also wanted to give the audience something unexpected. Turn the news on its head, so to speak.

Once I returned to my office, I threw myself into the week's preparations. Seeing as I'd spent the majority of Sunday night awake, putting my brain to good use was therapeutic. Alastair had flown to London this morning and decided to keep me occupied most of the night. I smiled. My enigmatic Englishman did not have an off switch. Turning my attention to the files the intern had dropped off, I sifted through some of the pages. I'd barely read through the first one when my desk phone rang.

"Lia Meyers."

"Don't kill me but I have to cancel lunch. This day sucks balls

and I'm not just talking about the non-stop cold and rain outside."
Stephanie sounded agitated.

"What's the emergency now?"

"These layouts are stressing me out and I'm going to go cross eyed if I stare at them another second. Why did I take this job again?"

"Because you're awesome and talented and you love it."

She sighed. "I would give anything to go sit out in the sun for, like, the rest of the day. Can we fly back to Orlando this weekend? Alastair has a zillion planes. He won't mind if we use one."

"You ask him."

"The guy can't say no to you. We'll have a more positive outcome if you do it."

"Go back to work, Steph." I laughed, ending the call.

A few minutes later, Meredith entered my office grinning widely and carrying a small box. "This just arrived for you," she said, leaving the box on my desk.

My heart fluttered as I admired the warm, caramel colored wrapping paper. This was Alastair's call sign. He liked to use this particular shade because he'd always told me how much he loved the rich, amber color of my eyes. I picked it up, smiling as the familiar pleasurable rush flowed through my body.

Opening it, I was mesmerized by the gorgeous platinum cuff bracelet nestled inside. Diamonds swirled in an elegant design, sparkling in the light.

"Wow," I whispered, wanting nothing more than to kiss him endlessly. And it had nothing to do with the jewelry. Alastair Holden was the love of my life for far better reasons. To the rest of the world he was the wealthy orphan and heir to a mind numbing fortune who never let anybody see behind his well-crafted stoic exterior. Only I knew the true man behind the mask. And he was all mine.

I noticed a small slip of paper in the box and unfolded it. Written in his unmistakable, perfect block penmanship were the words WEAR THIS TONIGHT AND NOTHING ELSE.

A yearning filled me so fast and furious that I almost forgot to breathe. Flustered, I placed the cuff back in the box and focused on getting back to work.

* * *

I powered through lunch and into the late afternoon going through most of the files the intern had dropped off. A chiming echoed through my office, disrupting my flow. Confused, I looked for the source of the sound. It was my cell phone.

**3:54pm How's your day, kitten? Did you get my special delivery?**

**3:55pm I did. Meant to text you earlier. So beautiful.**

**3:57pm Yes, you are**

**4:00pm Still the charmer. How's the board meeting?**

**4:01pm Still happening. I'm afraid I'll be home very late tonight.**

**4:03pm That sucks. Everything OK?**

**4:07pm Mostly.**

Frowning, I tapped a pen on my desk. I knew there had been some issues within the music division of Holden World Media recently. Sales were much lower than Samuel Holden thought were acceptable. Even though he was retired, he still gave Alastair an earful whenever he could. The company's other areas -broadband, television and cell phones- seemed to be performing above expectations. I didn't even pretend to understand what it took to run a huge corporation like that. All I knew was it weighed heavily on Alastair and forced him to work long, unforgiving hours.

I hadn't noticed it as much when he was in Orlando with me because I'd been so wrapped up in my own drama. Since I'd moved here, seeing how much stress he was under broke my heart. I'd often wondered why his uncle, Jason, hadn't been named CEO.

**4:15pm Don't work too hard, chief. Love you xx**

**4:22pm xx**

* * *

The taxi dropped me off at Alastair's house a little after seven. I still thought of it as his house because I hadn't been here long and, well, it still felt like him. Translation: it remained pristine and sterile and lacking in any personal effects.

I plopped my handbag onto the couch in the living room and sighed. An idea hit me so fast I bounced up and down with excitement. Scurrying off to the bedroom, I flung the door to the walk-in closet open. A couple of boxes that had been shipped out here from my apartment in Florida sat beneath a wall of my clothes. I dragged them to the center of the floor and ripped off the packing tape. Inside were some of my framed photos that I'd had hanging on the wall in my living room. I rummaged through them and picked out a few. I also grabbed the flash drive that I'd filled with pictures before I'd tossed out my old laptop.

Trotting down the hallway to Alastair's home office, I grinned like an idiot. Everything was in its place on his dark wooden desk. I moved a few files out of the way, making sure not to disrupt their order. I was pretty sure he'd arranged them in a specific way for the countless meetings he had each week. Pausing momentarily, I glanced at the cluster of photos hanging on his wall, focusing on the one of him as a sad little boy throwing leaves in the air. *How far you've come, Holden.*

After flicking on his laptop, a picture of him and me from the county fair we'd gone to in May appeared as the wallpaper. I melted. His gorgeous green eyes practically sparkled. So did his genuine smile. He was so beautiful it made my heart hurt. I looked content snuggled into his side. My smile matched his in brightness and almost muted the yellow sundress I'd worn.

"Okay, Meyers. Enough with the gawking," I muttered to myself, sliding the flash drive into the USB port.

Craning my neck, I searched around the room to see where the printer was set up. After scrolling through dozens of photos, I printed out some of my favorites and put them in the frames. Back out in the living room, I placed a few frames on his end tables and a couple on the fireplace mantle. They warmed up the room and softened the impersonal aura that had lingered here for far too long. Inspired by my progress, I dashed to the home office and printed out one more photo. By the time I'd finished, his living room finally started to feel lived in.

Satisfied, I changed out of my work clothes into some yoga pants and a tank top, grabbed some leftovers and flopped onto the couch.

I wasn't sure how long it would take for me to get used to Scottish programming. Sure, there were American shows sprinkled in but I wasn't really into watching reruns of The Big Bang Theory or Frasier.

*Oooh, reality shows.* Fortunately, they were as popular here as they were back home so I settled in to revel in the food and mindless television. The couch was so comfy and the food was so carb heavy, I stretched out on the cushions.

The skin near my collarbone warmed from the gentle kisses brushing against it. I moaned softly, opening my eyes. The TV was off and the room was dark but I could see the outline of a figure hovering over me. I could also smell shampoo and body wash.

"Alastair," I whispered, lifting my hands and finding his warm, damp body close to mine. He was naked. Wait, no, he had on a towel.

"Hello, beautiful," he said in a low, seductive voice directly into my ear. "Sorry I woke you."

"What time is it?"

"Late."

"Did you shower?" I asked, distracted by his mouth on my neck.

"Yes. I see you've been busy."

*I have? Oh, right. The pictures.*

He lowered himself so the full weight of his body pressed against mine and continued to kiss along my neck and shoulders. I attempted to hook my legs around his waist and inadvertently dislodged his towel.

"Do you like what I've done?" I asked, knotting my fingers through his damp hair.

His lips brushed mine, setting off all sorts of tingles and shivers. "Do I like that you've gotten me naked? Yes. What do you plan to do with me?"

He kissed me long and slow, running a hand along my curves. My mind drifted into a wonderful, fuzzy oblivion as I traced my fingers down his athletic body, pausing just above the curve of his backside. His kisses became more insistent.

A low groan vibrated in his throat when I pushed the towel to the floor.

"My Lia." The humid warmth of his breath tickled my skin. "Tell me all about your day."

"Not much to tell," I mumbled, stroking his lower back. The

lovely kisses came to a halt as he lifted his head. My eyes were slightly more adjusted to the dark and I could see him staring at me. "Why are you stopping?"

"I missed you."

I laughed. "So you'd rather stare at me than kiss me?"

"Cheeky. No present for you."

The divine heat of his body disappeared when he pushed himself up off the couch. I watched him wrap the towel around his waist, wishing he'd left it on the floor. Seeming to read my mind, he grinned and draped it over his shoulder instead.

"You mean the one you sent me at work?" I asked, not making an effort to tear my eyes away from his naked body.

"No. I'm up here."

I flicked my eyes up. "And your point is?"

He folded his arms with a wicked grin. "Give me two minutes and we'll finish what we've started here."

He flipped on a light before walking to the bedroom. I stared at his bare backside until he disappeared around the corner. I sat up, flustered and turned on and curious as to what he was up to. He reappeared, as promised, two minutes later dressed in boxers and a t-shirt.

"Why are you wearing clothes?" I asked, failing to hide my disappointment.

Fixing a dark stare on me, he flashed a sexy smile, reaching out his hand. "Come here, love."

Spurred on by his quiet demand, I followed him to the back patio and out into the yard. Goosebumps scattered themselves all over my arms when the brisk September breeze rushed through the night. I tried my best not to shiver.

"Look up."

I snuck at peek at him first before turning my sights to the skies. A few clouds disrupted the various clusters of stars glittering overhead. I smiled, allowing the serenity of the moment to wash over me. There wasn't too much light pollution from the city interfering, which was a nice surprise.

"Pick one," he whispered.

I looked at him, confused. "A star?"

"Yes."

"Um," I paused, staring into the heavens. They all winked at me, vying to be the one I chose. A particularly bright star caught my attention. I watched it for a few seconds to make sure it was actually a star and not a planet. Planets don't twinkle.

"That one," I said, pointing to the shiny one directly over our heads.

"Are you sure?"

"Yep."

I felt his body behind me, standing close. He hooked his arms around my waist and rested his chin on my shoulder. "Which one is it again?"

Baffled and extremely amused by this little game we were playing, I pointed again towards the star. "See it?"

Raising his hand next to mine, he pointed with me. "That one?"

"Yes, Holden. It's ri—"

Something glinted off his index finger. I squeezed my eyes shut and re-opened them to make sure I was actually seeing this. Yep. It was there. Instead of the star winking back at me, a diamond ring sparkled in its place. Were those emeralds in there too?

Oh. My. God.

"I figured it was time we made this official, yes?"

I don't know if it was the accent, the smile or the way he was looking at me but I couldn't form a complete thought. My no-relationships-non-dater just out romanced every other guy in the universe.

"I thought we weren't doing rings."

He shrugged. "I changed my mind."

His expression was completely blank but his eyes flickered. I eyed the ring as though it wasn't real. It looked vintage. The diamond was round and huge and surrounded by a halo of emeralds in a platinum setting. There were even diamonds on the band.

"It's so beautiful," I said, reaching up to touch his cheek.

"Lia...I..."

Fiery passion ignited a glow in his eyes that I'd never seen before. Fisting his hand in my hair, he pulled me against his chest, kissing me with such fervor I couldn't breathe. Gasping, he broke the kiss. "You are my everything." His gaze, fringed by thick lashes, revealed an overwhelming vulnerability coupled with a never-ending intent to claim me.

Enclosed in his magnetic sphere, I took his hand and placed it over my heart. "Always."

Swallowing hard, he slid the ring off his own finger and slipped it onto mine.

"Promise you'll never leave." His request hovered somewhere between a plea and an order. Knowing how hard it was for him to become emotionally attached to anyone, I ignored the slightly demanding tone.

"You're stuck with me, chief. You couldn't get rid of me if you tried."

I lost myself in his intoxicating scent the second he pressed his forehead to mine. I loved this man so much. From the top of that gorgeous head of dark red hair down to his toes, he was perfection. And right now, surrounded by the sight and scent of him, all I wanted to do was...

His emerald eyes darkened a bit, giving me a rush. "What are you thinking about?"

"If you don't know the answer to that question by now, then—"

He hovered his mouth over mine, essentially halting me from continuing. So help me, the level of seduction he operated at was out of this world. His come-hither stare and kissable sculpted mouth made my pulse race. He wasn't even touching me, yet my skin warmed at the mere thought of it.

A devilishly hot grin pulled at his lips.

"I know, I know," I breathed, too wrapped up in his sexually charged haze. "The look."

"My favorite."

A rush of anxiety surged through me, filling me with a sense of foreboding. I shoved it away as fast as possible but not before Alastair noticed.

"Hey," he whispered. "None of that. You're here with me now. You're safe. I will never let him near you."

"It's not that, trust me," I said, flicking my wrist to ward off the mention of my ex-boyfriend. "Can we go to bed now?"

Alastair studied me for several seconds to make sure I was really alright. I didn't want him to worry over what was probably just my self-doubt rearing its ugly head at the most inopportune time.

Placing my hands on his chest, I smiled. He smiled back, melting my heart. "What do you want to do in bed?"

"You."

Nuzzling into my neck, he hugged me soundly, as though holding me in his arms was the only thing he was meant to do for the rest of his life. I wanted to bottle this moment up for as long as I could.

"You're mine, Alastair," I declared, tightening my arms around him.

"Always," he said.

# CHAPTER TWO

I stretched under the blankets as best I could, not wanting to disrupt Alastair's vice-like grip on me. A delicious, satisfied soreness hummed between my legs and down my thighs. His gloriously naked body pressed into mine as he grunted in response to my movements.

"It's not time to get up yet, is it?" he muttered in my ear.

"Almost. It's just after six."

I managed to free an arm and shut off the alarm on my phone before it buzzed. Alastair turned me so I faced him, opened a sleepy eye and grinned. "Good morning, beautiful."

"Good morning, yourself. Did you sleep alright?"

"Never better." He kissed my forehead, nose and cheeks before pulling me into his chest. The last thing I wanted to do was remove myself from this amazing cocoon of comfort. Pieces of his messy hair tickled me like they always did. Waking up with him never failed to put a smile on my face. It was one of the perks of us sharing a bed.

"You feel good," he said, sliding his hand over my backside. *And there was the other perk.* "Come shower with me."

Untangling his body from mine, he pushed back the blankets and stood up. I drank in every absolutely stunning naked inch of him. His toned, athletic physique was second to none. That body was made to please a woman and thank goodness I was on the receiving end. Lifting an eyebrow, he gazed down at me. "Look at you, all sexy and gorgeous on that bed."

I stared at him through a lusty fog. "Why did you leave?"

"Good question." He crawled back on the mattress. "You smell good," he said, leaving a trail of kisses up my stomach. "So beautiful. And sweet." Lacing his fingers through mine, he held both my hands over my head against the mattress. "And mine."

I parted my lips, welcoming his kiss.

"I love this look," he said with a note of satisfaction, "and seeing you this turned on." He angled his head so his mouth hovered near my ear, making it easier for the velvet tone of his accent to slide through my bloodstream. "You're always so ready for me. Tell me what you're thinking about."

Forming a coherent sentence wasn't possible. Neither was breathing.

"Alastair," I moaned, arching my back. "Stop talking."

"And do what?"

"Whatever you want."

Letting go of my hands, he wet his lips. On impulse, I nipped at the bottom one.

"Tempting," he said, sitting up. "But what I'd like to do to you would make us both miss work and I have a full day of meetings."

*WHAT?*

My expression must have dropped like a lead balloon. I sat up and pouted. Cupping my chin, he kissed me firmly. "Tonight."

Something was off. I could see a subtle change in his demeanor.

The diamond shimmered on my finger as I stroked his cheek. "Is everything really okay with work after that board meeting?"

He tensed, retreating behind the all too familiar protective shield. "Mostly."

"Talk to me."

He'd made leaps and bounds in the sharing department but still hid behind the mask whenever he felt overwhelmed or flat out didn't want to explain what was happening in his head. I brushed a few messy pieces of his hair back, waiting patiently for an answer.

"Just the usual, kitten. You know, the Holden way."

I really didn't know. I could only assume he was referring to his uncle.

Running both hands through his hair, he sighed. "Can we keep all talk of my family out of the bedroom? I'd rather this be a place for us to escape the outside world and lose ourselves in one another." Tracing the edges of my lips, he aimed a white hot stare at me. I could tell he was agitated and didn't want what little time we had together this morning to end on the wrong note.

"That sounds good to me," I said, smiling. His expression softened, giving me that amazing, fluttery feeling in my stomach after breaking through his walls.

*  *  *

Alastair kissed me a little too long in the backseat of the Mercedes SUV after Paxton pulled to the curb in front of my building.

"I want you spend all day wondering about all the different things I'm going to do to you tonight," he whispered on my lips. "I want you to anticipate every touch, every kiss, every move."

I swallowed hard, glancing at the driver's seat to see if Paxton heard any of that. He seemed oblivious, staring out the window.

"Amelia. Look at me."

I met his heated stare and shifted on the leather seat. "This is the second time you've gotten me hot and bothered this morning without following through, Holden. I think you're enjoying it."

His sexy grin only made it more difficult for me not to tear off his expensive, three piece suit and have my way with him in the back of the car. Seeming to read my thoughts, he cupped my chin. "Control it. Channel what you're feeling right now and save it for later. Just think how much more satisfying it will be."

"You're a piece of work," I muttered, squeezing his thigh. "But I love you anyway."

"I know."

"That's all you have to say?"

Eyes darkening, he angled his body closer to me. "What I feel for you is more powerful than love. It's consuming and relentless." Our lips brushed together briefly. "You *will* think of me all day and you *will* be just as overwhelmed by this feeling as I am." His kissed me again, long and slow. "Go to work."

Resigned to the fact that he'd captivated me with his words yet again, I climbed out of the car and walked into the building. Shaking myself out of this seductive haze proved to be challenging. I twisted my engagement ring around my finger as I rode up in the elevator. Since I wasn't alone, I made it a point not to flash it out in the open. I waited until I was safely at my desk before admiring the way the diamond and halo of emeralds sparkled in the light. A smile tugged at my lips as I thought about what he had planned for me tonight.

"Lia." Julian burst through the door, scaring the crap out of me. "I have to reschedule our lunch today. My apologies. I've been asked to give a quick talk at one of the schools for some…*thing* that I had no idea I was signed up for."

His frown matched the dour look in his eyes.

"That's okay. I'm sure we ca—"

"We'll meet for cocktails after work tonight. I have a table at Pulse any time I need it. Be there at eight."

There wasn't time for me to give a response. He left too fast. Only the echo of his words lingered behind.

"Lunch? Cocktails? You've certainly managed to charm him." Robbie leaned against the doorframe. "Can't say he ever spent time outside the building with Gemma."

Gemma? Oh, right. The person I replaced.

"Was she really that bad?"

Robbie walked in and left the door partially open.

"It's not that she was bad, per se," he said, sitting across from me. "She just didn't have the temperament for Julian. As you know, he's a handful but he's not a horrible person. However, if you're unlucky enough to land on his bad side it's over."

"Hmm."

"You don't have anything to worry about. If he's offering you alcohol consider yourself bonded to him for life. Listen, while I've got your attention, I wanted to talk to you about the interview with Brent Garrison."

My eyebrows shot straight up. I'd been so wrapped up in my personal utopia I'd forgotten about that. Plus, he owned Pulse, the destination that Julian tossed out for our cocktail meeting.

"You know him, right?"

"Uh, well, sort of," I stammered, remembering our brief encounters all too well. "We've bumped into one another socially a few times."

"You're dating Alastair Holden so you will find yourself in the company of the city's upper echelon."

Keeping my hands hidden under the desk, I twisted the ring again. My personal life had been a hot topic at my former news station in Orlando thanks to the fact that Alastair's company purchased our rival. But here? It was always on display no matter the circumstance. People were so curious about me and how I'd managed to tame Britain's most eligible bachelor.

"Just so you know, Julian is ripe with questions for you. He's been dying to have Alastair as a guest for ages. Tonight's cocktail adventure could be his way of loosening you up."

"He knows enough to back off when it comes to my relationship. Don't worry about me."

Once Robbie left my office I set to work. A couple of the correspondents stopped by to review their package scripts with me and discuss placement in the show. I'd managed to stack the first twenty minutes by lunchtime and ran the segments by Sam to get any needed feedback. So far, so good.

At one, I decided to take a break and grab something to eat. Plus, I had to call Stephanie and tell her the news. Even though we'd technically been engaged since July, Alastair and I had kept it between us. The summer had been such a stressful time for both of us that we decided to stay quiet until I was settled here and we were ready to let everybody else in on the secret.

I stopped myself mid-dial. My parents. I had to tell them first. And my sister. Lowering the phone back into the cradle I considered my options. It was early back home, barely past eight in the morning. My mother was probably having her third cup of coffee and debating whether or not to meet her circle of friends for a leisurely lunch. My dad was most certainly working. Even though he'd retired a few years ago he still did consulting work for the bank on the side.

*I should do a video call.* A small laugh escaped my lips. Trying to explain Skype to them would be nothing short of hilarious if I wanted to tell them face to face.

My dialing was interrupted a second time by a knock on my door.

"Sorry to bother you. These were just delivered." Meredith walked in carrying a sizable bouquet of red roses.

"They're lovely," she said, placing them on the desk. "You're quite lucky."

Not saying anything further, she left. I searched for a card and found one nestled in with the baby's breath.

If my calculations are correct, these will make you smile.
Looking forward to tonight.
Yours, ARH xx

Oh no. Tonight. Dammit.
I grabbed the phone and dialed his office.
"Holden World Media."
"Hi, Simone. It's Lia. Is he busy?"

"Hold please."

His assistant sounded miffed at my familiarity on the phone. Or maybe I was just being paranoid. I stroked the pretty petals while listening to some rather dire sounding hold music. *They should probably play some of their own artists' music instead of this*, I thought, twisting the phone cord.

"Holden," he answered, irritated.

"I'm not bothering you, am I?"

"Amelia." The desirous way he said my name gave me an unexpected rush. "Not at all, kitten. Did you get my special delivery?"

"I did. They're beautiful." I paused. "Is everything okay? You sound stressed."

Silence permeated through the phone before he answered. "Everything's fine. I'm about to go sit with the finance team so you caught me just in time." He lowered his voice. "Have you been doing as I asked all day?"

The phone nearly slipped out of my hand from the tremor of yearning that shot through my body. I composed myself before lowering the boom about tonight. "Um, so, I've been invited out for cocktails tonight with Julian. Well, invited is too kind. He sort of told me it was happening and where and when to meet him."

"Did he?" he asked, clearly annoyed. "What time?"

"Eight. He said he has a table at Pulse already reserved so—"

"Will Garrison be there?"

I could hear the scowl in his tone.

"Not that I'm aware of. Do you want to come with me?"

"This wasn't quite what I had in mind for us," he muttered. "I should stay here later seeing as you'll be out. Maybe I could stop by around nine?"

"If you're not too tired. Julian likes to harass you into appearing on the show every time he sees you."

"I'm never too tired for you. Plan on seeing me at nine then."

The taxi arrived to pick me up at quarter to eight. I gave my hair one last fluff and checked my lip-gloss. I'd read a little bit about Pulse and my impression was that it was fairly swanky. I did another quick check in the hall mirror at my black sparkly tank dress and was off.

As the cabbie drove me through Glasgow's West End, I soaked in the city. Old world charm weaved itself through modern flair. It was loud. It was quiet. It was bright. It was romantic. This was certainly a far cry from the brightly colored print shirts and never-ending flip-flops that defined tourist central, otherwise known as Orlando, and I loved every last bit of it.

Pulse was located inside a large stone building. It looked rather nondescript on the surface, more like an old bank than an ultra lounge. From what I'd heard, Pulse had become quite the hot spot since Brent opened it over the summer. I noted with pride a glossy advertisement by the entrance that Stephanie had designed. She'd certainly found her calling, and her passion, with graphic design work.

A rather large, intimidating looking bouncer walked over to me.

"Miss Meyers?" he asked.

"Yes."

"Follow me please. Mr. Archer is waiting inside."

I pulled out my cell phone and checked the time as he led me inside the building. It was only five past eight. Apparently, I was late. When I looked up from the phone, I gasped. This place was incredible. Dimly lit in shades of blue, cream and lavender, the whole room gave off a cool, modern vibe. White leather couches shaped like trapezoids were chaotically organized throughout the space. Small, cube shaped chairs flanked dark wooden tables. I couldn't help but stare at the ceiling as we weaved our way through the crowd. It was made entirely of lights that were fragmented into triangles but were perfectly positioned to look like a huge stained glass window all in white.

Every person I passed was better dressed than the last. I appreciated this being a high-end bar but found myself wishing it was a little less pretentious and a little more relaxed.

"Ah, Lia." Julian stood up from the reserved table and kissed both my cheeks. "Gorgeous dress. Have a seat. What do you fancy for a drink?"

"Um," I glanced at the drink menu, "I'll have the Secret Crush please."

He grinned at me slyly after giving our drink orders to the server. My brows lifted a bit as I smiled back, anticipating what could possibly come out of his mouth.

"Is there a specific reason why you negotiated your contract to last only three months, which incidentally, is the length of your temporary visa?"

My stomach dropped and I did that really attractive fish mouth thing where my lips parted but nothing came out.

"Well," I started, finally finding my voice, "I wanted to see if this job was a good fit for me. For us. For the show."

"I see." His blue eyes narrowed slightly. "And if it is?"

"Then I suppose you'll be stuck with me." I smiled at the server as she placed our drinks on the table. Grabbing mine, I took a long sip of the raspberry flavored cocktail. The shrewd look Julian still aimed in my direction led me to believe he wasn't satisfied with my response.

"I've had a revolving door of executive producers over the last four years. Creative differences, incompetence, laziness, you name it. You came highly touted not only from your station in America but also from Sam and Robbie. If I'd known they were going to agree to such a short contract I would never have let you in the building."

This must be the bad side Robbie warned me about. I sank further into the plush cushion, nursing my drink and feeling more than a little bit guilty.

"Wait a second," I said, snapping out of my funk. "You didn't know that I'd only signed on for a few months?"

"No."

"They told me you knew. They said you'd be okay with it."

"Did they," he grimaced. "Sneaky bastards."

"I'm so confused."

Julian downed his bourbon like a champion and leaned forward. "The two of them have been scheming behind my back for months. They kept Gemma on for much longer than was necessary just to watch me slowly implode. They want me out. There's some younger, hot shot presenter from London making the rounds. His ratings are astronomical and the fine people at our parent company want to jump on the bandwagon. We'd be used as a satellite location for interviews and such but The Archer Hour would essentially go away."

The alcoholic fruity goodness of my drink slipped down my throat way too easily. I stared at the bottom of the empty glass, ordering another one through telepathy. I should have known being offered a three month contract in a different country without any pushback was too good to be true. Clearly, I was part of Sam and Robbie's master plan to watch it die a slow death.

*Good thing I didn't sell my car and kept the apartment in Orlando.*

Another cocktail appeared on the table in front of me.

"Looked like you needed a refill." Julian smiled and squeezed my knee with more affection than was necessary.

"Thanks." I drank this one a little slower not wanting to give off the impression I was an uber lush. For some reason the drinks in Scotland tasted much better than the ones in Orlando.

"Sorry I laid all that out on you. You've been with us a month and I just assumed you were the savior I'd been waiting for. My job has meant everything to me and the thought of it being given to some little tit who's nothing more than a glorified tabloid reporter pisses me off."

I felt bad for the guy. I really did. If I'd learned anything from my former night team it was to always stay ten steps ahead of the next generation. That rang especially true for the on-air talent. I could practically hear Cynthia Steele's strong, melodic voice in my head saying there was always someone younger with no morals waiting in the wings. I was fairly certain she'd been exaggerating about the no morals part but there had to be a grain of truth in there somewhere.

"Well, I'm not going to spend my time there going through the motions," I asserted, taking another sip of my drink. "I'm working my ass off to make sure you have the best produced news magazine show in all of Great Britain. If Sam and Robbie don't like it, tough shit."

"Lia Meyers," Julian said loudly. "You are amazing. If they do end up sacking me, you and I will start our own program."

I laughed, enjoying the level of passion he exuded for his craft. Grabbing my drink-free hand, he squeezed it.

"We're going to get on just fine, you and I. And by the way," he paused, "nice ring. I had a feeling we'd be celebrating an engagement soon enough. If you can melt the notoriously frigid Alastair Holden, you can work magic with my television show."

Shocked, I stiffened a little. I shouldn't be surprised though. The ring was like a beacon.

"Not to worry. I won't pester you to get an interview with him for me right now. I'm a bit of prat but I'm not that callous."

# CHAPTER THREE

"And then," I said, perching on the edge of the desk in Alastair's home office, "he called himself a prat and ordered another round of drinks."

Alastair half-smiled, looking up from the computer screen. "Sounds like you two got along quite well."

"We did. Most television personalities aren't as horrid as they appear."

"I'll keep that in mind," he responded dryly. "Sorry I wasn't able to meet you there."

Swinging my legs around so they draped over the arm of his chair, I grinned. "You're forgiven, chief. This time."

He sighed, running a hand along my left calf. I hadn't changed yet and the fuzziness from all the fruity drinks I'd had suggested that I give him a strip tease in the middle of the room. I would have if he hadn't been staring so intently at the open file on his desk.

"Hey," I said, nudging him with my foot, "come to bed. It's late." I sensed he was stressed and bothered by his day at work but I knew better than to pry. He'd tell me when he was ready, if he wanted.

Silence spread through the room. I tried to see if I could get a read on what was going on in his head. Obviously, that didn't happen. Hopping off the desk, I hitched up my dress and straddled him on the chair.

"Amelia."

The strained way he said my name triggered an immediate response in me. I kissed him desperately, feeling him shudder in my embrace.

"Come with me," I requested, skimming my lips over his.

I melted when he smiled.

"You like stealing my phrases."

"What can I say? You're quotable."

Squeezing my waist gently, he laughed. The sound of it always filled me with such joy. Leaning his forehead to mine, he closed his eyes. Bit by bit, the protective shield locked into place. I ran my hands down his chest, disheartened to feel him stiffen beneath my touch.

"Sorry, love," he said flatly. "I have to be in London for the rest of the week. I leave early tomorrow morning. Paxton will be here to make sure you get to and from work safely."

I swallowed down my disappointment like it was a spoonful of salt. "Why do y—"

"My fucking uncle," he snapped. "He's trying to undermine my decisions regarding the music division. He set up an investor meeting behind my back and now I have to go talk everyone off a ledge."

"What happened?"

Scrubbing his face with both hands he grimaced. "My grandfather is trying to convince me to dissolve the music end of the business and use the extra funds to launch a production company. I told him no and gave him my reasons but fucking Jason keeps," he paused, scowling. "My uncle and I don't see eye to eye on this and he's constantly up my grandfather's ass about it."

Not really knowing what to say, I could only play with his hair in the hopes it would calm him down. He never talked about work and I never asked so I knew nothing of the intricacies involved with running a worldwide media empire.

"Well," I said, "you're the boss. Jason has to answer to you and your grandfather is retired so he really has no say, right?"

Alastair laughed bitterly. "If only it were that simple."

"I'm sorry. I don't know—"

"My dad created the music division about a year before the accident," he interrupted. "I was so young, I had no idea what it was but I do remember him being rather excited about it. He'd play records really loud on the weekends and my sister and I would dance around the living room. I think," he paused, swallowing hard, "I think this was my dad's dream. I think maybe he'd started it because he wanted to step out of my grandfather's shadow. Jason was strictly the business minded one and yessed Samuel to death. My dad was the creative one."

He looked up at me. "Since Jason and Katherine have no children, I'm the last one in line. If I fuck up the business, it dies along with all the hard work my dad put into it."

"You're not going to fuck up the business. You're too smart to let that happen."

His frosty exterior thawed. "I shouldn't have snapped at you."

"No, you shouldn't have. Watch those sore spots, chief."

"Fair point." He pulled me closer so our faces were inches apart.

I kissed him because I could and because that's really all I'd been wanting to do since I returned home.

"Tell me to stay here with you."

His quiet words ripped through me, shredding my soul into a thousand pieces. *Oh, Alastair.* I hugged him, marveling again at the tremors shaking his body. He never failed to surprise me with the strength of his affection.

"I love you so much, it hurts," I whispered against his neck.

Gently breaking our embrace, he looked at me with clear, bright eyes. We didn't have to say anything for us both to know what I'd meant. "Come with me to London. I don't want to be away from you for one second."

I smiled, completely aware of how easy it was for him to disarm me. "You know I can't."

"Then come down this weekend. I'll have the plane ready and waiting for you after work on Friday. We'll go stay at the May Fair and never leave the room" -he kissed me- "or I'll send you to the spa and do whatever else you want."

"Tempting," I murmured, tracing my fingers along his jaw. "Why don't we go to your cottage here instead?"

He frowned. "I may not be back for the weekend, Lia. I don't want to leave you alone here."

"I won't be alone. I have Stephanie and Darren."

"Maybe your sister would like to see you. She does live in London, you know."

"Wow." I laughed. "When did you turn into my mother?"

A sharp squeeze at my waist made me flinch. "I see your smart mouth also made the journey across the Atlantic."

"It's a package deal, Holden."

Uncoiling a bit from his annoyance, Alastair kissed me firmly. "We could get married this weekend," he said, playing with my hair. "Have a civil ceremony at Islington Town Hall. It would be just the two of us."

The thought left me breathless. Every cell in my body, from my toes to the tips of my fingers, hummed with anticipation. Images of us exchanging vows and spending the entire weekend blissfully alone and entwined with each other filled my mind. It was perfect. It was…

"My family will kill me," I blurted.

Alastair raised an eyebrow. "Not if I have anything to say about it. Besides, they'll get over the shock. We'll have a massive party back in the States. That's why everyone has a wedding anyway, right? For the party."

"But don't we need, like, paperwork and licenses? And witnesses? We can't just walk in and—"

He kissed me quiet and essentially halted all talk of eloping. "You really need to do something about this habit of overthinking."

The smile in his eyes and on his lips sealed the deal for me.

"Fine. You're right." I tugged on his tie. "Is there a reason why you're still in CEO mode at home? I mean, the suits are hot and stuff but it's well past quitting time."

"There's no rest for the wicked." He smirked. "Would you rather I sat here naked?"

I slung my arms around his neck and grinned. "It would be an improvement."

"Cheeky." He felt his way down my body. "We do have some unfinished business to attend to, don't we?"

Capitalizing on his softened mood and flirty playfulness, I nuzzled into his neck, kissing his warm skin and enjoying the low groans vibrating in his throat. "That depends."

"On what?"

I loosened his tie and slid it off his neck. "Did you think about me all day?"

Yearning filled what little space there was between us as he knotted his fingers through my hair. We were so close our mouths nearly touched. "Trying to turn the tables on me, kitten? If I remember correctly, it was *you* who had all the thinking to do."

The gentle but firm tug he gave my hair resonated deep within me. A little smile pulled at his mouth when I tried to move.

"I have you just where I want you, Lia. Tell me" -he nipped at my bottom lip- "every thought that crossed your mind."

I'd have figured by this point in our relationship I'd be a little more immune to his level of seduction but I wasn't and he knew it. If that satisfied grin on his face wasn't so damn hot I'd have been able to form some sort of response. Leveling a dangerously sexy stare at me, he wet his lips.

"Are you going to tell me?"

"I'm going to show you," I replied in a much lower, much more seductive tone than I normally used. Alastair's grin grew larger but he wouldn't loosen his grip on me.

"Fancy a shag on the desk, do you?" He pulled on my hair

again. "I'd rather you come to my office building for that." He sucked on my earlobe, making me squirm with pleasure. "I'll spread you out on my big desk and have you for lunch. I do like the way you taste."

An animalistic, guttural moan rushed out of my mouth so hard I clutched onto the back of the chair. I swear, his level of sexy should be illegal.

"Is my kitten enjoying herself?" he asked, keeping his mouth so close to my ear I could feel his lips brushing against it. I'd be lying if I said no. This more aggressive side of his had me firing on all cylinders.

Peeling my fingers off the chair, I ripped his shirt open. Blinded by the raging lust that overpowered me, I couldn't move my hands fast enough to undo his belt. If I didn't have mind-blowing sex with him right now, I'd go insane.

I stood up and yanked my dress over my head, dropping it to the floor in an unceremonious heap. Pushing himself off the chair like a predator about to strike, he pulled me against his body.

"You're wearing too many clothes," I said, grabbing at the waistband of his pants.

I was a split second away from shoving him back onto the chair so I could mount him when I was halted by the detached way he looked at me.

"What is it?" I asked.

Shaking his head, he lifted my left hand and turned it towards the light so the diamond and emeralds sparkled. Immense sadness seized his beautiful face for the briefest of seconds but it was enough to deflate my mood.

"This was my mum's ring," he said in hushed tone. "It's been sitting in a box at the house in Ascot for years. My aunt told me it was mine to give to the girl I wanted to marry."

*Oh my God…NOW he wants to get all emotional?*

"She would have liked you."

Partly controlled by my ravenous libido and partly by my fierce love for him, I lunged forward, knocking him back onto the chair and climbed on his lap. Holding both sides of his face, I covered him in kisses before hugging him tight. I knew how difficult it was for him to talk about his parents. Running my knuckles down his cheek, I tried to compose myself. I think he sensed I was having a problem with that and smirked.

"Did I interrupt your saucy ways by being too soppy?"

"Yes."

He arched an eyebrow.

"Shit. I mean…you didn't but…" I was so wired and flustered that nothing was coming out right. "You just have me so turned on and I'm a little buzzed and then you drop that on me out of the blue and it…what you said is so sweet and romantic and I just… I'm so focused on wanting to…to fuck your brains out that—"

"You thought it was sweet and romantic?"

"I…yeah. Who wouldn't? It's your mom's ring. And coming from you that means a lot to me."

"Does it?"

"Of course, Alastair. But you could have given me a plastic ring from a toy dispenser at a bowling alley and I would have loved it all the same because it's from *you*."

He looked thoughtful. "So I've finally conquered being cheesy, then?"

I couldn't help but laugh. "For now, Mr. No-Relationships-Non-Dater."

"You," he grabbed my waist and squeezed, "are asking for trouble."

"No. You are. I was all ready to—"

"Fuck my brains out?" The dominant spark returned to his eyes, which drove me wild.

"If you keep interrupting me, then no."

He squeezed my waist harder, making me jump. "I'm going to keep you up all night, kitten."

"You don't have an off switch, do you?"

"Not when it comes to you." Running the pad of his thumb along my mouth, he remained quiet for several seconds. The same sadness that ghosted across his face before returned.

"Hey," I said. "What's going on in there?"

My pulse revved up as he caressed my cheek. A suffocating aura of want enveloped us. Hovering his lips above mine he said, "I love you."

The vulnerable edge to his tone hit me hard. Hearing him say those words to me was a rare occasion. Sure, he showed me in so many ways all the time but hearing it? I never thought three little words could light up my entire being the way they did coming from him.

Without saying a word, I stood up and led him to the bedroom where I peeled off the rest of his clothes. He finished undressing me, brushing his fingers over every inch of my hyper-sensitive flesh before pulling me down on the mattress.

We remained tangled together in comfortable silence for awhile. I thought maybe he'd nod off seeing as I kept running my fingers through his hair and his breathing had become deep and heavy.

I knew on some level he was still struggling with finding a balance between trusting his emotions and keeping them protected. Shifting slightly on the bed, he inadvertently flexed his hips into mine kicking my heart rate up to a frantic pace. I heard a small moan vibrate in his throat. We were breathing in unison now. When he opened his eyes I inhaled sharply. Gone was the sadness. It was replaced by a craving so powerful I could feel it cloaking my body.

"All night, Lia," he growled, rolling on top of me, the muscles in his face taut with lust and want.

At the rate we were going, we'd never sleep another full night for the rest of our lives. Not that I particularly cared. Feeling him inside me and knowing all of his love and attention was focused only on me was intoxicating. So were his soft moans and the unfiltered way he looked at me as we possessed one another, grabbing, caressing and claiming.

We were so connected now, so completely whole as a couple that we were unbreakable.

* * *

The next morning we showered together and spent our time talking, laughing and enjoying one another's company. I loved watching Alastair when he was carefree and smiling. The way he carried himself with such quiet control always hit all my hot buttons but seeing him relaxed and sated made him even more beautiful.

I rode with my handsome Englishman to the airport and hugged him with all my might on the tarmac before he boarded the plane. For a brief moment, I considered ditching work and flying to London with him. The steely, all-business look in his eyes was the only thing that had stopped me. Dressed in a dark blue double breasted suit, Alastair had morphed from insatiable lover into CEO-mode on the ride over. It was sexy as hell but I knew better than to poke the bear.

Grabbing me and kissing me briskly, he promised to be back by Friday evening.

When I arrived at my office I was in a great mood and felt indestructible. Noticing a small silver envelope on my desk, I sat down and opened it. Inside was a rather expensive looking invitation. I hadn't lived here long enough to be invited to anything so my curiosity was well and truly piqued.

**You are cordially invited to a Bridal Shower**

**honouring Olivia Garrison**

**Saturday, 17 September 2011**

I stopped reading and dropped the fancy piece of paper like it was on fire. All the blood in my body had run cold. The girl who nearly turned Alastair's carefully controlled world upside down wanted to socialize with me? At her *bridal shower*? This had to be someone's idea of a sick joke. *What the actual fuck?*

# CHAPTER FOUR

I didn't have a chance to dwell on the invitation thanks to Julian's demands and Robbie's constant interruptions. Wednesday went from awesome to annoying no less than twenty minutes after I sat at my desk. When I finally had two seconds to myself I called Stephanie.

"What are you doing for lunch?"

"Spending it with Brent Garrison," she said. "He loved my work for Pulse so much he wants my help on a campaign for a new residential complex he's preparing to open. Why? Did you need something? Is everything alright?"

I leaned back in my chair and added this to the list of things that had officially annoyed me today.

"Everything's fine."

"No it's not. You forget that I can see through your bullshit even on the phone. What's going on?"

I glared at the silver envelope. "I've been invited to a bridal shower."

"Really? Who do you know here that's getting married?"

"Brent's sister."

Stephanie was quiet for a full five seconds, a record for her. "Interesting. Want me to do some digging when I see him for lunch? I can be discreet."

I snorted. "Sure."

"Lia! How long have you known me? I have a way with getting information from unsuspecting people. Besides, Brent will think I'm flirting with him. He loves that."

"Does he?"

"Yeah. I'll tell you all about it later." She paused. "Darren doesn't have any lunch plans. I'll tell him to meet you in the lobby in twenty."

* * *

I'd barely walked out of the elevator when Darren hugged me and spun me in a quick circle before we walked outside. He might have been Stephanie's friend since they were teenagers but I adored him as if I'd known him for years and years. His sunny disposition always put a smile on my face.

The cafe wasn't too far from our building. Timid rays of autumn sunshine poked their way through some clouds, then had second thoughts and were eventually swallowed up.

"I hear this place has one hell of a mozzarella and tomato panini," Darren said, holding the door open.

The cafe was so warm and cozy I thought we'd mistakenly walked into someone's home. Several patrons were ordering at the mahogany counter while others were chatting at various tables spread throughout the dining area. The aroma of freshly baked bread filled the air. Darren motioned for me to grab a table and offered to place our orders. I found a table by the dark brown brick wall and people watched.

"So," Darren said, placing our sandwiches down, "how's everything at the new job? Is Archer on your nerves yet?"

I chuckled to myself. "Not yet. Ask me again next week."

"Steph says you went for cocktails with him last night. You should have thrown a drink in his face." The sour expression

Darren employed shocked me. I'd never heard him talk so negatively about someone.

"Alright. Spill it MacCourty. What did he do aside from being an overzealous, loud mouth TV guy?"

"My ex-girlfriend used to work for him as an associate producer. He likes to get friendly with the ladies on his staff. A little touching here, a little bum slap there. She didn't like it and when she called him out on it, he fired her. The twat." He took a large bite out of his sandwich and stewed in the anger of his distant memory.

I was shocked but not overly surprised to hear this. Julian did like the hands-on approach when he talked to me. I didn't think much of it because it never went further than a shoulder squeeze but I made a mental note to keep an eye on him.

"Sorry that happened to her," I said, sympathizing. "What does she do now?"

"She moved to France and works on some detective show there. I haven't talked to her in a couple years but she was really turned off by Archer. That guy is a massive knob. I'd—" He stopped and stared at my left hand.

I held the sandwich in front of my wide open mouth and stared back at him. We both must have looked like mental patients.

"You *are* engaged," he said with a smile. "That's brilliant, Lia. Congratulations."

"Thank you." I put my sandwich down and showed off the ring. "He gave this to me the other night but we haven't said anything publicly yet. Well, he actually asked me to marry him in July when you guys were in Orlando but we've kept it quiet."

"July? How have you both managed to keep it quiet?"

"Well, you know Alastair. He's a man of few words."

"True that. But if I scored a looker like you I'd shout it from the mountain tops."

I laughed. "It hasn't been easy not saying anything, trust me. We both decided after the summer we'd had that we just wanted to have something for ourselves."

Darren studied me with astute eyes. "The press over here is going to love you. You're pretty, smart and loads of fun to be around. They're so fascinated with Alastair and every little move he makes. He dodges them pretty well though, only giving his requisite face time and then disappearing from sight."

That had been Alastair's M. O. for years. He lived as private a life as one could, being the heir to a billion dollar mega corporation. When his grandfather retired and he was named CEO over the summer, the spotlight shined a little brighter on him. As his girlfriend, that also meant some of the light focused on me. I was used to it to some degree thanks to my previous relationship with a U.S. senator's son. I had a feeling this time around, the media attention would be more intense.

"There haven't been too many issues yet, knock on wood," I said. "Only an occasional photographer here and there. Having Paxton with me most of the time seems to help. I'm such a nobody anyway. They probably look at me as just another piece of eye candy for him."

"Once the news of your engagement gets out you won't be a nobody." Darren looked at me solemnly. "The gossip sites are already feasting on your taste in shoes and how you like to wear workout clothes while buying groceries."

The more I listened to Darren, the more uncomfortable I became. I'd had a sneaking suspicion the handful of photographers I'd seen were only hounding me for fluff pieces like that. For the most part, it didn't bother me but I knew it was only the tip of the iceberg. Alastair and I hadn't discussed how our lives would be affected by public scrutiny too much. He just made sure I was always under the watchful eye of Paxton or someone from his security staff. He also knew how much I disliked having babysitters and made sure they were inconspicuous. Most days I was oblivious to the bodyguard detail.

"Our boy is quite protective of you. We both know the lengths he'll go to keep you safe."

I swallowed another bite of my sandwich and nodded. If there was one thing everyone knew about Alastair, it was how close he kept me to his vest.

"Anyway," Darren said, brightening the room with his infectious smile, "Steph will go ballistic if you don't tell her about this engagement straight away." He winked and took another bite of his sandwich.

"I know. I was going to tell her today but she's off with Brent Garrison."

"She's been seeing quite a bit of him recently." The look on his face spoke a million words after he said that. "Damn. I wasn't supposed to say anything. She'll kill me if you tell her I told you."

I'd made it no secret that Brent wasn't one of my favorite people on the planet. He'd never been mean or horrible towards me but his history with Alastair was so salty and tense that I'd made a conscious decision not to bother with him unless it was necessary. Hearing that my best friend might be dating him threw a wrench in that.

"Like, 'seeing' him seeing him? Or just business lunches?"

"It started as business but they've been hanging out on the weekends and what not. I'm surprised she hasn't told you yet."

*You and me both.*

"He seems like a decent guy," Darren said, clearly trying to play the peacemaker. "I've done some work for him in the past and got on with him quite well. Alastair knows him from years ago." He paused and smiled sheepishly. "That's not news to you though. They went to university together at Oxford."

I stopped mid chew. "They did? I didn't know that."

"No? Brent was a year ahead of him. They played rugby together and were pretty friendly until something happened." He shrugged. "I always assumed Brent was jealous of Alastair's social ranking what with the family business and all. He seemed quite determined to make a success out of his real estate venture to steal some of the thunder from the Holden clan. Not sure why though, since they do media and what not. Seemed a bit odd to me."

I kept eating my sandwich in the most nonchalant way possible as Darren continued spilling details about Brent. Nothing about it was earth shattering, just interesting enough to fill some of the holes that Alastair left out. I felt better having a clearer picture of their past interactions outside the sphere of Alastair's relationship with Olivia.

"Your fiancé is a frosty one to try and be friends with Lia. And I say that with no disrespect. Whatever happened between him and Brent must have been huge because they were like brothers at university. At least that's what I hear."

The fact that Darren loved to gossip could work in my favor. My curiosity was insatiable and anytime I learned a new nugget about Alastair it left me craving more. For the time being, I chose to stifle the questions and just enjoy the rest of our lunch.

"You have exactly twenty-four hours to tell your best friend about that ring, lass," he said on our walk back to the building. "I can't keep a secret like that from Steph forever. We live together. She's up my arse all the time wanting to know if Alastair has told me anything. I'm surprised I haven't gone mad yet from all her pestering."

I laughed heartily as we walked into the elevator. "You're a saint, Darren."

"True that." He winked and gave me a little wave when we reached his floor.

Even though my dealings with Brent had always been a little stressful, I decided to have a little fun at Stephanie's expense and texted her when I returned to my office.

**1:43pm How big is it?**

**1:47pm ?????????**

**1:48pm Brent's wonder stick**

My desk phone rang within seconds.

"Yes?"

"Amelia Grace Meyers," she hissed, "you're not funny."

"Sorry." I laughed. "I couldn't help myself. What are you doing after work?"

"Finding a new roommate."

I laughed even harder. "Aw, don't be mad at Darren. You know he can't stay quiet about big news like that forever."

"There is no big news. We've hung out and stuff. It's really nothing."

"Alright. Whatever you say."

"Lia," she whined, "he's not even my type. He's too buttoned up and proper. I like 'em carefree and wild."

"You're protesting too much."

"Fine," she sighed. "We had dinner a couple of times. That's *it*."

I tapped a pen on my desk, wanting to be judicious with my words. "Listen, um. Just, you know, be—"

"I know," she snapped. "You hate him and Alastair hates him so I have to hate him too."

"That's not what I was going to say. I just…I know how you are when people say negative things about—"

"Oh my God," she grumbled. "Do you really think we sit around and talk about Alastair like he's some fascinating subject? Jesus Christ. He's your boyfriend. He has a bad history with Brent and his sister. I could give three flying shits about all that because it's really none of my business. You need to stop convincing yourself that your relationship with Alastair fucking Holden is the end all, be all of the world."

I sat in stunned silence, confused as to how this conversation took such a sour turn. When she was heated, Stephanie could be irrational.

"Fuck," she muttered. "Look, I didn't mean to fly off the handle like that. I'm PMS-ing and this deadline for creative is stressing me out and" —she sighed— "you know I love Alastair. And I love you. And you're far from being the girl who thinks their relationship is the most important thing on the planet to everyone else. Did I cover them all?"

"I'm coming down to bring you Pamprin."

"Smart ass. I'd rather have ice cream." She paused. "I really am sorry."

"Wow." I snickered. "You hate apologizing so that PMS must be severe."

"And yet you continue to test my limits, Amelia Grace," she said. I could hear the smile in her voice. "We should get together this weekend and do something fun. Maybe we could take the train into Edinburgh for some lunch."

"Sounds good to me."

"Fantastic. I gotta run. We'll talk later."

Shaking my head at Stephanie, I placed the phone in its cradle and emailed my sister to give her a quick update on how I was doing. I also promised to come visit her soon. I flirted with the idea of calling my mom but decided to wait until this weekend. She'd most likely want a detailed report on how everything was going here and wouldn't take too kindly to being ushered off the phone after a brief conversation.

Eyeing the silver envelope again, I finished reading the invitation for Olivia's bridal shower. The Hotel du Vin? I did a quick search online and learned it was a luxury boutique hotel in the West End. It looked quite lovely from the photos.

*Maybe I should go.*

I exorcized the thought from my mind before it had a chance to fester and grow. The last thing I wanted was to spend time with that girl.

* * *

Steady rain tapped against the windows, its delicate rhythmic dance relaxing me as I walked into the living room. Being alone in this big house put me on edge a little but only because I was still getting used to its size and some of the weird noises it made late at night. I decided against watching TV and chose to be nosey. Seeing as Alastair kept decorations to a bare minimum, there wasn't much to see. Yes, the earth tones that drenched the room were gorgeous and luxurious but aside from the framed photos I'd put out the other night there wasn't much here that screamed *him*.

I ran my fingers along a gold key that sat in a small crystal dish on one of the shelves while looking at some of his books. They were mostly reference books about various financial topics. Almost lost among them was a book that appeared to have no title on its spine.

"What's this," I mused, pulling it off the shelf. The soft, dark leather was old and worn, so I assumed it had to be a favorite novel of his or something. Opening it, I discovered it was an old diary. I saw the name Rose Taylor Holden handwritten in the front. Though small, I felt its weight in my hands after seeing his mother's name. I scanned the shelf again, hoping to find another hidden treasure. One by one, they made themselves known; a tattered children's book, an old photography manual, a comic book about someone named Moven Marvin.

The closer I looked, the more I could see that he did keep pieces of himself in this house. He just kept them hidden and protected, like he did with everything else.

A surge of love flowed through me as I returned the books to their proper places. What I first assumed to be nondescript decorations must have belonged to his parents. Every little figurine or bookend or delicate vase must be something from his childhood home.

His well-versed ability to show the world only what he wanted them to see extended to the privacy of his own house but was so subtle it went unnoticed. I trotted off to the bedroom and grabbed my phone.

10:49pm I miss you

11:02pm The plane is fueled and ready. Fly here now

11:03pm Wish I could

11:07pm You can. I'll handle Archer

11:10pm Next time, Holden. You're busy with work anyway. I'd be bored

11:11pm Not if I can help it

11:14pm Now you're just teasing me

11:16pm Are you in bed?

11:18pm Yep

11:21pm Dream of me x

Curling up on the mattress, I hugged his pillow tight and smiled.

# CHAPTER FIVE

"*Why didn't you call me as soon as it happened?*" Stephanie shrieked, staring at my hand. The handful of people standing to our left on the sidewalk gave her a dirty look. She didn't care one bit and carried on. "Jesus Christ, it's Friday. You've known all week and didn't say anything. I mean, what's the point of being your official-best-friend-unofficial-big-sister if *you don't tell me the important things?*"

Shivering, she pulled the jacket around her body tighter and shook her head. Her jet black hair had grown even longer, nipping at her shoulders like a swath of sultry, dark silk.

I gazed at the diamond, not bothered by her dramatics. "I'm telling you now. *Before* telling my actual flesh and blood sister and *before* telling my parents."

"But you told Darren?"

"Hey, I called to see if you were free for lunch and you sent him in your place. Don't blame me."

She started to say something then stopped, knowing full well I was right. I smirked.

"Darren is so dead," she muttered. "Did you set a date?"

"No."

She flailed her arms. "Why not? We need to start planning this wedding immediately."

I didn't have the heart to quell her excitement…yet. She rummaged through her purse while spouting off all sorts of suggestions for a venue, a dress, a DJ, honeymoon destinations and photographers. When she ventured into the realm of having two weddings in two countries I had to put a stop to the insanity.

"I have an idea," I interrupted her, putting my hands up. "How about Alastair and I enjoy being engaged for awhile before I scare the crap out of him with your cyclone of ideas and suggestions?"

"You've been engaged since *July*. How much longer do you need to enjoy it?"

"Steph." I gave her a stern look.

"Fine." She folded her arms. "But I'm throwing you an engagement party and there's nothing you can do to stop me." Her eyes widened. "Your birthday is next week. Two parties!"

"Oh my God," I snorted. "You're out of control."

She threw her head back in an exaggerated sigh and followed me toward the cafe to grab some coffee. Before I reached the door half a dozen guys holding cameras jumped up from one of the small tables out front and blocked my path. They all started snapping photos and talking at once.

"Let's see the ring," one shouted.

"When's the wedding?"

"Are you pregnant?" another one yelled in my face.

Frozen with shock, I stared at them.

"Hey, leave her alone douche nozzle." I heard Stephanie's voice from behind me, then felt her grab my arm and yank me into the cafe. "Don't those ass hats have any concept of personal space?"

Some of the people inside the cafe pointed and mumbled God knows what to each other. I shoved my left hand into my coat pocket. *So this is how it starts.*

A hard knock on the window startled me, rattling my now frayed nerves. I turned and saw yet another photographer snap pictures through the glass. When he finished, he smiled and walked off. Every eye in the cafe was now on me.

"Show's over people," Stephanie said, glaring at some woman in a brown pantsuit. "Don't you all have jobs to get to or something?"

I heard a few people mutter and was relieved to see them all returning to their morning routines.

Stephanie, the gem that she was in situations like this, diverted my attention from the paparazzi by filling me in on her job. Not only had her campaign designs for Pulse been a huge hit, she'd also been tapped to design the ads for a new perfume and a new clothing boutique. She practically glowed telling me all about it.

"Cassie told me if I keep going at this pace I'll have her job in six months."

I laughed. "Try to remember us little people when you're skyrocketing to the top."

"Stop it. What about you? How's everything at the show?"

"So far, so good. Julian's a trip." I tapped my nails on the counter. "I think he's paranoid though. He seems to believe Sam and Robbie are out to replace him with some guy from London. I can't see why he would think that. Sam is very focused on improving the show and Robbie is one of the most talented producers I've come across."

"Paranoia runs deep with those on-air people. You know how I feel about their constant neediness and always having to be reassured that they're the best and nobody else compares and blah, blah, blah. I've said it before. You're a saint to put up with that crap day in and day out. I'm surprised you don't keep a bottle of wine at your desk just in case."

"Maybe I should."

"So, do you think you'll stay there once your contract is up? I mean, you were pretty adamant about only wanting it to be for three months but that seems a little weird to me. You can't *not* work. You'll go insane from the boredom." She paid for the coffee and we walked back out onto the sidewalk.

I did a quick scan of my surroundings to make sure no other photographers jumped out at me. A few people still stared a little too long.

"I don't know. I like doing the whole television thing but I'm starting to get burned out, you know? I never thought I'd be doing this for as long as I have."

"Six years isn't that long."

"Oh no? Working in TV news can be soul sucking, trust me."

"What else do you want to do?"

"I haven't a clue." I shrugged.

"What does Alastair have to say about that? He did make you move here and take that job."

I stopped short and gave her a look. "First of all, he didn't make me move here. I wanted to. Second, I took the job because I thought it would be a great stepping stone for my career."

"Okay, okay. PMS." She put her hands up in retreat. "I suppose it's convenient that he has dual citizenship if he wants to relocate and work out of the New York office though, right?"

"I don't know if he'll do that. It's not really something we've ever talked about."

"Keep the option open," she said, pushing through the revolving doors. "What are you doing tonight? Come over and hang out until Alastair gets back from London. I'll be home alone."

"Um, sure. I don't know what time he's coming back though." *Or if he is.*

"Then leave him a love note and tell him you're at my place, naked and tied up on the couch."

I lifted an eyebrow. "So you either want him to think he's walking into an orgy or I've been kidnapped?"

Stephanie laughed good and loud as we waltzed through the lobby toward the elevators. "I suppose I should have worded that better. What time do you go off the air again?"

"Six. Unless I royally screw up and they throw up bars and tone in the first segment."

"You'll be amazing," she smiled. "Come by the townhouse whenever. I'll order Chinese."

More magical words had never been spoken. I could already

picture myself diving into a carton of egg rolls and shrimp lo mein. At some point I should really get back into my jogging routine. To say I'd been lazy since moving here was an understatement. Then again, I've more than made up for the lack of jogging with bedroom activities.

"I'll be there with bells on," I said as the doors swished open.

"Fabulous. Oh, and call your mother," she yelled over her shoulder walking out of the elevator.

* * *

"Lia." Meredith burst through the door breathless and flushed. "Julian is on his way. He wants more time for the interview."

"We're stacked pretty heavy," I smiled, amused at her blatant fear of the man. If she wanted a career in television she'd have to shore up her intimidation factor and face these people with more confidence. "Tell him no."

She paled and ran out. Seconds later Julian strolled in.

"Lia," he smiled. "Love, I need an extra five minutes."

"Five?" *He must be drunk.*

"Yes, five. We only have three in the segment. It was originally longer and I don't see any scenario that will enable me to accomplish my interview in a responsible, informative manner that doesn't include an additional five minutes."

"So, you want to subject the viewing public to eight minutes of you and Brent Garrison?" I rolled my eyes. "No offense but neither one of you are that interesting. Besides, he's only here to promote himself and his real estate accomplishments."

"I've already looked at the next segment. There are stories in there you can bump or kill or whatever," he said, ignoring my remarks. To humor him, I scrolled through the rundown as he continued to butter me up with flowery language and pearly white smiles. He even worked in a brief shoulder massage. There were a couple of stories I could shuffle and one I could bump to next week. I managed to finagle them without destroying the program's flow.

"I can give you an extra two but that's it. Don't waste the time."

Julian grinned triumphantly. "You're an angel." He rubbed his hands together and left with just as much zeal as when he entered. Leaning back in my chair, I sighed. Meredith appeared at my door, looking unsure of herself.

"Come on in," I grinned.

"You handle him so well. I wouldn't know what to say because he's always talking so fast and moving from one topic to another."

"He's all bluster. I've learned over the years to let them spout off whatever they feel is so important to say and then tell them what's actually going to happen. Being straightforward and firm with them will get you far. It all comes with time."

Meredith flopped onto the chair in front of my desk. Conservatively dressed in a tan pencil skirt and dark blue blouse, she looked the part of a hopeful network employee; her dark hair was pulled back in a low ponytail, stylish glasses rested on her nose and her gorgeous mocha complexion glowed. She didn't wear much make up, just a little gloss on her lips and a touch of mascara to bring out her round, dark brown eyes. She was unassumingly pretty with a shy, quiet way about her.

"Did the files I dropped off on Monday help with preparing for Mr. Garrison's interview?"

"Absolutely. I really appreciate it."

"Oh, good. I've done some additional research on him if you need to fill the extra time Julian requested."

"I think I'm all set, unless there's something else about him I need to know."

"Well," she looked down, "he's gorgeous." The blush that stained her cheeks was vibrant.

"I meant anything professionally."

Laughing nervously, she fidgeted with her skirt. "He's very charming, intelligent, direct and to the point." She thought for a second. "He rarely does interviews like this. I suspect that's why Julian is so excited."

In all of my encounters with Brent he'd seemed quite outgoing and not opposed to being the center of attention. Or maybe that was just when Alastair was around and he felt the urge to needle him whenever possible.

"You're exactly his type, you know," she continued. "He's only thirty-two and you're what, twenty-seven? He'll probably ask you out."

"I'm actually in a serious relationship," I said, twisting my ring.

"I'm sorry. That's right. You're engaged to Alastair Holden." Her blush deepened. "I shouldn't be talking about this at work anyway."

* * *

'Hurry up and wait' should be painted in large letters on walls in every single newsroom and television studio in the world. Sure, the hectic times were insane but for the most part, we waited. We still had about an hour and a half before going live so I decided to see what Julian was up to. He was relaxing and reading through scripts when I popped into his office for a brief meeting.

"You are becoming the toast of the town," he announced, swiveling his monitor so I could see the photos of me from the coffee shop that had been posted online. One caption in particular made me cringe: **HOLDEN'S AMERICAN ARM CANDY WINS THE DIAMOND**

"Everyone wants to know about you. These idiots don't know how to handle a story of this magnitude. I say we do an exclusive with you next week—"

"Stop right there," I interrupted. "Hell will freeze over before I say one word to the media about my relationship. It's not for sale and it's not a story. People will get bored with me soon enough when they realize—"

"They will never tire of Alastair Holden. Don't you understand? He's the golden child of a billion dollar media empire who also happens to have one of the most tragic back stories I've ever heard. People are fascinated by him. They can't get enough of him because he's so goddam private. You're their window into his life. Just think of the—"

I stormed out before he could finish. What an ass. I expected photographers to jump out at me and strangers to stare but not my own co-workers. Fuming, I locked myself in my office. A silver piece of paper caught my attention. *The invitation.*

Grabbing it, I glared at Olivia's name. To think I had to fake pleasantries with her brother in a little while gave me a headache. I could handle it though. I'd been in worse situations.

After my mood cooled off, I spent the final thirty minutes before the show went on the air in the control room. It was the heart and soul of any working station. Monitors covered an entire wall, all of them glowing with moving images. A massive board of lights and levers blinked, waiting for the technical director to give them a press or a pull. Of course, a giant digital clock ominously ticked the minutes away as a reminder for me and everyone else to remain on time. I found my seat, said my hellos and plugged in my headset to listen to the pre-show chatter between the director and his crew.

Once the opening music sounded and the final countdown given, I was in full-on producer mode. Robbie sat to my left, diligently working.

During a pre-packaged piece toward our final segment, I noticed the floor director motion for someone to walk on set. I watched curiously as Brent moved into view. I hadn't seen him since our unexpected meeting at dinner in New York. Tall, broad shouldered and, yes, handsome, he made his way to the chair. Piercing, hazel eyes darted around the set as he waited to get mic'd up. Wavy chocolate brown hair framed his angular face. There was no hard edge to him, no hidden agenda, just a powerful energy that radiated off him.

"Thank you for coming in today, Mr. Garrison. I appreciate it," Julian greeted him with a smile.

"My pleasure. I hope I can enlighten your audience."

Hearing his rich Scottish accent come through my headset caught me off guard. I'd only ever talked to him at a normal, human distance. This seemed a little too intimate for a guy who despised my fiancé. Shaking off the weird feeling, I glanced at the clock. The show was coming back live in one minute and I needed to focus.

"Okay, Julian. We're coming up on you cold in sixty. You have three minutes, then toss to the package."

"Thanks, Lia. Oh, be sure either you or Robbie get in my ear when we're thirty away. I don't want our guest to be cut off mid thought."

"Will do."

Robbie nodded in my direction to signal he'd take care of the timing.

"That was Steve Berman reporting. We're pleased to be joined now by Brent Garrison, owner and CEO at Summit Enterprises. Good evening, Mr. Garrison. Thanks for being here."

"Mr. Archer." He nodded politely.

The two men chatted about the changing climate in the real estate industry and how it was affecting jobs in the city.

"Have any of your properties suffered due to the sluggish economy?"

"Not at all," Brent answered. "Fortunately, people still enjoy going out on occasion even though they've tightened their belts, so to speak. I look forward to opening a few more establishments in the coming year. New businesses mean more jobs."

I sort of zoned out a little during their interview. Finances, business plans and all that weren't my cup of tea. When Julian tossed to the package on job growth in Glasgow and throughout Scotland I made a mental note that we'd be off the air in less than ten minutes.

"Lia," Julian's voice floated through my headset.

"Yes?"

"How much longer is this?"

"One-thirty."

"How does it look from in there?"

"Fantastic. You're doing a great job. Although…"

"What? Although what?"

"Your tie is crooked."

"Bloody hell," he grumbled. "Jim, punch me up on two."

Julian preened and fixed his tie while staring into the monitor mounted beneath camera two. Robbie cued him at ten seconds for the remainder of his interview.

"You founded Summit at such a young age and broke out onto the business scene rather quickly. To what do you credit your success?"

"Success is subjective. I look at where am I now and think there's always room for improvement. But I do credit the success I've had so far to my dedicated team at Summit and to the support of my family."

"You're constantly listed with other notable young businessmen in Great Britain, including Alastair Holden. Obviously your background is quite different from his but do you see his success as something you'd like to emulate?"

I sat immobile, clutching a pen. That question wasn't listed on our sheet of talking points. Sneaky bastard.

Brent smiled slightly. "As you said, our backgrounds are quite different. I wasn't born into an established, worldwide conglomerate but I can certainly appreciate how he's contributed to the ever-changing atmosphere of the media industry."

"Tragic childhood aside, he's had it pretty easy when it comes to his career. Do you see your success as more satisfying because you weren't handed a company like he was?"

It took every ounce of my strength not to leap out of the chair and run into the studio. Livid was too weak of a word to describe what I was. *This is what he wanted the extra time for? Ass.*

"Now Julian, we all work hard at what we do," Brent answered smoothly. "Nobody's success is more satisfying than another's. Alastair Holden is a smart and savvy businessman. Being handed a company or building one from the ground up has no bearing on whether or not one's success is more deserved."

Breathing out slowly I was thankful and more than a little shocked at Brent's diplomatic answer. When the interview concluded and the show went off the air at six, I relaxed.

"Great show, Lia," Robbie said, patting me on the shoulder. "I could tell you were caught off guard by those last couple of questions. Not many people would have handled that with such grace."

"Don't be so sure about that," I muttered, rising to my feet. Visions of Julian being catapulted toward the sun put an extra spring in my step as I walked into the studio. Brent stood just to the left of the desk, waiting patiently to have his lavalier mic removed. A broad smile curved his mouth.

"Hello, Lia."

"Hi, Brent."

"I heard you'd started working here. How's it going so far?"

"Fine." I plastered on a fake smile. "Thanks for coming in for the interview. You did a great job."

He shrugged, fixing his suit jacket once the mic was removed. "Interviews are generally boring. I could recite all that in my sleep." He angled toward me. "Those last questions were Archer's way of goading me. Regardless of my history with your boyfriend, I hope you know I'd never embarrass him or myself like that in the press."

His admission came as a surprise. Nodding, I thanked him. Reaching into his pocket, he pulled out a business card and handed it to me.

"If you ever get tired of Julian, give me a call. I'm always looking to add good talent to my media relations team."

I took the card and stuck it in my notebook. Standing here

chatting with him like it was no big deal felt weird.

"I'm having a few people over to my place tonight. You and Alastair should come. I've already invited some of the staff at Finley's, so your friend Stephanie will be there. Nice seeing you, Lia."

More than a little suspicious at his invitation, I thanked him again. Tonight? Stephanie didn't say anything about this earlier. I decided to text her after I dealt with Archer. He was still at the anchor desk, writing intently and ignoring my presence. Laying my hand on the paper, I blocked his furious scribbling. He looked at me with a noticeable level of dread.

"If you ever pull a stunt like that again without telling me, I will sound a foghorn into your IFB. Are we clear?"

The right corner of his mouth ticked up. "It wasn't intentional. Lots of people have thought the same thing."

"Leave Alastair out of your on-air curiosities unless he's sitting in front of you. And even then, keep your mouth shut."

"You are fiery," he assessed, leaning toward me. "And protective. That's admirable."

"You're on my shit list. That's not."

Turning on my heel, I stalked back to my office.

# CHAPTER SIX

"Finally."

I whipped around, startled by the voice and let the door slam behind me. I swear my heart skipped at least twenty beats. Leaning against the desk smiling, hands tucked in his pants pockets, was Alastair. The casual stance did not fool me at all. He leaned against that desk like he fucking owned it. The site of him knocked me for a loop.

"What the— Jesus, Holden. Stalk much?"

He lifted an eyebrow. "I'm just waiting for my fiancée. Have you seen her? Pretty girl. American. Brown hair, amber eyes. Usually nice. Definitely cheeky."

"You're supposed to be in London. How did you get in here?"

"Sorry to disappoint you with my return." He grinned. "The lovely young lady at reception let me in. I made her promise not to tell anyone I was waiting for you. Judging by the look of terror of your face, I'd say she kept her end of the bargain."

My smile was artful as I placed my belongings on a small table next to the door. "I'm not terrified, smart ass. You surprised me."

"Good."

"Why didn't you call me?"

"And miss this priceless reaction?" He unbuttoned his suit jacket. "I wanted to come here as fast as I could. The plane landed and

56

I could only think of two things."

Little shivers nipped at my skin as I watched him remove the jacket with calculated ease and drape it over the chair. "What were they?"

"You," he said, pushing himself away from the desk.

"That's only one thing."

He positioned his well-dressed, great smelling body in front of me and played with a loose tendril of my hair. I steadied myself against the door. Being seduced in my office wasn't quite what I'd expected to happen today. The crazy-sexy smile curling his sculpted mouth sent tremors down my spine. When he wanted something, he went after it with full force.

"Use your imagination for the second thing."

"You are unreal with this charm and seduction combo thing you've got going for you."

"I try."

"So," I said, looking up at him, "how long have you been snooping around my office?"

"Snooping? I've been waiting patiently for the last fifteen minutes. I even got to enjoy your show."

Oh no. That meant he saw the…

"Garrison handled himself rather well when Archer tossed those questions at him," he said, pausing to kiss the tip of my nose. "It's a good thing nothing surprises me that much anymore." He cocked his head to the side. "What's wrong?"

"Oh, nothing." I sighed.

"You're a bad liar," he whispered, brushing his lips to mine. I shoved my hands through his hair and kissed him with reckless abandon. I'd missed the warmth and softness of his mouth on mine. I deepened the kiss, tasting and savoring him. He groaned, placing his hand on my hip and pulling me closer. Heat radiated off his taut body. I loved the way he felt against me. He broke our mouths apart, sliding a hand along my jaw.

"Lia." The animalistic way he said my name made my knees

buckle. So did the way he looked at me with eyes as dark as night. "I want you."

Not much separated us from the rest of the newsroom, just a door and some glass windows covered with blinds. The thought of having sex with him so close to the people who would give anything for a juicy exclusive turned me on in a way I didn't expect.

"What are you waiting for?"

A low growl vibrated in the back of his throat as he flexed his hips into mine, the friction from his erection teasing me with the promise of what I knew was to come. "I can't be quiet when I'm with you. They'll all hear me shout your name. Do you want that?"

"I'll be quiet if you will."

Fisting his hand in my hair, he ran his tongue along the edge of my bottom lip. I let out a long, breathy moan.

"See? You can't do it either."

"Take me home. Now."

The left corner of his mouth quirked up. "I will, as soon as you tell me what's bothering you."

"Alastair," I exclaimed. "Don't do that. Don't rile me up with your irresistible kisses and touches and say those things to me and not follow through. You're a fucking tease and I've had a long day. I'm not in the mood for your games."

"You're hot when you're angry."

"Ugh, you're impossible," I grumbled, pushing him away and stalking toward my desk. I didn't make it far. He caught me by the waist and spun me around.

"Hey, I'm sorry. I don't like seeing you stressed and knowing something's bothering you. Is it Archer?" His eyes flashed. "Is he still hounding you for an exclusive on me?"

I exhaled, leaning my head back. "Yeah but now he wants the story to focus on me. Apparently I'm the public's window into your life."

The muscles in his jaw twitched as the rest of his body tensed. "Dammit. I knew this would happen. Th—"

I pressed a finger to his lips to halt whatever it was he wanted to say. "Drop it for now. It's Friday night. I haven't seen you in days. Let's go home."

Staring intently at me he remained quiet. I could almost see the cogs turning in his head.

"Have the paparazzi been on your tail? Paxton said there's been more than usual this week."

"Half a dozen photographers leapt out at me this morning when Stephanie and I were getting coffee down the street. The pictures ended up online with headlines about our engagement."

"Then we should probably beat them at their own game. I'll have Simone draft a release with an official announcement."

I wrinkled my nose as his suggestion. "No. That sounds too impersonal and stuffy. Besides, don't you think we should tell our families first before they read about it on the society pages?"

"My family already knows." He paused. "And so does yours."

My mouth dropped open. "What?"

His throaty laugh filled my office. "I called your parents last weekend and told them my intentions. I also made them promise not to say anything to you. Your mum is quite excitable."

"Alastair Reid Holden." I shoved him playfully. "You are sneaky."

A glowing smile brightened his entire face, melting my heart. "You know you love me anyway."

"I do." I kissed him hard, hooking my arms around his waist.

"Now that we have this settled, there's one more bit I have to tell you."

"Oh?"

Dread consumed his expression so subtly I almost missed it. "My aunt wants us to go to the house on Sunday for brunch with her, Jason and my grandfather." He scowled. "They're not taking 'no' for an answer."

His body stiffened in my arms until he became almost statuesque. Never in my life had I seen someone grow so agitated over the thought of spending time with their family. After all, these people did take him in when his parents and sister died and provided for him. His cold reaction to their generosity didn't sit well with me.

"Brunch with your family sounds like a good idea to me. I didn't get to spend much time with them at the garden party and—"

"We won't stay long. We'll eat and then leave."

"Stop with the interrupting. I'm not saying we have to move in with them but it would be nice if I had the chance to spend more than two minutes with your aunt and uncle. I'd really like to get to know them."

Alastair backed away and ran both hands through his hair. I knew that meant he was over this conversation. "You've made a fair point, Amelia." His frigid stare chilled my blood. "But I'm only doing this because of how I feel about you. It's not for them."

Thoughts swirled through my brain, trying to figure out a way to make this visit at least tolerable for him. "Just think how happy your aunt will be to spend time with you."

Narrowing his brows so the little patch of skin between them wrinkled, he sighed. "You're right again. How do you do that?"

"You forget that I know the truth about you, chief. You're nothing but a big 'ol softie underneath all those scowls and icy stares."

"I see." He ran a finger along his lips. What that little movement did to me. *My. God.* "About that second thing on my mind." In an instant he had me caged against the door. I gasped, not from his searing kiss but from the blind sticking in my ass.

"Alastair, stop. There's a piece of plastic in my butt."

Amused, he let me go, craning his head to see the offending material. "Not a fan of that then?"

"Not particularly," I deadpanned. Grabbing my belongings I led him through the now quiet newsroom towards the elevator bank. Out in the hallway, he walked in front of me. I got a nice eyeful of the way he moved with such fluid control. I caught his eye when I hit the call button. A second later he was on me, his hands holding my face as he kissed me unapologetically. My mind scrambled and drifted to that amazing place it went when we were lost in each other. Not seeing him for a few days enhanced the steady ache that grew at my core. My skin reveled in his firm grasps, warming quickly the more he touched me. We stumbled closer to the wall.

"What if someone walks by?" I asked between kisses.

A loud tone sounded signaling the elevator's arrival. We barely pulled away from one another in time to walk in. Thank goodness nobody else was in there because as soon as the doors closed Alastair had me pinned in the corner and curled my right leg around his hip.

"I hated being away from you," he said, cupping my backside. The way his lips glided over mine with such love and passion made me lose all sense of time and space. "My Lia," he whispered, pushing my skirt up. "What you do to me."

Our interlude was rudely interrupted by the elevator's annoying tone yet again, signaling we'd arrived at the lobby. Alastair grinned and ran a hand through his disheveled hair, looking pristine and perfect and not like he'd just been making out in an elevator. I must have looked a mess but really didn't care.

The doors swished open and in walked none other than Brent Garrison. Embarrassed, I glanced at the digital display and saw we weren't at the lobby but on the fifth floor. I smoothed my skirt down to make sure I was covered.

Brent looked at me, then Alastair and smiled. "This is unexpected."

"Garrison," Alastair muttered.

"I was just talking to your lovely girlfriend earlier," he said, ignoring Alastair's tone. "I'm having a few friends over tonight. I've already extended the invitation to Lia. Has she told you?"

I noticed Brent kept the 'doors open' button pressed as he spoke. Alastair aimed a suspicious gaze in his direction.

"Thanks for holding the—" Stephanie trotted in breathless

and stopped short. She looked from Brent to Alastair to me and remained silent.

The elevator had turned into a portal to the Twilight Zone. Only Brent's movement and the sound of the doors closing clued anybody in that we weren't in an alternate universe.

"So, I guess this means no Chinese food." My voice sounded normal but I hadn't a clue as to how I was able to form a complete thought.

Stephanie opened her mouth, then shut it. She scrunched her lips together and blew out a sigh.

"This is my fault," Brent said. "I had no idea you ladies had plans. I went up to reconfirm with Stephanie and wouldn't take no for an answer. Please, do me the honor of coming to my home for a little while tonight. It's just a casual gathering. I'll even order Chinese takeaway for you two." He smiled.

My hand warmed at Alastair's touch, simultaneously giving me a rush and making me nervous. Lacing his fingers through mine, he squeezed. "What would you like to do, Amelia?"

We arrived at the lobby before I had the chance to consider an answer. The four of us gathered by the exit. I was struck at how normal we must have appeared to everyone else but how uncomfortable it felt to be a part of this group.

"I totally spaced on this, Lia," Stephanie blurted. "I really do want us to hang out. Let's go for a little while. We'll toast to your engagement and have a fun night."

Since my hand was still knotted with Alastair's, I felt him stiffen.

Brent regarded both of us with surprise. "Engagement?"

"Oh shit," Stephanie mumbled. "I didn't mean to…oh shit."

"It's alright, Stephanie," Alastair answered with ease. Shocked to hear his calm tone, I looked up at him. He was enclosed in his protective shield, leveling a dispassionate gaze at Brent. "It's already been online today and the news was bound to spread eventually."

The muscles in Brent's jaw tightened as he held Alastair's stare. "Then it's settled. You'll both come tonight and we'll drink to your happiness." His smile was as effortless as it was taunting. The last thing I wanted was to spend several hours faking niceties with him and a bunch of strangers.

"We'll be over at eight," Alastair said, mirroring Brent's disingenuous smile.

Stephanie and I exchanged glances. If nothing else, this night would be interesting.

* * *

No matter how hard I attempted to engage Alastair in conversation on the ride back to his house, he remained stony and silent. I marched to the bedroom as soon as we walked in, tossing my bag on the bed. I knew he followed me into the room, I could feel his presence.

"Do you want to explain what the hell that was all about?" I asked. "You've been gone all week and now I have to spend an evening with Brent Garrison?"

He leaned against the doorframe and fixed a hard stare on me. "We can't avoid him forever, Lia. Glasgow is smaller than you think. We're going to be in similar social circles so the sooner we get this out of the way—"

"Get this out of the way?" I yelled. "This is our engagement, not a decree to be sent to some torture chamber. And it's also not a goddam game. I've told you already that what we have isn't some ace in your pocket to whip out when you want to make yourself feel superior."

"Enough," he said through clenched teeth. "I would rather stay home in bed with you all night than go to his house but we have to."

"Why?"

He steeled his expression, clenching his fists. "We just have to."

Frustrated at his lack of answers, I paced the room. "When did you become so concerned about what other people think?"

"I'm not. I don't give a shit what these people think of me but I do care what they might say about you."

"What could they possibly have to say about me?" I spread my arms in a grand gesture. "The headlines say it all. I'm just some piece of American arm candy who bagged Britain's wealthiest, most eligible bachelor who, up until this past spring, screwed women for fun until he got what he wanted and dumped them."

I couldn't stop the awful words from pouring out. The air was sucked right out of the room within seconds. Guilt surged through me at lightning speed. My mouth had a way of running off on a tangent when I became overemotional. I regretted every syllable.

"Alastair, I'm…it's just when you're quiet and shut me out like you did in the car it bothers me. You know how I get when I start overthinking."

Cloudy, tortured eyes held my remorseful gaze before shifting their attention to the floor. "Is that how you think people look at us? That you're just a conquest for me? Someone I don't deserve to have in my life?"

He paled, sending me into a panic. I bolted across the room and held his face.

"I shouldn't have said that. You know you deserve me."

He looked away, disbelieving my words. Nausea rolled my stomach. I could never stand it when Stephanie played on my deepest fears and here I was, doing exactly that to the man I loved. "Hey," I whispered, stroking his cheek. "Look at me."

Swallowing hard, he did as I asked. The love that burned in his eyes dimmed. "This isn't going to get any easier, Lia. The public curiosity will be insatiable. You're like a new toy for the press to play with."

"I can handle it."

"You're not in Orlando anymore. This isn't some online blog run by a small time reporter. These people are relentless. They'll use you to get to me because they know I'm vulnerable now."

"Are you saying you don't want to marry me?" I couldn't even get the words out.

"Amelia." He cupped the back of my neck. "At some point you might be wondering why *you* want to marry *me*."

"That's ridiculous. I'd marry you tonight if you wanted. You need to stop it with the paranoia about my leaving you."

He scowled. "One headline called you a piece of arm candy and you couldn't handle it. The skeletons in my closet will always be there for you to use as ammunition." He stared at me with no emotion. "Get changed so we can leave soon." With that, he left the room.

Well, this night was getting better and better by the second, wasn't it? He had a point though. I went right for the jugular the second I felt threatened by his silence and the unknown. Grabbing a dark red cotton dress from the closet, I changed and went to the living room. Alastair stood by the fireplace, holding one of the framed photos of us I'd put out. A weird sense of deja vu consumed me. I went over to him and placed my hand on his back, feeling the warmth of his skin bleed through the cotton shirt.

Turning, he lifted an eyebrow and looked right through me, leaving a chill in my bones. He was angry and rightfully so. Desperation to make things right bubbled through me. Leaning close, I kissed the corner of his mouth. "Do we have time to make up before we go?"

Placing the photo back on the mantel, he traced his dark gaze down to the hem of my dress and back up. The tiny hairs on my arm stood at attention when he skimmed his fingers along my skin. I wet my lips as a reflex, knowing it would elicit a soft moan from him. Hovering his lips above mine, he parted them. I did the same, anticipating his kiss. He pulled back just as our mouths were about to touch. The denial made my lower abdomen clench.

Stroking my cheek, his intense stare burned through me. He slanted his head and leaned in again. I trembled with want when his damp, warm breath tickled the edge of my parted lips. Tilting his head away, he denied me a second time. I could feel the tremendous vibrations of my heart in my throat. He was toying with me. I reached up to touch him and was halted by his firm grasp.

"Kiss me," I begged, arching my back so I pressed against his chest. "Please."

"Why do you doubt my love for you?"

"I don't. I would never doubt that."

"I know you're frustrated. So am I. Neither one of us handled this well." His eyes hardened to stone. "And I know you would never doubt how I feel about you but—" He faltered, catching himself and reeling in any trace of emotion. "I hate arguing with you."

Caught in his dark stare, I leaned closer, pulled to him by the unrelenting magnetic force that connected us. "I'm sorry."

Our lips were on the brink of touching but he restrained me with such force I couldn't get what I wanted. My arms ached from his powerful hold. I didn't fight him. I couldn't. He was in control and I had no choice but to pay for my words.

"Do you want me to kiss you?" he asked, releasing my arms and tracing his thumb over my mouth.

"More than anything," I whispered, losing myself in his feather light touch. "Please don't be angry with me."

Softening his expression, Alastair tipped my chin up. "I'm not angry." A wicked grin curled his sculpted lips, which he'd now poised dangerously close to mine. "I will kiss you. But not now. And when I do, it will be much more than a kiss. Let's go."

Following him out the door on shaky legs, I remained in a silent daze on the ride over to Brent's. I didn't register where he lived or pay much attention to the building. I was so hot and bothered by Alastair's impromptu game that I almost didn't greet Brent when he opened the door. Finding my composure, I smiled in the most pleasant way I could and walked into the foyer.

Brent led us through a large sitting room that was draped in sleek, modern decorations. Large French doors led out to a brick patio that must be great to use when entertaining on a warm summer night. Too bad it was a bit chilly out tonight. Music and laughter wafted in from another room.

"Everyone's in here," Brent said, leading us toward the rest of the guests. I noticed a gorgeous spiral staircase and wondered if he'd give us the whole tour.

The main living room had an open, airy floor plan that blended into the kitchen. I saw Stephanie chatting with her boss, Cassie, by the breakfast bar. The unmistakable sound of someone knocking a glass with a spoon or butter knife filled the air. I cringed, turning toward the noise and saw that Brent was the source.

Alastair stood next to me with a possessive arm wrapped around my waist.

"Everyone," Brent said.

The guests quieted down and glanced in our direction. All of them knew who Alastair was but looked at me with growing curiosity.

"I know this was just going to be a quiet little gathering but I have exciting news." Brent smiled at me and I almost bolted out the door. "Someone has tamed the elusive Alastair Holden. This is Amelia Meyers, the new executive producer for The Archer Hour. Let me be the first to congratulation her and Alastair on their engagement."

Quiet shock filled the room for several seconds before some of the guests whispered to each other. A few of the women looked me up and down and shook their heads almost in sympathy. I stiffened, knowing that Alastair's reputation still preceded him. Brent signaled to a young man dressed in all black. He scurried over carrying a tray with two filled champagne flutes.

Concentrating as hard as I could, I lifted a glass for myself and waited for Alastair to grab his.

"A toast," Brent said, raising his glass, "to the soon to be Mr. and Mrs. Holden. Here's to a lifetime of happiness."

This had to be the most awkward, insincere toast I'd ever witnessed. People sipped and stared and then went about their business, throwing quick glances at me over their shoulders. I downed the champagne in one gulp, wishing the floor would swallow me whole. Now I knew why Alastair would make an appearance at these things and leave after only twenty minutes.

"Congratulations."

My heart froze upon hearing that light, airy voice. Olivia walked into view seconds later, smiling at both of us.

# CHAPTER SEVEN

I thought maybe I was being punk'd or having one of those lucid dreams where I was aware of everything happening around me but couldn't fully wake up. Olivia stood in front of us, smiling as though this was as normal as breathing.

"This is really very exciting," she gushed. "Have you set a date?"

"No," Alastair answered, shooting her a warning glance.

She moved closer to me and placed her hand on my arm. Her fingers were so cold and bony it made me uncomfortable. "If I were you, I'd run off to the Maldives or somewhere gorgeous and warm. Sergio wanted an autumn wedding in Italy otherwise I'd have it on a tropical island."

I smiled, I think, and made a little noise that I hoped sounded like a laugh.

"Did you get my invitation, Lia?" Olivia released my arm and looked at me with her big, round blue eyes.

Alastair's grip on my waist tightened. I inhaled slowly, hoping to keep an impassive expression on my face. "I did. Thank you for inviting me but—"

"I hope you can come. I don't have many girl friends and Brent always says such nice things about you. Besides, it could be a chance for us to get to know one another better. I feel horrible our meeting in New York was so," she paused, "brief."

I couldn't get a definite read on what her end game was. She sounded genuine and wasn't looking at Alastair in that wistful, lovesick way she'd done at the restaurant in New York. In fact, she barely acknowledged his existence.

"At least consider it." Her smile added a soft glow to her already ethereal aura. Maybe the champagne bubbles had gone to my head too fast.

"There you are." Stephanie descended on us like an angel from heaven. "That was awfully nice of your brother to say those kind words, wasn't it?" she asked, dazzling Olivia with her brightest smile.

"Absolutely," she grinned. "I'm going to mingle a bit but hope to catch up with you all later."

She hadn't been gone more than five seconds when Alastair planted a brusque kiss on my temple and excused himself. I watched him disappear around the corner and fought an urge to follow him.

"What's up with Stony McStoic?" Stephanie asked, folding her arms.

"Oh, let's see. He's at the home of a guy he doesn't like who took it upon himself to announce our engagement to a room full of snobby people. And, wait for it, his ex-girlfriend is also here and decided to chat with us like we're all a bunch of old college friends at a reunion. Pick one."

"Okay, okay," she held up her hands, "it was a stupid question."

"So how did this party slip your mind?" I gave her a look.

Chewing on her bottom lip, Stephanie searched the room for an answer that wouldn't come. "I really wasn't planning on coming. He asked me last week and I told him maybe. Then he asked me again at lunch the other day and I said maybe and then he showed up at my office and…he doesn't really take too well to hearing 'no.'"

"I know that all too well," I muttered.

"This will be painless. You can hang out with me all night if that helps."

I rolled my neck in the hopes it would relieve some of the tension. Stephanie sighed and put on her I'm-going-to-make-it-all-better face.

"You're handling yourself really well, Lia. I'm serious. I mean, I can tell you're pissed off and uncomfortable because I know you but these other people have no clue. You're almost as good at the blank look as Alastair."

I snorted. "Really? I pretty much assumed I looked like a deer in headlights."

"Nope. You only get that look when you're thinking of sexy time with your man."

My jaw dropped. Stephanie laughed so loud some people nearby gave her a dirty look.

"It was just a hunch. Thanks for confirming it."

Shaking my head, I laughed with her. The absurdity of this night began to outweigh the stress. "I'm so glad you're here. It was bad enough when I had to rub elbows with all the hoity-toity people Nathan knew. I mean, I can talk to anybody but I was not in the mood for this tonight."

"I hear ya," she said, slinging her arm around my shoulders. "Sorry I opened my big yap about your engagement in front of Brent. I know how private Alastair is."

"It was bound to come out sooner or later."

"Will you two be leaving early? I know you said he was away all week. I'm sure this wasn't how he wanted to spend his Friday night."

"I'm keeping my fingers crossed we can leave in the next half hour." I sighed. "Tonight has just completely gone off the rails."

"What happened?"

I flicked my wrist to ward off her question. "Nothing. Just a misunderstanding."

"Try not to let it bug you. I know what a massive over thinker you are." She gave my shoulder a quick squeeze. "This is a hot little dress. Go find that fiancé of yours and loosen him up. I'm going to shake some hands and network."

I smiled at my vivacious best friend as she glided across the room, greeting complete strangers with ease. Her idea of finding Alastair and loosening him up was great one. Making my way through the room I was stopped a few times and congratulated by some of the people. They were mostly employees at Summit and some of them seemed nice enough. Although one woman gave me such a sour look my mouth almost puckered.

"I know you."

I turned toward the unfamiliar voice and found myself face to face with a young guy in jeans and a sweater.

"Yeah," he smiled, "we met at some cocktail party last spring. I bought you all those martinis and then you disappeared. Broke my heart."

Remembering that night was a bit of struggle thanks to 'all those martinis' so I couldn't for the life of me place this guy.

"I'm really sorry, I don't—"

"Remember," he finished for me. "That's understandable. You've been swept off your feet by the billionaire playboy. Although I do remember you fancied rubbing my head. Should've grabbed you and kissed you when I had the chance." He sauntered away and started talking to a group of guys. I remained frozen in place for a few seconds.

*Rubbed his head? Oh God…Bill-Jack.*

I was stopped by another one of Brent's employees named Tania who worked in his media relations department. She joked with me about how Brent always hands out his business card to television or radio people when he goes on interviews.

"It's his version of recruiting," she laughed.

"That's not a bad way to find new talent. Nobody knows the media like someone who works in it."

"Very true. In all seriousness, if you ever get sick of Archer, give us a call. One of our account executives is going on maternity leave at the end of the month. We're thinking of bringing someone in to handle her accounts and then hire on full time after she returns."

"Well, thanks but I'm okay where I am now."

Tania regarded me shrewdly. "You know Archer is a right prat. Likes to feel up the ladies when nobody's looking. You're a pretty little thing. He'll have his hands on that hourglass figure of yours in no time. I'd be careful."

Great. What started out as a fun conversation had gone downhill fast. I politely excused myself to regroup in a corner. I almost wished I was in a room filled with politicians instead of these people. Not all of them were bad but the staring and the whispers were getting on my nerves. I helped myself to a glass of sparkling wine and scanned the room for Stephanie and Alastair. Both of them had vanished.

"Fantastic," I muttered, leaving the empty glass on an end table.

"Lia."

I turned, coming face to face with none other than Sarah Everett, the vice president at Stephanie and Darren's agency.

*Could this night get any more awesome?*

The blonde with the over-glossed lips grinned at me in the same disingenuous way she'd done at the charity benefit when I bumped into her in the ladies' room. Images of that picture with her wrapped around Alastair from his grandfather's retirement party saturated my memory. I clenched my hands so tight my fingernails dug into the skin.

"You've done the impossible. I thought Alastair would remain unattached forever." She frowned, looking me up and down. "You've broken quite a few hearts in this city."

I bit back an acrid response for two reasons: she wasn't worth it and I didn't want to make a scene in a room where every eye was focused on me.

Her chin lifted. "Your friend Stephanie speaks very highly of you in the office. I'm sorry you and I haven't run into one another yet in the building. We should plan to have lunch one day next week. We're considering partnering with The Archer Hour for some magazine adverts in the coming months. I'd love to hear your thoughts on the direction of the program."

*I'd rather dance barefoot on hot coal.*

"Sure. Give me a call on Monday." I hoped to God that didn't sound forced.

"Brilliant." She smiled. "And really, my sincerest congratulations. You must be one special woman to have melted the ice man."

Sarah sauntered off, leaving me annoyed and fed up with this damn party and these people. I knew she'd been trying to land Alastair for years. Being here played on my insecurities more than I anticipated. Knowing that Olivia and now Sarah were hovering close to a man they lusted after made my skin prickle with jealousy. I became suspicious of every woman in the room, wondering which one had spent a hot night with the billionaire orphan. I shouldn't feel this way at all but it was impossible to ignore his *I-don't-date-I-just-get-laid* reputation.

*Stop it. He's marrying me, not them.*

Brushing off the self-doubt, I made my way toward the front hall.

"I wonder what the grandfather thinks of her," I overheard someone say as I walked past a group of partygoers. "He might not be too keen on leaving his precious empire in the hands of some American who spread her legs for his grandson."

I whipped around to see which one of these pretentious assholes said that. Too bad none of them had the balls to look me in the eye.

"That's what I thought," I said, glaring in their direction. "No class cowards."

A couple of the guys fidgeted with their ties and broke away from the group. One woman smiled at me in sympathy before walking toward the bar.

Slipping out into the main foyer I exhaled and gathered my wits. I was letting all of this external noise affect me too much. It wasn't like I hadn't been scrutinized by high society men and women before. Maybe I just didn't notice it as much because I'd been so damn dazzled by Nathan and all the parties he'd brought me to had hundreds of attendees, not a couple dozen. Then again, I was in Alastair's world now. I hadn't been subjected to it yet and really didn't know what to expect. The Holden World Media spotlight burned bright and I was the newest attraction in the center of the ring.

I sat on one of the steps on the spiral staircase and wondered what my friends in Orlando were doing. A pang of sadness swept through me. I did miss them but knew this was where I belonged now.

As I stood up, I could hear voices coming from upstairs and figured maybe that's where Stephanie and Alastair went. When I reached the landing at the top I didn't see anyone. The second floor was just as beautiful as the main one. I had to hand it to these guys, they knew how to live the good life. I noticed the bathroom was to my left so I took the opportunity to use it. The voices I thought I'd heard sounded again. They were coming from an open window next to the sink. Curious to know who it was, I went closer to the window. The voices became clearer. I peeked out and noticed a balcony but couldn't see anybody.

"I want her to be there."

My heart seized. *That's Olivia's voice.*

"You had no business inviting her. I asked you to respect the boundaries we agreed upon and still you defy me."

*Alastair.*

"I don't see the harm in this," Olivia whined. "I like her. She seems nice and I think we could become friends."

I heard the bitterness in Alastair's laugh. "Do you know how fucked up that is? You and I aren't even friends. I sure as hell don't want you anywhere near Lia."

"You're being paranoid. I'm not going to say anything to her about our past, remember? You made that crystal clear when you flew out here in a panic this summer."

I clutched onto the windowsill. I'd always suspected that was why he'd disappeared to London for two days. Hearing it still stung though.

"Christ," he muttered. "I'm not discussing that again."

The sound of heels clicking on stone resonated through the night. She must have been pacing.

"Just stay away from her. Please."

The pacing stopped.

"Why does it have to be this way between us, Alastair? So much time has passed. Can't you just—"

"I am not risking my relationship with the only woman I've ever truly loved just because you want me to forget about everything that happened with us. It *has* been a long time yet you still find ways to antagonize the situation. I'll say it again. Leave her alone."

"You mean to tell me she satisfies you in every way?"

Thick silence bullied its way through the night, reaching in through the window and suffocating me. *I should go before I hear anything I don't want to know.*

"Do you miss it, Alastair? Do you miss the excitement and lack of inhibition of what we did? I can't even count how many weekends we never left the bed—"

"That's enough," he snapped.

"You'll get tired of her. I know you. Being with the same person isn't your style. It's not something you can survive on for the rest of your life." Her heels sounded off the stone again. I could only assume she was moving closer to him. The thought made my skin crawl.

"Tell me again, what you said to me that night in the French Riviera." Her words oozed with seduction and temptation.

"No." I heard shoes scuffle and scrape. "This conversation is over."

"I'm the one who should be with you, not her. After everything we shared together, I should be your fiancée." Her loud declaration filled the night air. "Don't you ever forget about that, Alastair. You asked me first."

I sat down hard on the edge of the bathtub. *Asked her first?*

I looked down at the diamond ring he'd given me. The ring that belonged to his mother. The ring that he'd said sat at the Holden Estate until he was ready to marry. I couldn't stop the tsunami of thoughts that drowned me. Any rational line of thinking failed to break through my panic.

He wanted to marry *her*?

All the hurt and anger I'd felt while being used by Nathan bubbled to the surface. I knew I shouldn't project that situation onto this one but it was hard not to. *I'm so tired of being screwed over by these rich assholes.*

I nearly ripped the knob off the door when I opened it and stormed into the hallway. Rooms extended to the left and right. I had half a mind to go in all of them until I found Olivia and yanked every piece of blonde hair out of that head of hers. Jealousy and fear whittled my vision down to one specific beam of light: I had to get her away from the love of my life. Alastair was mine, not hers. She lost any claim to him when she blackmailed his family.

The voices had been coming from the left so I went into the nearest room on that end of the hallway. It was dark. I thought I heard a sigh and turned my attention to a set of French doors. They were ajar and led to a balcony.

*This girl is going to wish she never met me. The little bitch.*

I heard another sigh and a voice as I pushed the door open. "Tell me again." The quiet stillness of the night was interrupted by a plea. *Olivia.*

A moan of pleasure echoed on the breeze, taunting me. My throat went dry. According to my brain, Olivia and Alastair were now fucking on the balcony. Rage and horror shook my entire body as I forced myself to walk outside.

There were two people fucking alright: Stephanie and Brent.

# CHAPTER EIGHT

Bursting out into the hallway I ran nose first into a cotton, button down shirt.

"Amelia, watch out. Are you alright?" Alastair's rich voice slid through my bloodstream.

Snapping my head up, I backed away but didn't go very far thanks to the rather tight hold he had on me. "I'm all set with this party. I'm leaving."

"Okay," he said, studying me with caution. "First you need to tell me what happened and why you came tearing out of that bedroom. If I hadn't been coming this way you'd have launched yourself right down those stairs."

"First, you need to let me go." Exasperated, I wrenched my arms out of his grip. What I saw on the balcony paled in comparison to what I'd overheard. "As for what happened in there? Just Stephanie and Brent screwing each other's brains out. No big deal."

Alastair's eyebrows shot up. I glared at him.

"I'm going outside. Maybe you should go back to Olivia and continue reliving that night in the French Riviera." I took off down the stairs before he had a chance to respond. The cool night air coasted over my red hot skin. I was half way down the block before I realized I had no clue where the hell I was going. Footsteps pounded on the cement behind me seconds before a hand clamped down on my arm.

"Don't run away from me like that," Alastair snapped, turning me to face him. "Dammit, Lia."

I held his ominous emerald gaze with my own penetrating stare. "Let go of me."

His expression faltered when he dropped my arm. "I didn't mean to grab you…I just…what the fuck is going on?"

"I heard everything you guys said. I was in the bathroom and I heard Olivia telling you that I can't possibly satisfy you and that you'll get bored with me and…" The more I rattled off every disgusting detail of their conversation the more upset I became. I shook so violently I could barely stand.

"Amelia," he whispered, cupping my cheeks, "calm down."

"I will not calm down. She said you wanted to marry her," I yelled.

Pulling my forehead to his, Alastair tightened his hold on my face. "Fuck," he hissed. "It's not true. I told you she wanted more when I broke it off. She couldn't handle it then and she can't handle it now. She only said that to get under my skin. I'm so sorry you heard it."

"I don't believe you."

Alastair bared his teeth and swore under his breath. "You're overreacting. She loves nothing more than to goad me on and get a reaction. I never wanted to marry her. Never."

Unbridled love burned in his eyes, making it hard for me to look away. He was right about my overreacting. He knew me better than I knew myself sometimes. Relief swept through me with such power that I collapsed into his arms and let him hold me for as long as he wanted. Burying his face against my neck he sighed.

"My Lia. You are the only one I want to marry. You are the only one I love."

Lifting my head, I gasped when he crushed his lips to mine. This was not a gentle kiss. This was spine-tingling and lip-bruising. He kissed me as though his life depended on it, like he'd wither away and die if he didn't. Breaking our mouths apart he ran his knuckles down my cheek.

"Come with me."

Lacing his fingers through mine, he led me back to the car. He didn't let go of me while he sped through the streets of Glasgow. Every few minutes he'd kiss my knuckles or the back of my hand as he drove. I stared at him under the lights and shadows of the street lights, captivated by the determined look in his eyes. The only time he let go of my hand was to make a phone call.

"We're on our way now. Have it fueled and ready."

Minutes later we pulled through the security gate at the airport and parked. Helping me out of the car, Alastair kissed me again and then led me into the hanger where his plane waited. I didn't even ask where we were going, I was just so happy to be away from that party, those people and Olivia.

*   *   *

*Long, lazy bubble baths cure everything*, I thought as I slipped into a white, fluffy robe. I glanced around the hotel suite, charmed by its unassuming glamour and mesmerized by the gorgeous views of London. I would have remained frozen in place if not for the promise of cheeseburgers and ice cream waiting for me in the suite's living room. Alastair was standing by a massive picture window, arms crossed, staring out into the night.

"Have you been standing there the whole time?" I asked, hoping I didn't sound as nervous as I felt.

"Yes." He flicked a curious gaze in my direction. "Are you feeling any better?"

I fidgeted with the robe's belt and shrugged. Our eyes remained locked as a cloud of uncertainty hovered above us. The usual electric connection that bound us together seemed muted. My heart fluttered.

Tonight had been disastrous on all fronts. If I could, I'd press a giant reset button.

Alastair paced the room, raking both hands through his hair. His strides were full of purpose, measured and strong. When he stopped, he stared right through me. In an instant, he was in front of me, hands firmly on my hips. "I love you. I shouldn't have forced you to go to Brent's tonight. I shouldn't have put you through that." He cupped my jaw. "I've lived my life a certain way for so long. There are certain expectations that come with being in my position. That's not an excuse, I know. Having you here…I'm… all I want is for you to feel safe and loved and happy."

His smile lit my soul on fire. That was my smile, the one he saved only for me. I relaxed in his embrace, finally feeling the stress and tension of the night sliding away.

"We're both adjusting as best we can, Holden. I promise not to fly off the handle if you promise not to be so closed off."

"Sounds fair enough."

"Good." I looked up into his big green eyes and smiled. "Now where are those cheeseburgers?"

The room filled with the sound of his throaty laugh. "You have a one track mind. We'll eat in a little while." He tugged at the belt holding my robe together. A rush of cool air tickled at my bare skin when it fell open. "We've had too many interruptions this week."

Goosebumps scattered across my arms and shoulders when he slid the robe down to my elbows.

"All I could think about every day we were apart was you." The damp warmth of his lips glided down my neck. "Come with me."

Without much effort, he pulled me toward an oversized chair and sat. I straddled him, combing my fingers through his disheveled hair.

"I want to start tonight over. Can we do that?" he asked, nuzzling his nose along the curve of my breasts.

"I'd like to."

"There is no one else for me but you. The outside noise is just that. Noise."

I swallowed down a hot, salty lump. "Did you ever love her?"

"No." He brushed his thumb over my lips.

"And do I—"

Fisting his hand through my hair, he pressed his mouth to mine. I parted my lips, sighing into his kiss. The quiet stillness of the suite was amplified by Alastair's soft moans, kick starting my pulse with a vengeance. I pulled his hair, eliciting the low growl that drove me crazy. Like a woman possessed, I grabbed at the waistband of his pants, unbuttoning them and tugging down the zipper. I stood up long enough to yank his pants and boxer briefs off, tossing them to the floor with little fanfare. Staring at him, I let my eyes move slowly along his body. There had never been a more beautiful man created. *Perfection*. Sitting like a king on his throne, he pulled me onto his lap, pressing his fingers into the flesh of my lower back, holding me in place. I shifted, unable to move.

"Lia." The quiet, lust-fueled way he said my name matched the heated glow in his eyes. "Let me." He removed the robe, leaving a trail of kisses in its wake.

Slipping further and further into his magnetic sphere, I submitted to him, losing myself with every caress. Unaware of anything but his mouth on my skin, I shivered when my back touched something cold. Looking to my left in a foggy, lust-filled haze I barely registered that he now had me plastered against the picture window.

A steady ache grew at my core when he ran his tongue along his lower lip. Blood pounded in my ears, seeming to echo through the room.

Using both hands, and starting at my shoulders, he traced along the contours of my body with slow, deliberate strokes. His fingers moved around the curves of my breasts, pausing to brush against the nipples before gliding down my stomach. I shuddered and clenched my thighs together as he knelt down, caressing my hips and pressing a light kiss just below my bellybutton. Every touch was more gentle than the last, sending jolts of pleasure cascading through me.

"Alastair," I whispered.

In a split second, his lips hovered over mine as the warmth and strength of his body pressed me against the window. Lost in his scent and the security of feeling him so close, I ran my nails on the curve of his backside.

"Don't stop."

"*Lia*," he hissed, thrusting into me hard and deep, over and over until my body quaked.

Keeping our bodies connected, he walked to the bedroom and placed me on the mattress. Blanketed by the strength, both physically and sexually, of his body, I focused on nothing but his sounds and the way he felt moving inside me. As gentle as he'd been by the window, he was now ravaging me, transforming into the unbridled lover I craved. I grabbed at the glistening flesh on his back, reveling in his animalistic movements.

"Come with me," he panted, feverishly pumping his hips. "I need you to come with me."

I sank deeper into the plush bedding, enclosed by the full weight of his body. An intense tingling surged through me, signaling that I was almost ready. As his thrusting grew faster and harder, I rolled my hips to match his rhythm.

"That's my girl."

I felt him swell inside me and clutched his ass, digging my nails into his skin. He grunted, pushing harder. I arched my back, gasping and clawing at the sheets.

"You feel too good," I cried out. My mind went blank, wiped clear of any conscious thoughts. A sharp, rapid throbbing pulsed through me, almost as though my body was trying to turn itself inside out. Alastair pushed himself up onto his forearms, locking a molten emerald stare on me.

"Now, Lia," he said in a husky groan. "Come with me now."

An explosive orgasm shook and gripped me, not letting go. The world shut off. I couldn't hear if Alastair was finished. I was just so lost in the paralysis and complete euphoria of this moment that I didn't even realize I'd been holding my breath.

Exhaling, I knew every muscle had been rendered useless. The utter lack of control I had over how my body responded to him in bed was amazing. If I wasn't so spent, I'd ask him to do it again. I was so relaxed. So. Relaxed.

"Open your eyes." Alastair's silky accent coaxed me back to the real world.

"They're closed?"

"Yes, love."

I heard the amusement in his voice and was pleased to see a smile on his lips when my lids fluttered open. "You're so goddam beautiful, Alastair Holden," I said before closing them again. "If I could move, I'd kiss you."

He chuckled quietly. "Would you like some water?"

"Yes, please."

The bed shifted when he climbed off. I had enough presence of mind to open my eyes and watch him walk toward the small bar to grab the water bottles. *I will never get over how freaking hot he is.* My body responded with a subtle tingle and a faint pleasurable throb.

"That smile will only encourage me to give a repeat perfor-mance." He smirked, handing me the water.

"Must be nice to be able to walk around freely after all that."

"You dozed off for a few minutes so you clearly missed me lying paralyzed next to you."

"I did?"

"Yep. Passed out cold."

Alastair had a sip of his water and curled up close to me, resting his hand on my stomach. Sporting the ruffled hair and satisfied expression of a guy who'd just had great sex, he lowered his heavy lids, his long lashes splaying out above his cheeks. A faint smile curled his mouth.

"You're still staring," he said, pressing his fingers into the soft flesh of my stomach.

"You're still so goddam beautiful."

"Mmm." He wrapped himself around me like a vine. I loved being draped in him. I felt so protected and safe. And he smelled amazing. He nuzzled into my neck, squeezing me tighter. "Stay close to me."

"Any closer and we'd be conjoined twins."

"Cheeky." He opened his eyes. "And gorgeous. What have I gotten myself into with you?"

"Nothing you can't handle, chief."

The sight of his genuine, effortless smile lit up my soul. I knew, without question, I was the reason for his happiness.

"What this look does to me," I said, touching his cheek.

"So that's all it takes, huh? A soppy grin after a roll in the sack?"

"Among other things, smart ass."

He pressed a kiss to my nose and laughed. My God, it was such a wonderful sound. I didn't want to say anything more. I didn't want to tarnish this moment with superfluous words that couldn't possibly explain how I felt.

"You're so deep in thought, kitten." His husky tone had me firing on all cylinders once again.

"I just really love seeing you this way. You're so happy and playful and carefree and…" I struggled to find the right thing to say. "There's so much to love about you and…I hope you hold onto this feeling whenever you want to withdraw or shut out the world."

His eyes opened wider and wider the more I spoke. Flustered, I sighed.

"I'm not saying any of this right. That's why I must have looked so deep in thought. I can't find the words, I can only lose myself in the feeling."

Cupping my jaw, he swallowed hard and blew out a shaky sigh. For a split second I was terrified I'd let my mouth run too wild and he'd shrink back into his shell like he always did. To my immense pleasure, he secured his hold around me, resting his forehead to mine.

"I was thinking we could visit your sister tomorrow, seeing as we're in town. Would you like that?"

I hadn't seen my sister Dayna in months. I'd love nothing more than to spend some time with her.

"Sounds like a plan," I said, raising an eyebrow. "Does she already know about our engagement, too?"

"Maybe."

"Is there anybody in my family that you didn't tell and then swear to secrecy?"

"No." He flashed his megawatt smile. "They're all quite excited for us."

"You stole my thunder, Holden. That's a no-no."

"I'm sure I can find a way to make it up to you." Desire burned in my throat as he drew nondescript shapes on my stomach and devoured me with dark, molten eyes. "Have I told you how absolutely exquisite you are? I could admire you like this for hours."

"Flattery will get you everywhere. So will those cheeseburgers you promised me."

"I have a better idea." He stood up, slipping on some cotton pajama bottoms. "Feel free to join me."

"Sure thing." I hopped out of bed and rummaged through the closet for something to wear. As per usual, Alastair had an arsenal of clothes at the ready for both of us. I'd long since given up asking where it all came from. Instead of choosing one of the little silk nighties he liked so much, I opted for one of his button down shirts. There was something indescribably sexy about wearing his clothes. The shirt hung on me like a mini dress. I even had to roll up the sleeves.

I trotted out to the main sitting area and perched on the back of the oversized chair. "Hey, can I ask you something?"

Alastair raked me with his eyes before answering. "Of course."

"While you were away I was sort of looking through that book shelf in the living room." I paused, gauging his reaction. As usual, there was none. "Anyway, I found an old journal that belonged to your mom."

"Did you read it?"

"What? No. I only opened the front cover and saw her name."

"What do you want to know about it?" Tension clung to each word.

"Nothing. I was just wondering what other keepsakes you had at your house, aside from the old books. Do you have any family photos lying around from when you were little? I could have them fra—"

"Everything is boxed away in Ascot." His hands were clenched. "I only have those few items with me in Glasgow. It's more than enough."

"Oh. Okay." I decided to cease all discussion of his parents, keenly aware of how agitated he'd become. It frustrated me on so many levels. At some point, he had to stop blaming himself for their deaths and move on. I'd never say it to his face though, at least not yet. I feared it would ignite an argument that I'd lose hands down.

Determined not to lose the relaxed, blissful atmosphere we'd created in the bedroom, I smiled and hopped off the chair. "Come over here, Holden."

Sizing me up cautiously, Alastair folded his arms. I went to the window and waited. He hugged me from behind, nuzzling into my neck. "I'm really trying not to be such an ass when you ask about them," he said after a few minutes, his lips brushing along my skin. "It's getting easier with you even though it may not look that way."

I kept my focus locked on the London Eye as it glowed against the midnight sky. "Remember the night you took me on there?"

"How could I forget?"

"Do you still have places you want to show me here in England?"

Tightening his arms around my waist, he sighed. "Yes."

I turned to face him, enraptured by the way he looked at me.

"Why don't we do some of that tomorrow? We can have dinner with my sister and Andrew but I'd like to spend the day with you as my tour guide."

"Tour guide, huh?" He arched a brow. "Not sure how exciting that will be for you."

"It'll be as exciting as you make it. Get planning, chief."

"Alright. But I have one condition."

"Of course you do."

Grinning, he squeezed my waist. "You are not allowed to ask me where I'm taking you."

"Why not?"

He tipped up my chin and gave me a quick kiss. "You know why. I like surprising you. See? Even now those big, beautiful eyes are filled with curiosity and mischief. I enjoy this look almost as much as the one you have when you want to do filthy things to me."

"But I always want to do filthy things to you. I don't have time for other 'looks.'"

I got the reaction I wanted from him: a hearty laugh that filled the room. I made a silent vow that this weekend would be the one where he finally turned the page on his past and fully opened himself up to the bright future that he deserved.

# CHAPTER NINE

Quiet conversation hummed through the cozy, warm pub. I loved how the interior looked more like someone's living room than a restaurant. All the creature comforts of home oozed from each corner; a fire crackled to ward off the damp chill of the outdoors, plush chairs beckoned to be curled up on for those lucky to nab one, and there was enough carb heavy food to satisfy the most ravenous of cravings.

"Am I succeeding at my tour guide duties?" Alastair asked, sipping his beer. He looked nervous which was impossible. The guy had ice water in his veins.

"So far. What's the story behind this place?"

He shrugged slightly, avoiding eye contact. "I'd come here all the time when I was at Oxford. It was sort of my place to go when I didn't want to be around people."

"You must have been here a lot then," I teased.

Fidgeting with the glass, he kept his eyes downcast. His usual expressionless demeanor was betrayed by the uncertainty clouding his features. "Aside from the cottage, this was the most out of the way place I'd go to get away."

"Why?"

"I don't know. It's just what I do, kitten. I avoid people, you know that."

"You avoid becoming emotionally attached to people. That's different." I caught his eye. "You didn't drive me out here in a torrential downpour just to have a beer and tell me you used to come here when you were in college. Spill it, Holden."

"Look who decided to come in for a pint after all these years," an unfamiliar voice with a heavy English accent boomed.

Alastair looked up and smiled, clearly aware of who had approached our table.

"Graham. Good to see you, mate." He stood up and shook his hand, turning on the Holden charm that he normally reserved for someone he didn't know. "Was in the neighborhood, so I thought I'd stop by."

"Likely story, son," Graham said with a twinkle in his eye. "And who is this lovely young woman?"

Not wanting to be rude, I stood up to introduce myself. Alastair reached for my hand, pulling me into his side. He appeared more relaxed now, which made me smile.

"This gorgeous creature is my fiancée Lia."

The blush that stained my cheeks must have been spectacular. I felt my body temperature rise. In all fairness, this was technically the first time he'd introduced me as his fiancée. I had a feeling I wouldn't ever tire of hearing him say that.

"You've got yourself a fine young man here, miss. Congratulations to both of you." Graham smiled. "Drinks are on the house along with whatever you'd like from the menu."

"Does he own this place?" I asked after Graham walked off and we sat down.

"Yes." Alastair slid onto the chair next to mine and draped his arm over my shoulders. "There haven't been many people who've treated me like a normal person in my life. Graham is one of the few who has. He's never pestered me about my family or wanted anything from me other than some good natured conversation. That's why I came here so often while at university."

His fingertips brushed the nape of my neck, sending a shiver down my spine. I watched him casually enjoy his beer and imagined him sitting here as a college student, desperate to find some uninterrupted moments to just breathe and escape the precision and control of his life. Then again, he was always in control.

"I can see the wheels spinning inside that pretty head of yours." His warm breath tickled my temple. "Are you okay?"

Enveloped by his scent and the closeness of his body, I had a hard time forming an answer. The rest of the pub seemed to disappear, fading into the backdrop of a distant world. Only Alastair remained in sharp focus.

"I'm perfect," I said, squeezing his thigh.

"Can't argue with that." He grinned, kissing me softly. "I like having you here. It feels…right."

"Were you not expecting it to feel that way?"

"I don't know." His brows furrowed. "Being with you always feels right. I guess it's just different now that I'm seeing Glasgow and London and home through your eyes. You sort of gave it all new life for me."

I kissed him. Hard. Those words meant so much that all I could do was show him how they affected me. In the months since we met, he'd become such a different person in the best way possible. At first, everything about him had screamed 'I'm going to take you and make you forget your own name.' And yes, that was true. Boy, was that true. And yes, locked in this kiss with him, I still felt his unbridled desire and that urge to dominate me in every way. But I also felt the one thing he'd shied away from for so many years: his emotion.

"Kiss me like that again in public and I won't be able to control myself," he said, placing a possessive hand on my hip. "You know what you do to me, kitten."

"Promises, promises."

A sly grin curled his lips. "I know this pub well. There's an office in the back. Tempt me again and I'll have my way with you in there."

I didn't have a chance to respond. Graham showed up with two more beers and a platter of food. As hungry as I was for what Alastair offered, the sight of the food made my stomach growl impatiently.

"I didn't follow through on my cheeseburger promise last night so I thought it best to make it up to you today."

"Thanks, chief." I smiled, grabbing a burger. He watched me eat with that little sparkle in his eye he gets anytime he sees me enjoying food.

"So you'd really come here all by yourself and just sit and have a few beers?" I asked after several minutes.

"Yup."

"You never brought a friend with you? Not even Brent?"

The question tumbled out of my mouth so easily it took a second for me to regret my words. Alastair stared at me blankly.

"Why would I socialize with him?"

"Oh. Well. Darren told me you guys were close friends in college so I assumed—"

"MacCourty told you that?"

"Yeah."

"When?"

"The other day at lunch. We were talking about the engagement and stuff and he…I don't really remember how it came up."

Alastair's discomfort bled from his pores. "We were friends for a time, if you want to call it that." He shrugged. "Then we grew apart. It happens."

"Because of the stuff with Olivia."

"Yes, Lia," he said through clenched teeth. "We've been through this."

"I know, I know. I'm sorry." I smiled sheepishly. "You know me and my curiosity. It doesn't know when to stop."

Lifting an eyebrow, he leveled a hard stare in my direction. "You're lucky I find you irresistible. I'm more focused on wanting to shag you than be annoyed with you right now."

I leaned into him, nuzzling my nose to his. "My Alastair. My moody, enigmatic, unbelievably sexy Alastair. Thank you for taking me here today and sharing another part of your past with me."

Softening his demeanor, he tucked a strand of hair behind my ear. "I love your curiosity. I love that you want to know everything about me because you have no ulterior motive. You just see me. You've always just seen me." He shifted in the chair and held my face with both hands. "You make me…" Stopping himself, he swallowed. "I can't ever imagine my life without you. The very thought of it tears me apart. You are my lifeline. Without you, I have no reason to exist."

Kissing the corner of his mouth, I whispered, "Again with the dramatics, Holden?"

"Whatever it takes."

I ruffled his hair and turned my attention back to lunch. We ate in comfortable silence, sharing a smile every so often when our eyes met. I noticed how nobody seemed to care that the billionaire orphan was enjoying a leisurely lunch with his American girlfriend. It was a nice break from the swarming photographers and nonstop internet gossip. The clientele seemed more enthralled with their own conversations and meals to bother with anybody else's business.

When I couldn't possibly fit another morsel of food in my stomach, Graham appeared at our table with a generous serving of warm, gooey chocolate bread pudding. My entire body flushed.

"Best dessert in Oxford," he said, smiling. "A favorite of yours, right Alastair?"

"Has been for years." He winked at me. "Thanks, Graham."

Two spoons sat on the table but I knew without question only one would be used. At least I hoped so. *And then maybe we could visit that back office.*

"Not this time," Alastair said, handing me a spoon. "We'll share but I want to feed you in private." He ate a spoonful and I had to steady myself watching the way his mouth wrapped around the spoon.

"Right. Point taken."

His throaty laugh quickened my already frantic pulse. "You have the most adorable little frown when you're frustrated."

"Do I?" I pursed my lips.

"Yes." He leaned in and kissed me.

"You taste like chocolate." I held onto his shirt so he remained close to me. "Can we have this wrapped up to go? I'm sure we can finish it in the hotel room."

"We're due at your sister's in a few hours. We'll never make it."

"The back office then?" My grip tightened on the material. I was raring to go and only asked as a formality.

"I think," he said, touching a spoonful of dessert to my mouth, "you should eat this."

"Are you turning me down?"

"Not quite." He slid the spoon along my lips. "Open."

As per usual, I had zero control over how I reacted when he spoke to me in that low, sensual tone. The warm, buttery chocolate bread pudding was so good that for a split second I couldn't decide what I wanted more; him or another spoonful.

"So much for wanting to feed you in private," he muttered, offering another taste. "More?"

"You have no willpower, Holden."

"Not when it comes to you." He scanned the dining area. Our table was tucked close to the corner so we were barely visible to most of the room. The few people that had been seated near us were gone, so for all intents and purposes we were alone.

He continued to feed me the bread pudding, pausing every so often for a kiss or to help himself to a scoop. He appeared so relaxed, so at peace with himself. I'd only ever seen him this way when he slept.

"Why the serious look? You're staring at me like you're never going to see me again."

"I just love your face. That's all."

"This boring old thing?" He scrunched up his nose in the cutest way. "You haven't gotten sick of it yet?"

"Shut up." I shoved him, pleased to see a wide smile spread across his face. It made him look much younger than his already youthful thirty-one years. "Finish that last bite before I do."

More than happy to oblige, he ate the rest of the bread pudding and we made our way toward the back exit. Or so I thought. Alastair grabbed my hand and pulled me into a small office so quickly I needed a second to get my bearings straight. Thank goodness I was anchored against the desk otherwise I would have toppled over from his searing kiss.

Adrenaline spiked through me. I groaned into his mouth and wrapped a leg around him. Tearing his lips from mine, he stared at me with white hot animal intensity.

"You make me lose control," he whispered, sliding his hands along my jaw. "The things you make me feel."

He fused our mouths together again, lifting me away from the desk. We stumbled through the exceptionally tiny space, bumping into filing cabinets and a potted plant while tearing each other's clothes off.

"Whose office is this?" I asked, dropping his shirt to the floor.

Pinning me to the door, he locked it before raising both my arms over my head. "Does it matter?"

"Not really."

Heavy lidded emerald irises latched onto me. "Tell me what you want," he ordered, flexing his hips so the hot stiffness of his erection pressed against me.

"You know what I want."

The sexy, confident smile of a man who knew he had complete control over the situation spread across his face. "I want to hear you say it."

"Seriously," I hissed, straining against his grasp. "Stop with the games, Holden."

"Tell me."

His mouth was so close to mine I could almost taste the chocolate. The sweetness of the dessert mixed with his natural scent and it drove me to the brink.

"I want you," I said, holding his flashing stare. "Only you."

The feel of him entering me was nothing short of spectacular. I shoved my hands through his hair, grabbing it and pulling his head back.

"Lia," he growled. Next thing I knew, he pulled out, led me to the desk chair and sat. I straddled him, gasping at the fullness and pressure as he filled me. Perspiration misted over my body with each deep thrust. Alastair grabbed my hips, holding me in place. Nothing about this screamed romance. This was pure, unadulterated fucking.

"You feel so good." He buried his face into my neck, increasing the intensity of his movements. Keeping one hand at the small of my back, he held the nape of my neck with the other. Being so connected to him in such a hidden, yet public, place sent a surge through me. Instinct took over as I dictated the pace. No matter how much he tightened his grip on me, I was in control.

With a gasp, he laid his head back. Seeing him so vulnerable, so gloriously spread beneath me was empowering.

He came with a sharp yell, snapping his head up and covering my mouth with his own. I shook from the tremors of my own orgasm, kissing him and sucking on his bottom lip.

"Jesus Christ, Lia," he panted. "I fucking love you."

"Ditto, chief."

He was still inside me and as spent and throbbing as my body was, I wanted him again.

"We have to go, kitten," he said, seeming to read my mind.

"Oh?" I slung my arms around his neck. "And who made you the boss?"

He smirked. "I just am."

"Mmm." I kissed him. "Sexy beast."

Standing up slowly, I reveled in how mind-numbingly awesome

he felt pulling out of me. I enjoyed a lingering glance at the magnificent body that I was just connected to. God help me, he was still hard. Flicking a mischievous glance in my direction, he rose to his feet with all the grace of a king and started redressing. I searched for my clothes as nonchalantly as possible but couldn't find my underwear. *Guess I'm going commando for the rest of the day.* A small mirror hung on the wall so I checked myself out. Aside from overly bright eyes and a flushed face, I looked as normal as one could after a quickie in a restaurant office. I turned and noticed my cotton panties in a heap on the floor. They were torn and left for dead.

Alastair stood by the desk watching me. "Sorry about that."

"These?" I asked, shoving the ripped undergarments in my purse. "I have more."

He grinned, picking up a nameplate off the desk. "Mary Beth Dunleavy. Assistant Manager. If she only knew the shenanigans that happened in her office on the weekend." A pained expression blanketed his otherwise sated features, making my heart seize. Running a hand through his messy post-sex hair, he cleared his throat. "Ready?"

I hooked my arms around his waist, pressing my cheek against his chest. The rapid beating of his heart hypnotized me. We stood like this for several minutes, mostly because I had a bad feeling that if I let him go, he'd shrink back behind the mask. I don't know why I felt that way, I just did.

Shoving my concerns away, I chose to focus on Alastair's soft caresses. He tilted my chin up, a small crooked smile curving his mouth. It was disarming and sweet. Seeing it set off a wave of pleasure through me.

"I love you," I said, squeezing him. "And your blatant disregard for this woman's office."

"I told you, you make me lose control."

"Good."

Opening the door, he poked his head out to see if anyone was nearby. Lacing his fingers through mine, he led me back through the pub and right into the orbit of an overzealous guy talking with Graham.

"Holden," he called, sauntering over. "Can I have a min—"

"No," he said with all the warmth of a lion who'd just been woken from a sound sleep.

"But I ha—"

"I said no." Placing a protective arm around my waist he stared down the man.

"I'm on deadline. Just one question."

"Not. Now."

I watched the guy physically shrink from intimidation, shoulders slumping in defeat. When Alastair Holden didn't want to be bothered by the press, he had no mercy. I'd been so spoiled by his softer side all day I'd almost forgotten what a hard ass he could be.

Regaining some of his composure, he straightened his spine. "Still an ornery bastard." He sized me up before continuing. "I hear there's discord among the ranks at Holden World Media. Company's about to fall apart according to my source. Care to comment?"

Stony silence filled the space between us and the reporter.

"Any comment on the accusations your uncle is—"

"Enough," Alastair growled. "Another word and I'll call your editor and have you fired."

"I struck a nerve. Then it must be true." His smug brown eyes lingered on my face for longer than was acceptably comfortable. "He's going to make you sign a pre-nup, you know. Too much money is in play."

"I said enough." Alastair moved close enough to the guy to make him lose his bravado for a second time. The last thing any of us needed was a public brawl. I'd only seen Alastair lose his temper like this around one other person.

"Told you he wasn't going to talk to you, mate," Graham said, pulling the reporter back. "Time to leave now, yeah?"

Shooting one last glance in Alastair's direction, the guy left.

"Do you know who that was?" I asked Graham.

"Local guy named Michael. He writes for the Times and likes to sniff around here when Alastair comes in." He turned to my agitated fiancé. "Haven't seen you scare the shit out of someone like that in a long while."

Scowling, Alastair muttered something under his breath before we said our goodbyes and thank yous to Graham.

The car heaved with tense silence for the entire drive to my sister's. I had half a mind to say forget it and just go back to the hotel. When Alastair's mood went dark, it stayed there for hours.

# CHAPTER TEN

Dayna flitted about the living room, placing a platter of pastries on the coffee table and filling our mugs with hot water for tea. She'd made the most delicious roasted chicken dinner with a side dish of tagliatelle in truffle butter that put me in the most awesome food coma. Having a sister that writes for a food magazine certainly had its advantages.

Her husband, Andrew, had Alastair engaged in a spirited discussion about rugby. I didn't really know what they were going on and on about, I just liked seeing Alastair with a smile on his face even if it was somewhat forced. He'd been charming and personable all through dinner but I knew his mood was still sour.

"Mom is beside herself about this wedding, you know that right? If you thought she was unbearable planning mine, just wait." Dayna joined me by the picture window. The views from her house in Gypsy Hill were stunning. The London skyline glittered in the distance.

I nodded, sipping my tea. She regarded me curiously. "Are you okay? You guys have both been on edge since you got here."

"I'm fine."

"Lia," she sighed. "You can't do the smoke screen thing with me. I know something's bothering you." She leaned closer. "Is everything okay between you two?"

"Yeah. I think there's something going on at his company though. He's been working crazy hours and going back and forth to London. He won't talk about it. Believe me, I've tried. I'm just worried that brunch with his aunt and uncle tomorrow is going to be a challenge."

"Don't obsess. His relationship with his family is what it is."

"Easy for you to say."

She pursed her lips the same way our mother did. "Stop inserting yourself into his personal drama. Whatever issues he needs to work out with them is his business. If he wants to open up and talk to you about it, he will. Until then, keep doing what you're doing. It's working. He's a much different person now than he was when you guys were here in June. He's softer but don't tell him I noticed."

I sighed, glancing across the room at my future husband. "I just wonder how he's going to process all this. He's an orphan consumed by survivor's guilt who chose to barricade himself from emotion and getting close to anyone. And now, he's on the verge of having not only a wife but an extended family. It must be so overwhelming."

"Wow. You are the worst over thinker in the universe."

"Thank you, Captain Obvious."

"Seriously. How do you function with that brain?"

I knew she was teasing me but everything she'd said was so spot on. "We all have our cross to bear."

Nudging me with her elbow, Dayna grinned. "Can we just talk about how friggin' exciting it is that I'm going to be Alastair Holden's sister-in-law? People at work are already peppering me with questions."

"Have you been contacted by any newspapers or reporters or anything?" I asked with a hint of concern. Having the paparazzi chasing me was one thing but if they went after my family I'd have a serious problem with that.

"Nope. They haven't gone all Pippa Middleton on me yet. Of

course if you put me in one of those butt hugging bridesmaid dresses that could all change."

"Oh my God," I snorted. "He's just some guy, not royalty."

"And that, my dear sister, is why he loves you."

A calming warmth spread through me as I remembered his words from the pub. *You've always just seen me.* On cue, he looked in my direction, gaze darkening. Andrew excused himself, giving Alastair a chance to meander over to the window where we were standing.

"You both look like you're up to no good," he said, kissing my forehead.

Dayna chuckled. "Nah. Just some sisterly conversation. Have you and Andy dissected the rugby league enough for one night?"

"Reckon we have."

"Do you still play on the weekends? I remember Lia saying you were part of some amateur league."

"Work's been busy, so no. Next weekend looks promising though, if you sister doesn't mind seeing me muddy and sweaty." The gleam in his eyes hit my hot buttons in a way I wasn't expecting.

"Mud and sweat look good on you." I smirked. "The dirtier, the better."

Leaning close, Alastair lowered his voice. "Well then. Rugby next Sunday it is."

*Christ, he smells so good.* I blinked myself out of this seductive haze, hastily reminding myself that not only we were in my sister's house, she was standing six inches to our left.

"Yep. I'm the third wheel. I'll leave you guys to do…whatever."

"Sorry." I smiled, blushing.

"That is one thing you should never apologize for." She laughed.

"Your sister is right," he said, squeezing my waist. "Thank you again for dinner, Dayna. You'll both have to come to Glasgow so we can return the favor."

"Absolutely," she beamed. "You're part of the family now so don't be surprised if we show up at your doorstep unannounced all the time."

Alastair's pleasant smile was betrayed by the barrier blocking any warmth from reaching his eyes. He slid his arm low around my waist, cupping my hip. The intimate embrace thrilled me but didn't distract from his masked discomfort.

"I have one more little dessert to get out of the oven. Be right back." My sister waltzed off to the kitchen, leaving us alone by the window.

"Enjoying yourself, chief?"

Pulling me closer, he rested his chin on top of my head. I figured this was as close to an answer as I was going to get. When Dayna and Andrew came back into the room we rejoined them on the couch for an assortment of cookies, small cakes and pastries. I watched as Alastair interacted with ease, turning on the irresistible Holden charisma. Draping an arm over my shoulders, he tucked me into his side as we leaned against the cushions. His gentle caresses made my skin tingle and pulse race. But I knew this was all for show.

They couldn't tell how shrouded behind the protective shield he remained but I could. And it broke my heart.

* * *

I walked through the elegant lobby of the Savoy a few steps behind Alastair. We were still staying at the hotel so, in the words of my stubborn Englishman, 'we don't have to spend any more time at the Holden Estate than was necessary.'

His controlled, purposeful strides were watched and admired by almost everyone who could see him. A few women stood a little straighter as he passed them without a sideways glance. Their greedy, wanton eyes sized me up with envy. Much like the snobby people at Brent's party, I imagined these women whispering amongst themselves, asking each other how I could have landed such a hotly desired man like Alastair Holden.

I pushed my shoulders back and passed them with as much ease as I could muster.

Once we were in the suite, Alastair flopped onto the couch. A rather normal, unspectacular move for a guy who just strolled through the hotel like he owned the place.

"You're handsome when you're tired," I said, sitting on the arm of the couch. He smiled up at me.

"Is that the only time?"

"Maybe."

He had me on the couch and in the grips of a severe tickle attack before I knew what was happening.

"Oh my God, Alastair," I shrieked in between giggles.

"I do love hearing you say that." He tickled me faster, smiling and laughing in a way I didn't think was possible after the mood he'd been in all night. When I thought I wouldn't be able to take it anymore, he stopped, seeming to know I'd had enough.

"You're mean," I gasped, ruffling his hair. "But I love you."

"My Lia." He pressed his forehead to mine. "I want to spend the rest of tonight lost in you. I haven't been able to stop thinking about it since I had you in that office." He kissed me, stoking the eternal flame that always burned deep inside. "Make me forget. Make me feel wanted."

"Hey," I whispered, holding his face. "You're always wanted. What's wrong?"

Not answering, he averted his eyes.

"Don't worry about tomorrow, Alastair. It's not here yet."

"I'm not worried," he grumbled. "I'd rather not waste my energy talking about that."

"Why do you get so agitated about them?" The words flew out faster than I could tell my mouth to shut the hell up.

Annoyed, he pushed himself off the couch and paced the room. I sat up, refusing to let his sour mood dampen my spirits.

"Look, I'm sorry it upset you but at some point you're going to have to explain it to me. They raised you. They gave you the best upbringing anybody could ask for. Your aunt adores you, so I know she's not the one you have a problem with." The flood gates were open and I couldn't reign in my curiosity. I had to know what the deal was.

"You're going to do this now?" he glowered. "After I told you I didn't want to talk about it."

I raked my fingers through my hair and sighed. "I don't want to argue with you. I just want to understand."

Staring at me with the same guarded curiosity as when we first met, he reached out his hands. "Come to me."

"I know this routine, Holden," I said, standing up and walking over to him. "You're very big on seducing me into silence."

"And yet you came to me."

"I can't help myself."

His small crooked smile melted some of the agitation from his face. "Is that why you put up with me?"

"We've been over this already. I put up with you because you're insufferably hot and a good cook. The fact that you're a master of seduction is nothing more than the cherry on top of a really, really delicious sundae."

Catching me around the waist, he pulled me in for a kiss. My insides turned to useless goo at every movement of his lips and stroke of his tongue.

"I should marry you." He grinned, his beautiful mouth still brushing against mine.

"Mmm." I ruffled his hair. "Too charming."

"You should get naked so I can do some really charming things to you all night."

"Not so fast, lover boy. I want to make sure I'm not sideswiped by one of your pendulum mood swings tomorrow."

Narrowing his eyes, he took a step back.

"Don't get all pissy just yet, Holden. We're in this together. If something happens and you shut me out I will *not* tolerate it. What affects you, affects me. I see your discomfort and your annoyance whenever you have to visit your family. I may not understand it yet but I'm not letting you hide behind that awful wall alone."

He stared impassively for several seconds as the mood in the suite shifted from playful to strained. I'd never been so vocal about his closed-off ways before so I figured he'd need some time to process what I said. If not for the love that burned in his eyes I'd have thought he transformed into an unyielding statue.

"Do you promise not to leave me this time?" he asked in hushed tone.

"What?" I asked, stunned by his question.

Clutching his stomach as though he might be sick, Alastair shook his head. "That time you left…I can't." His jaw tightened as he regained some composure. "That house doesn't hold many pleasant memories for me."

Swatting away the guilt that surfaced, I folded my arms and aimed my best determined stare at him. "You don't get to throw that back in my face, Alastair. You acted like a little brat that day. It killed me to leave you. We're beyond that now. It's part of the fabric of our relationship but it does not define us. It doesn't define how we should react to one another when things get tough. I know that and you know that."

He visibly uncoiled from the tension. Uncertainty clouded his eyes, wrenching my heart. After all this time, he still feared loss. As much as I sympathized for him, I was also frustrated.

"Do you see this?" I asked, lifting my left hand so the diamond ring glittered in the light. "It's an outward symbol of my promise to never leave you." I grabbed his hand, placing it over my racing heart. "Can you feel that?"

The dominant spark returned to his eyes full force. Fisting his free hand in my hair, he pulled. "You are all that I feel, all that I am and all that I'll ever need."

I leaned close, trapping his bottom lip between my teeth and tugged. "I'm yours," I whispered. "Forever."

The sound of slow, ragged breathing permeated through the suite. His hunger for me was palpable. Gritting his teeth, he pressed his forehead to mine. "You make me—" he paused, scowling. His chest rose and fell in a heavy sigh. I waited, my body tingling with anticipation. He was on the verge of another breakthrough, I could sense it.

# CHAPTER ELEVEN

The Holden Estate loomed large in the distance, its imposing stone structure dominating the gray skyline. The only dots of color on this dreary day came from the strands of ivy that snaked around some of the windows. Driving up the long and twisting driveway, I took several cleansing breaths and fought off the unpleasant memories of the last time I was here. Alastair was quiet, lost in his own thoughts as we walked to the front door.

He grabbed me and planted a firm kiss to my lips. Searching me with veiled eyes, he sighed.

"Love you," I said, giving his hand a reassuring squeeze before ringing the bell.

"Amelia." His aunt Katherine greeted me with a warm hug. She beamed at her nephew. "It's so lovely to see you again." She ushered us through the foyer and into a large, formal dining room. I remembered walking through it briefly when I was here for the garden party. The table was loaded with a variety of foods fit for an extravagant brunch. My stomach snarled, always ready to indulge.

Already seated at the table were Alastair's uncle, Jason, and grandfather, Samuel. Both were casually dressed and chatting comfortably amongst themselves. I'm pretty sure I heard Jason mutter something about the premier league. If not for the cavernous house and opulent surroundings, this felt like just an average family gathering for an average Sunday brunch. Except that it wasn't.

They both regarded me with interest.

"Have a seat, please," Katherine said, motioning toward two chairs. I sat first, watching Alastair as he moved with fluid control to the chair next to me. His expression was unreadable and stony. He didn't even flinch when I squeezed his leg under the table.

"Amelia, my grandson tells me you're working for Julian Archer. How do you like it?" Samuel asked, his strong voice booming across the table.

"So far so good."

"He's an interesting fellow. I approached him years ago when I was thinking about adding his program to one of my affiliates." His gray eyes danced with mirth. "He scoffed at the idea and called me an old fool. I hear he may be in trouble now. His people have been ringing our affiliate department for the past month. Have Sam and Robbie said anything to you about merging with the weekly news magazine program here in London?"

*Maybe Julian wasn't so paranoid after all.*

Mindful to keep an impassive expression, I paused to gather my thoughts before answering. Retired or not, it should come as no surprise that Samuel's finger was still on the pulse of the media industry.

"I haven't heard anything concrete. Just office rumors."

"It's my understanding you only signed a three month contract with them. That was wise." He swirled what appeared to be a mimosa in his glass before taking a sip. "Our offices in New York City will be looking to hire a public relations director at the start of the new year. My grandson also tells me you're quite the talented young woman. I'll have Jason make a recommendation on your behalf to the board at our next meeting."

I hadn't even glanced around the table yet to see what we were eating and already I was being propositioned for a job at Holden World Media. This was going to be one hell of an afternoon.

"We agreed not to talk business." Katherine scolded him with a smile. "Honestly, you have a one track mind, Sam."

"Just trying to make the newest member of the family feel welcome."

He said it with a smile but wow, the stern look in his eyes made me think twice about relaxing in his presence. He was a force to be reckoned with wrapped in the guise of a cuddly eighty-five year old grandpa. I wasn't too concerned though. I could stand toe to toe with the best of them. Samuel Holden was no exception. Still, I'd made a promise to myself not to inflame the already tense atmosphere between Alastair and his family. Besides, I had a feeling this assertion was mostly for show. The silver-haired patriarch kept his shrewd gaze focused on me.

"Speaking of that," Jason said, turning his attention toward us, "congratulations are in order." He looked pointedly at the diamond ring on my finger. "We'll plan for a summer wedding next year, then? You're free to use the grounds as you'd like. Katherine can coordinate with a wedding planner—"

"That's not necessary," Alastair interrupted. "Thank you for the offer but Lia and I can handle it."

"I'm sure you can. You and I will discuss the more intricate details privately after we eat." Jason leveled a hard stare at his nephew, causing my chest to constrict. I felt the warmth of Alastair's hand slide under the hem of the dress I was wearing. I looked at him, unable to catch his eye. He was too busy glaring across the table. I noticed Katherine bow her head and sigh. My heart went out to her. The tension between the younger Holden men was so thick it could break the blade off a knife.

Anxiety surged through my body. Real life certainly had a way of bursting through the doors with its middle fingers high in the air and a bounce in its step. Alastair has spent too much of his life blocking out all the unpleasantness with his family and as much as I loved how much progress he'd made, there was still a ways to go.

"What would you prefer, Lia?"

I snapped out of my head and stared right at Katherine's beaming face. Alastair's hand was still on my leg so he took the opportunity to give me a squeeze. I looked at him, confused.

His smile was forced but it loosened the granite exterior coating his expression. "Pancakes?"

"Oh. Yes, please."

"There's also some very naughty cheesy French toast with grilled ham and tomatoes."

"Naughty? Is that because you didn't make them?"

"Possibly." He leaned in for a soft, passionate kiss. I caught his aunt grinning at us like a proud parent and blushed.

"Don't mind me," she laughed. "There's nothing wrong with a little peck between two people so obviously in love."

Food seemed to have a way of easing a stressful situation. Or maybe it was because our mouths were full and nobody could get a word in edgewise. No matter the reason, I was finally able to relax a little and enjoy the scrumptious cuisine.

Observing the Holden clan fascinated me. Katherine was most certainly the soothing force that kept a level of civility between her husband and her nephew present. Samuel, though intimidating in his own right, was easy to talk to. He asked me endless questions about my time in Orlando, even admitting that my station was the one he'd wanted to buy and not our competitor.

"I thought we had them," he said, smiling at me. "Next time."

I laughed, admiring his tenacity. The more he spoke, the more I liked him. He was smart, driven and had a world of experience to share. His story of how he built the company from a single news-paper to the worldwide conglomerate it became was captivating and inspiring. Even Jason seemed to loosen up a bit, adding in his two cents about growing their company more in the American market. Before long, the two men were yammering on and on about Los Angeles, productions companies, and an online store for people to buy music and movies.

It dawned on me that the only one not participating in any of the conversations was Alastair. He remained closed off and silent as stone next to me, surveying the table with veiled eyes. I started to wonder if he brought all the unpleasantness he complained about on himself. His aunt, grandfather and uncle were nothing short of gracious. Either that or they were the best actors on the planet and this was their Academy Award winning scene.

I nudged him with my elbow. "You okay over there, chief?"

Nodding slightly, he slid his hand farther up my thigh until his fingers were dangerously close to my lace underwear. Not missing a beat, I put my hand on his, stopping the progression. This was neither the time nor place for these shenanigans.

Flicking his eyes at me, Alastair wet his lips. "You're helping."

"They're lovely, Alastair. I'm not just saying that." I squeezed his hand. "Relax. Enjoy yourself."

"Will you be in the London office on Wednesday?" Jason asked, gently interrupting us.

"Yes," Alastair answered, stiffening. "I'll fly down for the meeting but I won't be staying over. Lia's birthday is on Thursday and I want to be home to spoil her."

"And you should do just that." Jason looked at me. "If we had known your birthday was so close we would have surprised you with a cake. It's probably for the best though." His sapphire eyes shimmered with mischief. "My father can't ever say no to sweets."

Samuel's arched eyebrow reminded me so much of Alastair's expression, I laughed. "I'll take a rain check on that cake, then."

"You're welcome to visit anytime, Amelia. The door is always open for you and my nephew."

I didn't have to see Alastair to know he'd reattached the mask and had that listless look in his eyes. The warmth of his hand slipped from my leg, deflating my mood. I was almost at my breaking point with his frostiness.

"Now, if can steal your fiancé away for a few minutes?" Jason stood up and motioned for Alastair to follow him. Samuel excused himself as well. I assumed they were heading toward the study.

Alastair rose from his chair and paused to look at me. He brushed his thumb along my lips and softened his expression. "I won't be long."

Once they left, I offered to help Katherine clear the table so I could focus my nervous energy and stop fidgeting. I liked being around her. She reminded me of my mother minus all the theatrics.

"You have no idea how happy we are for you and Alastair," she said, placing a cup of tea on the breakfast bar for me. "All of us. We never thought we'd—" She stopped abruptly and shook her head. "I don't mean to embarrass you or make you feel uncomfortable. It's just that Alastair has been so distant for so much of his life. Jason and I tried everything. We thought we'd had a breakthrough when he was thirteen but something kept preventing him from letting go of what happened to Daniel, Rose and Grace."

The cup remained frozen in my hand in midair. The hot liquid vibrated with every beat of my heart. This was not the conversation I expected to have with her. I figured she'd fuss over dresses and flowers and shoes.

Pushing pieces of her satiny blonde hair behind her ear, she looked apologetic. "I've let my mouth run off again."

"It's okay. I have the same habit." I smiled.

"When he asked me for his mother's ring and said he wanted to propose to you, I…well, I was stunned to be honest. He's clearly quite taken with you but I never thought I'd see the day." Her voice trailed as she leaned against the counter. "He looks at you with such wonder and love and fear. It's enough to stop my heart."

I had to put the tea cup down. I was starting to shake. As much as I loved all the progress Alastair has made, I didn't want to shoulder all the responsibility. The pressure of being looked at as the one who may have changed him was too potent.

"I really haven't done anything. I've just let him find his own way."

"You've done more than you realize, Amelia."

Curious to know more, I paused for a second to gather my

thoughts. "Do you know why his relationship with Jason is so tense?"

*Okay, that was so not the question I should have asked.*

Katherine frowned and appeared hesitant. "Alastair loved his father very much, like any young boy would. He idolized him. When Daniel died and Jason stepped in, Alastair shut him out. At six years old, he knew what death meant and he knew that letting people get close to him would one day lead to heartache. He was different with me though. For whatever reason, he allowed me to care for him to a certain extent. But he never let Jason be a father-figure. He rebelled and lashed out."

I was so engrossed in Katherine's story I sat as still as a statue. These were the pieces of Alastair's past that I longed to know. These were the pieces he never revealed, even at his most vulnerable. I felt a little guilty for going behind his back and asking his aunt but she did volunteer most of it without too much prodding. I mean really, it was almost like she'd been dying to tell me.

Butterflies rustled in my stomach. The familiar electric sensation I had when he was near hummed through my body.

"There you are."

I turned toward the sound of his rich, silky voice and had to concentrate on not launching myself into his arms. Instead, he hugged me and kissed my forehead.

"You two were talking about me again, weren't you?" An impish grin curled his mouth. "I'm assuming you've said nothing but flattering things."

I sensed something was wrong. His body language was off-putting even though he painted a picture of complete ease. The second I touched his arm his muscles tightened. *Shit.* Memories of the last time he'd been in a dark mood while at this house flooded me. My heart beat a little faster as anxiety snaked its way through my body. I needed to focus. Letting my emotions and fears get the best of me was the last thing I should allow.

"Is everything all sorted for Wednesday, then?" Katherine asked, placing another cup of tea on the counter for Alastair.

He bristled. "For the most part."

"Why don't the two of you go to the sitting room? We'll join you in a bit."

"We really can't st—"

"That sounds like a great idea," I interrupted. "Thank you."

Grabbing Alastair's hand before he could protest, I led him into the sitting room. We lingered by the massive floor to ceiling windows and stared out into the backyard. The reflection pool cut through the yard, its water as still as glass. Without the giant party tent from June it appeared much more peaceful and pastoral. The enormity of this house had the potential to be suffocating but instead exuded a calm, comforting aura.

Alastair didn't move when I placed my hand on his back. His fixed gaze remained listless and remote.

"Talk to me," I requested softly, running my fingers through his hair.

Seconds passed by like hours as I waited for any type of response. The silence was deafening. Unable to stand it any longer, I sat at the baby grand piano and played a few notes. Since I only knew how to play by ear I just sort of messed around on the keys until a recognizable tune floated through the room.

"Do you still remember how to play that John Field song?" Alastair asked, straddling the bench next to me.

"Probably not that well."

"Try it."

"Why?"

He shrugged, skimming his fingers over the keys. "It's too quiet in here."

Looking up at him through my lashes, I was met with the same distant stare he'd had since we arrived. As frustrated as I was with him, I couldn't be angry and force him to talk about the thoughts he kept so well protected. That wouldn't be fair.

"Tell me what you want," I said. "Tell me what I need to do."

Positioning himself so his chest was flush against my right side, he wrapped his arms around my waist. "Amelia. All I want is to be alone with you. Away from this house. Away from these ghosts that haunt my memories every time I come here."

I felt his body quiver against mine.

"You can't keep running, Alastair. At some point you have to stop. Shutting your family out isn't the answer. They love you. I saw that today so clearly. I know you're afraid. I know you have a hard time trusting your emotions. It's time you let go and let them in."

"I can't."

"Yes you can, you're just being stubborn."

Defiance flashed through his eyes like lightning. I'd hit a nerve.

"I. Can't."

"You. Won't." I countered, arching an eyebrow. "That frigid stare doesn't scare me. Stop being difficult."

Parting his lips to exhale, he shook his head. "I don't want to do this now. Not here."

Laughter echoed through the hall moments before Katherine, Jason and Samuel entered the room. Alastair's grip on my waist tightened.

"Do you play the piano, Amelia?" Samuel asked. "Rose knew how to play. Right Alastair? She'd sit here with you and Grace for hours."

The room became a vacuum, depriving me of precious oxygen. Samuel's timing couldn't have been worse. Alastair squeezed his eyes shut momentarily before rising off the piano bench. The delicate balance I had with him regarding the death of his family shattered before me.

He stood, an immobile silhouette by the window. Panic seized me. I feared the worst was about to happen. Controlled by my unfiltered love for him, I stood up and banded my arms around his waist. If he hadn't taken a breath I would have sworn I'd hugged stone.

"I don't play very well, I'm afraid," I answered, keeping my voice as even as possible. "I can't read music. I just play the notes from memory."

"Rose loved playing for her little ones," Katherine said, smiling. "Especially on Christmas morning and for their birthdays. This room was always filled with music. That's probably why your brother formed the music division, right Jason?"

Alastair's muscles tightened, signaling he was about to bolt for the door. I held him closer, hoping to assuage his discomfort. Resting my head on his chest, I continued to chat with his family, careful to steer the conversation away from too much mention of his mom, dad or sister. As important as I believed it was for him to stop running from his past, I didn't want to bombard him with it in one afternoon.

I had the feeling they sensed it too and started asking me questions about my family. The longer we talked, the more rigid and unyielding Alastair's body became. He just stared out the window, ignoring everything and everyone surrounding him. As much as I knew he hated this, I held him closer and hoped to God he wouldn't lash out like he'd done in June.

"We should go, love," Alastair finally said, sounding tired.

Jason and Katherine exchanged glances before standing up to walk us to the door. Samuel embraced me in a firm hug and kissed both my cheeks. "You keep an eye on my grandson. He listens to you and holds you in very high regard." He leaned close, lowering his voice. "Losing my son, daughter-in-law and granddaughter has taken its toll on me as well. On all of us. He hasn't suffered alone. I hope he knows that."

Swallowing back a hot, painful lump I nodded and scurried off to the front hall. Alastair reached for my hand the second he saw me. We said our goodbyes and promised to stay longer next time. Neither one of us spoke on the ride to the airport or on the flight back to Glasgow. I'd learned by now that when Alastair was in this mood, the only person who could bring him out of it was himself. Seeing him so sealed off left me heartbroken and disenchanted.

He went straight to the bedroom when we arrived at the house. I flopped onto the couch and covered my eyes with my arm. Today's events raced through my brain, filling me alternately with hope and discouragement. At least he didn't force me out this time when he felt overwhelmed. That was progress.

"Lia."

My whispered name roused me from thought. I sat up, meeting his tortured gaze. He stood in the middle of the room, emotionally spent. He was a raw nerve desperately searching for protection.

"Sit with me."

Shaking his head, he paced the room, scrubbing his face with both hands. I hadn't seen him this agitated in all the time I'd known him. Composing himself enough to grab my hands, he pulled me off the couch.

"You make me," he said hoarsely, gritting his teeth.

"I make you what?"

Caught in his luminous tractor-beam stare, I waited for an answer that never came. He just studied my face as though he'd never see me again. Pressing his forehead to mine, he cupped my jaw.

"I love the way I feel when I'm with you." Vulnerability etched itself on his face and in his words. "But I also feel like I'm hanging onto the edge of a cliff and I'm losing my grip. I wanted to…being in that house is so hard and…" The more he struggled with what to say, the tighter I held him. And then, like slipping on a pair of familiar, comfortable shoes, he retreated behind the mask. The transition was so seamless I almost missed it.

"You're so close, Alastair," I said. "So close. I wish you'd stop running. I wish you'd stop hiding. Be in the present. Stop torturing yourself with the past."

Large green eyes darkened as fear, sadness and anger twisted through them. "I don't know any other way to be."

# CHAPTER TWELVE

Another group of photographers waited for me when I arrived at work Monday morning. This time, there were a dozen of them. They didn't jump in my face but hovered close enough while snapping pictures to make people stop and stare. I scurried through the main lobby and into an elevator, feeling the weight of reality as it settled in around me. Sleep was elusive last night thanks to Alastair's intense nightmares. He'd been nightmare free for weeks so the onslaught was unpleasant for him. He'd brushed them off this morning but I knew they weighed heavily on his mind.

Meredith greeted me with a huge smile when I walked into the newsroom.

"Social media has been buzzing all weekend over your engagement to Alastair Holden. You're a star. How exciting."

She followed me into my office talking non-stop about the photos and stories and speculations as to where and when the wedding will be. I sat with a thud and flicked on the computer to see the damage. As per usual there were more 'close friends' and 'sources from inside the Holden camp' than actual facts. Most of the online attention was here in the United Kingdom but I had to be all nosey and see if the news skipped across the pond yet. Yep, it did. The Orlando websites picked it up and touted me as 'their own.' Some of my former co-workers were approached for comment. The only ones more than happy to give their two cents publicly were Katie Vitale and Vanessa Jaxson.

I closed the browser and jetted off to the morning staff meeting with Sam and Robbie. They were in high spirits after last Friday's show, which put me at ease. Ratings were higher and some viewers even commented on the program's Facebook page how much they enjoyed the new style. There were a few dissenting voices but nothing too horrific.

Julian burst into my office seconds after I returned from the meeting.

"Brilliant work, Lia. You were the talk of the town all weekend." He grinned. "And you did a great job here on the program, too."

"Is that supposed to be charm you're using because you're still on my shit list."

"Lia," he said in an almost patronizing tone, "don't let what happened on Friday come between us. Admittedly, I was a little overzealous. I can't help myself sometimes." He perched on the edge of my desk and rifled through a file. "Let me make it up to you. There's this great restaurant called Two Fat Ladies at the Buttery that I've been dying to try. We'll do lunch there today. I'm off to the Bilberry for a meeting. I'll send a car to collect you at one." He stood up and practically waltzed toward the door, disappearing as quickly as he'd arrived. *Stephanie is right about all these needy TV personality types.*

Oh my God. I hadn't talked to or heard from my best friend since I saw her *in flagrante* with Brent. Rummaging through my bag, I dug out my cell phone. The battery was on its last leg since I didn't charge it at all over the weekend. There were about a zillion texts from Steph. I put the phone down and rubbed my temples. I should get to work. That way my brain would be occupied and not tempted to wander off and overthink anything.

I did manage to get some work done but only for about ten minutes. Out the corner of my eye I noticed the silver invitation still sitting on my desk. Snatching it, I tore it into tiny pieces and tossed it in the trash. The mere thought of Olivia turned my stomach. *Conniving little…*

The desk phone rang.

"Lia Mey—"

"What the hell happened to you? Where have you been? You disappeared from the party and ignored me all weekend. What the fuck, Lia?" Stephanie sounded pissed off which didn't help improve my mood.

"Slow down," I said. "Alastair took me on a surprise getaway to London. We hung out, saw my sister and then had brunch with his aunt and uncle. I didn't keep my phone with me or anything."

"Oh." She sighed. "I thought you were mad at me or something. You just vanished from Brent's without a trace. I was looking for you and nobody knew what happened. I almost called your parents but since you were with Dayna—"

"Tell me you didn't call them."

"Are you nuts? Your mother would have been on the first plane over here."

I leaned back in the chair and closed my eyes. "So, how was your weekend?"

"Fine. Darren decided he wanted to take up tennis and enlisted me as his doubles partner. I need to find that guy a girlfriend or something."

"Tennis? I thought you didn't like to sweat."

"I don't," she grumbled. "I just stood there and let the ball whiz by. Sports and I do not mix." She paused. "So, where did he take you? You sound totally Zen. Was it some swanky spa or something?"

"Nope." A knock at the door caught my attention. Meredith was standing there and she looked upset. "Hey, I have to run. Want to come over later?"

"Sure. I'll drag Darren with me to keep Alastair occupied so you and I can have some serious girl time."

Hanging up the phone, I waved Meredith in. Her eyes were swollen and red and she looked disoriented.

"What happened?" I asked, growing more concerned.

"I messed up some video one of the editors needed. I know I shouldn't get this upset but she was yelling and carrying on and told me I should stick to filing."

My heart went out to Meredith. She was a sweet girl who genuinely wanted to learn the news business but still had to grow a tougher skin. "Don't take it so personally. Everybody ends up on the receiving end of a screaming match at least once in the newsroom. Even me." I smiled as she relaxed.

"Sorry for being so emotional but I really want this work experience to be successful. I'm only here until—" She started becoming upset again.

"You're doing a great job," I said, reassuring her the best I could. "Why don't you come to lunch with Julian and me today? You can ask him anythi—"

"Lia." Robbie burst into my office appearing a bit harried. "Come to Sam's office. Now."

Meredith's wide eyes filled with panic. Uneasy, I jumped up and followed Robbie down the hall to our news director's office. Sam paced the floor, burning a path in the carpet with every step.

"Close the door," he ordered.

Robbie and I sat, waiting for whatever apocalypse was about to be announced. Sam's entire office was drenched with disquiet.

"Julian's been accused of sexual harassment." He stopped pacing, leaving the words to hang in the air for several seconds before continuing. "He supposedly sent a lewd picture to some girl via text."

"What?" Robbie asked.

"A dick pic." Sam's face turned bright red as he tried to compose himself. "That pain in the ass has caused nothing but trouble for years. I've a good mind to terminate his contract immediately."

I sat speechless, not quite sure what to do in this situation. Part of me wanted to laugh at the utter ridiculousness of what Julian had done but I knew better than to make a joke of this when my news director was so upset. Robbie and Sam carried on and on about what they had to do next to lessen the inevitable 'shitstorm' of unwanted media attention. I told them to do whatever they thought was right once they had all the facts and went back to my office. I could hear my phone ringing so I sprinted inside.

"Lia Meyers," I answered, breathless.

"Have I caught you at a bad time?" the unfamiliar female voice on the other end asked.

"No. Who is this?"

"Emma Whelan. We met over the summer at the Holden Estate."

*Does every one of Alastair's former flings have nothing better to do than bother me?*

"You're probably surprised to hear from me," she continued, sounding smug. "Or maybe not seeing as you've made quite the splash in the papers over the weekend. People must be ringing you like mad."

"Not really."

"Don't be modest. The British press is relentless. Which is why I'm calling. I'd like to offer my assistance."

My eye twitched.

"What assistance would that be?"

"Whether you want to believe it or not, you're now a public figure. You need someone to handle the press and any other annoyances that come with the territory. I've known Alastair for years so I know he handles his public life with precision. You, on the other hand, need a guiding force. Someone who can navigate through the shit. I can help you, Lia. I can make this engagement and wedding look seamless to the general public."

Today had turned into one of those days where the universe felt off center. Everything looked normal on the outside but, in reality, it had become one giant bucket of suck. I closed my eyes in an effort to dull the raging headache that materialized.

"Think about it," she continued. "Do some research on me if you feel the need. Ask Alastair. My clients are some of the most prominent in Great Britain so I know what I'm talking about."

She wished me well and hung up. I grabbed my purse and headed for the lobby.

* * *

The short cab ride to the financial district did nothing to settle my twitching nerves. I paid the driver and rushed into the impressive modern building that housed Holden World Media. I probably should have called before showing up but I wasn't really thinking straight. A security guard stopped me at the desk. Once he took a good look at me and saw my ID, he apologized for delaying me and ushered me to the elevators. I supposed it does pay to be dating -or engaged to- the head of the company.

When the elevator doors opened I saw Simone sitting at a sleek reception desk near Alastair's office. She regarded me with disinterest.

"He's in a meeting."

"I'll wait in his office then."

Her protests were interrupted when the doors opened and Alastair walked out with three other men. Seeing him in his element hit all my hot buttons at once. Watching him dress for work and wrap himself in those expensive suits at home was one thing. But seeing how it all looked here? God help me.

"We'll see you in Los Angeles at the end of the month," one of the men said while shaking Alastair's hand. "This is going to be a great partnership."

"Looking forward to it." My fiancé zeroed in on me with a look of concern as he guided them to the elevator. "Simone, clear my schedule for the next hour," he ordered once they'd left. He laced his fingers through mine and pulled me into his office, closing the door. Like everything else in his life, Alastair's office projected classic elegance.

124

"What's wrong?" he asked, leveling an intense stare at me.

"Nothing," I said, gazing out one of the huge windows that boasted a fantastic view of Glasgow.

"Lia. You've shown up at my building unannounced. Something happened. What is it?"

I sighed. "That girl Emma called me."

His eyebrows shot up. "Emma Whelan?"

"That's the one."

"What did she want?"

"She offered to be my publicist and help keep the press off my back now that our engagement is public." I folded my arms. "Are there any other ex-fuck buddies out there I should expect to hear from?"

Sitting on the edge of his glass top desk, he looked thoughtful. That wasn't quite the reaction I'd anticipated.

"It might not be a bad idea to let her help," he said without an ounce of irony.

"I'm sorry. Did I come to the wrong building? I was looking for Alastair Holden."

"Emma is the best at what she does. I've known her since we were teenagers so I trust her to keep our private life protected."

I stared at him, dumbfounded. This was the same woman who told me I'd never get him to love me back, that he was only good for a shag and that he always, *always* went back to her. How did she put it? Oh right. She was the closest thing to a girlfriend he'd had.

"Wow. Okay. I made a mistake coming here." I turned on my heel but was stopped before I reached the door.

"Knock it off, Amelia. You can't keep running away every time you're presented with an uncomfortable situation."

"Says the pot to the kettle." I glared at him.

The muscles in his jaw twitched. "Emma knows she shouldn't have treated you that way at the garden party. I told her how important and special you are and how much I need you in my life. She has a good head on her shoulders and won't interfere in

125

our relationship. As I've told you before, she didn't want anything from me. But she has been a constant in my life since I was thirteen. We went to school together. Grew up together. She knows me as well as one can."

I recoiled, moving away from him. "I thought I knew you."

He was in front of me in seconds, cupping my jaw. "You do. Why are you reacting this way?"

"Why? In a span of three days I've had to deal with Olivia, Sarah and now Emma. I don't feel good about asking someone you screwed around with for help. I don't trust her motive. I don't want to open doors that could pose problems for us. I don't want—"

"I love you," he interrupted. "I love this messy, complicated, impossible thing that we have and would never do anything to jeopardize it."

My knees almost gave out hearing those words and seeing the unflinching intensity behind his eyes. I relaxed, letting him hold me. I could feel the vibrations of his heart pounding through his shirt. Being in his arms never failed to calm my deepest fears and quiet any doubts.

"Feeling better?" he asked, combing his fingers through my hair.

I nodded. "Between the party on Friday and the weekend and Julian getting in trouble and now Emma…I…I lost my head a little."

"Julian's in trouble? What did he do now?"

I rolled my eyes. "He allegedly texted a naked picture of himself to some girl and she didn't like it. Sam and Robbie are up in arms."

Alastair's amused grin broke through the tension. "Freed his willy, did he?"

"Stop it." I laughed, shoving him.

"I've made you laugh. That's a good sign." He wrapped me in his arms again. "Let me talk to Emma and see exactly what she wants. I know she wouldn't risk her job to launch a crusade to destroy my relationship with you."

The look on my face must have spelled out my trepidations in capital letters punctuated by exclamations galore. Alastair smiled and kissed me.

"My Lia. Stop worrying. I wish you'd come to see me for different reasons, kitten. Want to stay for lunch?" He walked back to his desk and looked at the computer. Through all the stress and weirdness of this day, I still found beauty in how he moved. I'd only seen him work from home so being here was a treat for me. Standing with his hands in his pockets in the midst of this pristine office, he looked every bit like the powerful, smart and sexy CEO that he was. "You're staring." He smirked.

"So?"

"Keep looking at me like that and neither one of us will get any work done today." Coming around the edge of the desk, he approached me with deliberate strides. My pulse quickened. I knew that look in his eyes. I knew what he wanted and I knew he would most certainly get it. But through the carnal way he looked at me I could see his exhaustion. The emotional wear and tear of the visit to his family's estate and the ensuing nightmares had taken their toll on him.

"Are you working late tonight?" I asked as he reached for my hands.

"Yes. Why?"

"I invited Stephanie and Darren over."

"Good. I don't like when you're home alone."

"I don't like when you work late."

He sighed, running his knuckles down my cheek. "I'll try to be home by half eight."

"Try hard. You barely slept last night."

He scowled and shook his head. "I don't want to talk about it, Lia. I appreciate your concern but let's not push this any further."

Against my better judgment, I dropped it and kissed him good bye. The rest of my day passed without incident. Julian stayed out of the newsroom and Sam remained locked in his office. When I left for the night, I was so happy to see Paxton waiting for me that I practically skipped to the waiting Mercedes SUV.

"This is a nice surprise," I said.

"It was Mr. Holden's idea," he responded without cracking a smile. My stomach dropped. Usually when Alastair sent Paxton for me that meant something was up or someone was making him antsy.

"Is everything okay?" I asked after settling into the backseat.

"Yes."

Ah, well, there begins the one word answer parade. Deciding not to put myself through the mental carousel of questions, I leaned back and watched the city flash by before my eyes. Raindrops hit the windshield one at a time, then fell faster until the outside world was drenched. I ran up the front path after Paxton dropped me off and stood in the hallway. The house was quiet and dark and felt unwelcoming. The same sense of foreboding I'd had the night Alastair gave me the diamond crept through my body. Figuring it was just the weight of the past few days, I ignored it.

# CHAPTER THIRTEEN

"Hello, double standard," Stephanie grumbled, pouring herself another glass of wine. She and Darren had arrived about an hour ago and were making themselves quite comfortable in Alastair's museum-like living room. Darren even managed to discover an unused PS3 and promptly helped himself to a game.

"Don't be so dramatic," I said, giving her the side eye. "I trust him and know he'll do what's best."

She narrowed her eyes at me and sipped from the glass. "After everything that happened with Nathan this summer I would have thought you'd be more suspicious of ex-flames nosing their way back into your fiancé's life. I don't like it."

"I don't like it either," I snapped. "But it's not like this girl causes problems for him on the level Olivia does."

Stephanie rolled her eyes and gave me a look. "Olivia is harmless. She—"

"Just because you're fucking her brother doesn't mean I'm going to forgive or forget what she did to Alastair."

Her jaw dropped open. Flustered, she stared at me. "What are you…I'm not…"

"Save it, Steph. I saw you guys on the balcony at the party. You looked pretty into it so spare me the whole 'it's not what you think' speech."

Her alabaster skin turned crimson with embarrassment. This wasn't the way I'd planned to clue her in that I'd seen them but given the tone of our conversation, it just came out. Thank goodness Darren was wrapped up in his gaming session. He was missing quite the spectacle.

"So you're pissed at me now because I like Brent?"

"No, I'm not pissed at you. You can date whoever you want. But I refuse to give his sister the time of day."

She squirmed in her chair, tapping her nails on the wine glass. As outspoken as she could be, my best friend hated confrontation.

"What is it?" I asked, growing more irritated by the second.

"I'm going to the shower on Saturday" —she raised her hand to halt my protest— "and I think you should come with me as a sign of goodwill."

"A sign of—" I balled up my fists, unable to speak. "No. Not a chance in hell. That girl tried to seduce Alastair on Friday night. You should have heard the things coming out of her mouth."

"Lia, I think it's best for everyone involved if someone extends the olive branch first. She likes you. Brent likes you. Be the bigger person and turn a new page."

"What is your end game?" I shouted.

Darren turned his head to see what the commotion was all about. Stephanie gave him a warning glance so heated he focused his attention back to the television.

"This is supposed to be a fresh start for both of us. Holding onto baggage from the past won't help anybody. Whatever happened between Olivia and Alastair has to be water under the bridge by now. He's marrying you. She's marrying Sergio. If she said or did something at the party it wasn't intentional."

I stood up and started pacing. "You should hear yourself. You have no idea what their past relationship was like. Olivia is a conniving, lying, crazy person. She's like a female Nathan minus the hot temper."

"I spent a lot of time with her Friday night after you disappeared.

She's not a bad person, Lia. Give her—"

"I think you should go home before I say something I'll regret." I shook, glaring at her. How my best friend, the one person who I leaned on the most during a difficult time in my life, could push me into something she knew made me uncomfortable hurt like nothing I'd experienced. My head pounded so hard my eyes felt like they'd fly out of their sockets.

"Amelia."

I spun around and came face to face with Alastair. I hadn't heard him walk into the room. He looked from Stephanie to me, tilting his head to the side. "Is everything alright?"

"Everything's great," Stephanie said with a sugary smile. "Lia was just telling me all about the generous offer another one of your ex-girlfriends made today."

Alastair bristled at her tone and steeled his expression. Darren sauntered over and grabbed a beer off the table. "Want one, mate?" he asked, offering a bottle to Alastair.

"Cheers."

The four of us remained at the table as a black cloud of tension billowed over our heads. Darren attempted to lighten the mood with a funny story about a Photoshop mishap. Too bad nobody else found it amusing. More than anything I wanted to sink into a warm bubble bath, put on some music and forget today happened. Hell, I'd even go for a long jog in the pouring rain. For a fleeting second I wished I still lived in Orlando. Then I looked at my handsome, exhausted fiancé and wiped that thought clear from my mind. I wanted to wrap myself around him and shut out the world.

"I don't understand why you won't come with me on Saturday." Stephanie practically shrieked.

I clenched my fists and started to answer. Alastair raised his beer bottle and interrupted. "What's on Saturday?"

"Olivia's bridal shower."

Without missing a beat, he took a sip and glared at her. "Why are *you* going?"

"Because I'm fucking her brother." She folded her arms and glared back. "Is that what you wanted to hear?"

"No, Stephanie, it wasn't. You can go to any bridal showers you want. Lia won't be going with you."

I took offense to his bossy tone. "Hang on a second. I'm not going because I don't want to, not because you say so."

"What is it with this girl that has the two of you so up in arms over her? She's harmless."

I was not about to open that can of worms. "It's not important, Steph. Let it go."

"Then come with me." She pleaded before jabbing her finger at Alastair. "Your goddam past has such a hold on everything. Stop dragging my best friend into your black hole."

"This isn't up for negotiation. Lia isn't going."

"How dare you," she yelled. "The last time I checked, Lia was free to do whatever she wanted. You don't control her. You should thank your lucky stars that she ever gave you a second chance after you were such an asshole to her."

Her shrill voice echoed through the room. Darren winced and shrunk back into the chair.

"That's enough." I clutched onto the table so hard my knuckles turned white.

"Great. Defend *him*." Her ice blue eyes darted from Alastair to me. "What happened to you, Lia? He says jump, you say how high. I want you to come with me because you're my best friend and I want to spend the day with you. So you don't like the bride. I get it. Big deal. We'll make fun of the presents or whatever. Besides, I like her brother. A lot. Brent will be there and I want you to see what an awesome guy he is."

I didn't know what to say. Stephanie and I just stared at each other. After a couple minutes, she shook her head.

"That's it. I'm out." She jumped up and stalked toward the front door. "When you're ready to start acting like my best friend again you know where to find me." The door slammed behind her, resonating through the house. Darren excused himself quietly.

A hot, salty lump formed in my throat, burning my esophagus. We'd never fought like this before and I feared our friendship was forever damaged. Alastair wiped an errant tear from my cheek.

"I'm sorry, love."

I had no words. I just stood there like a weakling and cried. The one person whose comfort I wanted was also partly the cause of this argument.

"I can't bear to see you like this," he said, brushing his thumb on my damp skin. "Come. Lie down."

He led me to the bedroom and attempted to curl up next to me on the mattress. "Stop," I said. "I want to be alone for a little while."

Pain and guilt ravaged his features before they were locked away by a mask of impassivity. He walked away without saying a word.

*  *  *

The clock on the nightstand revealed it was a little after two in the morning. Alastair's side of the bed remained unused and there was a distinct chill in the room. I got up, looking for something to put on over my pajamas to ward off the cold. I found a soft, gray cardigan and wrapped myself in it before shuffling down the hall to Alastair's office. When he wasn't asleep next to me, this was the next logical place he'd be. But he wasn't there. Making my way toward the living room, I heard a noise coming from behind a closed door and stopped. I twisted the knob slowly, expecting it to be locked. This room was never open and I hadn't worked up enough nerve yet to ask what was in there. To my surprise, the knob turned and the door creaked open.

A single lamp sat on a nightstand next to a bed. Aside from a dresser and a small chest, the room was bare. Standing in front of a window, Alastair stared out into the darkness. He hadn't changed out of his suit yet. Turning to look at me, his callous, cold expression stopped my heart.

"You shouldn't be in here." The melodic beauty of his accent fell as flat as his words. "Go back to bed."

Desolation and sadness filled every corner of the room, suffocating me. I started to walk toward him but was halted by the deadness in his eyes. "What's—"

"Not now, Amelia."

I grasped the doorknob, steadying myself. I'd already fought with my best friend. I didn't need a blowout with the man I loved. "Come to bed with me."

A yearning filled his eyes so powerfully I could feel his love for me stretch clear across the room. I wanted to know what haunted him. I wanted him to lose himself in me, not this black hole.

"You said you wanted to be alone."

"I did, for a little while. Not all night. Alastair, please, don't shut me out."

Like an apparition, he appeared in front of me, pressing his lips to mine. "You make me feel…" He grimaced, shaking his head. "I can't."

I ran my fingers through his hair, unable to prevent him from drowning in his own personal hell. All I could do was wait.

"My Lia," he whispered. "Hanging onto that cliff is harder and harder each day."

Choking bad a sob, I held him so tight I thought I might crack his ribs. All his muscles tensed. I shivered as the warmth of his body left mine. He backed away, sitting on the bed. I fought an urge to run to him. Instead, I watched him withdraw so far into himself I feared he'd never be reachable again.

"Do you blame me for what happened with Stephanie tonight?"

"Of course not. She's been testy for days. This has been building, trust me."

Luminous green eyes met mine. Their brightness was tinged with the familiar dominant spark that sent my pulse racing. My lips parted. We stared at one another as the seconds morphed into minutes. He never broke free of the protective shield but his eyes kept their intensity.

"Come to bed," I requested again, holding out my hand. Without hesitating, he stood up and scooped me in his arms. I laughed in spite of the disquiet as he carried me down the hallway. To my surprise, he brought me into the kitchen.

"Wait here," he said, putting me down. I sat at the breakfast bar, watching him grab a pint of ice cream from the freezer and a couple of spoons. I still couldn't get a read on what was going on in his head.

"What's this for?" I asked.

He shrugged, sitting next to me. "Felt like having something sweet."

We ate in silence for a few minutes. The impenetrable shield was padlocked. His whole demeanor was unwelcoming and stiff. Stabbing my spoon into the ice cream, I sighed.

"Talk to me."

"No."

"You can't keep doing this. You can't keep tugging at my emotions and putting me on this roller coaster all the time. You're so hot and cold sometimes Alastair. I can't take it."

"Why are you pushing me?"

"Because I love you and I want you to be free of everything that you've been holding onto all your life. The guilt. The self-hate. The fear of letting people in. You lock yourself behind this wall and refuse to feel anything."

Dropping the spoon, he balled his hands into tight fists. "I feel *everything* when I'm with you," he said through clenched teeth. "I lose control of every emotion whenever you're near me. You make me feel..." He exhaled sharply. "Dammit, Lia. You make me feel like I can have it all with you. You make me feel so safe and loved. But it scares the shit out of me because I could lose you in a heartbeat."

I let the raw emotion of his words fill the space between us.

He'd bared his soul to me so unexpectedly I almost didn't believe it. Seeing him so exposed sent me into a tizzy.

Sliding off the stool, he cupped my jaw. "Tell me," he ordered. "Tell me what you're thinking."

"You feel safe with me?"

His eyes widened as the realization of what he'd admitted set in. "Yes," he answered in a strained whisper. "I've felt safe with you all along."

On some level, I'd always known he felt that way but I needed to hear it. And he needed to say it, to make it real. He needed to realize on his own and in his own time that expressing how he felt wasn't a death sentence.

"Maybe now you can let go of that cliff," I said, playing with his tie.

Grabbing my hand, he frowned. "I can't fix everything in one night. Can feeling this way and being with you be enough?"

"Of course, chief." I kissed him. "Come to bed."

"With you?"

"No. With the other tired chick standing in your kitchen."

I started to make my way to the bedroom and noticed he wasn't following. When I turned, I saw he was still seated at the breakfast bar, looking me up and down. "Are you coming?"

Lifting a brow, he smirked. "Invite me."

"What are you, a vampire?"

"Want me to suck on your neck?"

Words failed me, yet again. Folding my arms, I grinned. He looked so damn alluring sitting there with those come-hither eyes. "You have to catch me first."

I made it maybe three steps before I felt his arms around my waist. His body pressed to mine.

"When will you learn, kitten? I'll always catch you."

* * *

136

I sat in Sam's office flanked by Robbie, Julian and the company attorney. Apparently Julian's little sexting scandal was all a hoax set up by a woman he'd been flirting with online. The picture was deemed not to be of my host's unmentionables. The girl who accused him doctored the screen shot she'd taken of her phone to make it look like the photo was sent from Julian's cell number. His phone was searched and no lewd photos were found. In fact, the only photos on there were of food, ties, suits and his dog. I didn't even know he had a dog.

"We dodged this one," Sam said, rubbing his eyes, "but let this be a warning to you, Archer. In this day and age with social media and the internet and what not every little thing you do can become public in seconds."

Julian employed an impassive expression. "Can we move on to more pressing topics, like this week's program?"

I thought Sam's head was going to explode. Robbie shifted in the chair and shot me a look. All I wanted to do was wrap up this meeting and get on with my day. Thankfully, the attorney had the same idea and within minutes we were all free to continue with our lives.

The afternoon remained quiet so I was able to breeze through my tasks without too many interruptions. Of course that gave my mind permission to wander. Last night's fight with Stephanie still stung. I hadn't heard from her all at today. The whole argument had been so irrational and stupid. I sat up straighter. She'd cool off soon enough. I knew how she operated. By tomorrow night we'd be laughing over a bottle of wine.

"Lia?"

My desk phone started ringing. Ignoring it, I looked up and saw Meredith standing in the doorway.

"You have a visitor."

"Who is it?"

She turned and waved someone in. Sashaying in like the Queen of Hearts was none other than Emma Whelan.

"Sorry I didn't call," she said, sitting down in a swirl of perfume,

Burberry and smiles. "It's been a day."

I stared at her, not quite believing she'd just invited herself into my office and subsequently, my life. Her violet eyes gleamed with excitement as they studied every inch of my face and body.

"You look fantastic, Lia. Girl-next-door with a hint of sexy. Perfect for any run ins with the press."

"What are you doing here?"

"Strategizing. We have a lot to get through and the sooner we tackle everything on my list, the better."

She rummaged through her fancy Chanel bag, pulling out a notebook. All I could do was think about how nasty she'd been to me at the garden party.

"What are you talking about?"

"I'm your publicist, darling." Ruby glossed lips stretched back into a smile that was meant to be endearing but came off as fake.

"No you're not. I haven't decided—"

"I've just come from a meeting with Alastair. He decided."

# CHAPTER FOURTEEN

"Get out of my office." I slammed my hands on the desk, rising to my feet. "Now."

Emma sighed, shaking her head. "I told him to call you. That boy never listens." She crossed her legs, making it clear she wasn't going anywhere. "He asked to see me this morning so I flew in from London first thing. Sit down, Lia. You know how Alastair is. When he wants something, he stops at nothing until he gets it."

"This is insane. We can't work together. You still want him. You told me as much over the summer."

Her all-business expression softened. "He's not mine to have anymore. He never was. My relationship with Alastair isn't what you think."

"Oh no? Well he seems to think it's okay to sanction this… whatever this is without talking to me first." My stomach twisted into a knot.

"He's protecting you."

"From what?"

Tossing her raven hair over one shoulder, she leveled an intense stare at me. "That's just his nature. You know that."

"It still doesn't explain why *you* have to be the one involved."

She sighed again, waving her hand. "Sit."

My butt hit the chair with a thud. I folded my arms, giving

Emma my best don't-screw-around-with-me stare. "This better be good."

"I can count on one hand how many people Alastair Holden trusts. Really trusts. There is something about you that breaks down every barrier he has and as you know, those are infinite. You're his weakness and in turn, he is fiercely protective of you. I've never seen anything like it and I've known him for ages. That night at the garden party when we met? I was at the receiving end of a scolding so harsh I'm surprised I managed to walk away with my dignity."

"It couldn't have been that harsh. You were still able to throw me a bitchy look."

A swath of pink stained her cherubic face. "Natural reflex. Look, I'm sorry. I didn't come here to rehash anything. I want to help Alastair and that means helping you."

"No offense but I can handle a group of photographers waiting outside the building on my own. I don't need you for that."

The desk phone rang for the millionth time today. I ignored it, watching the wheels turn in Emma's head.

"How many calls are you getting?"

"I don't know. A lot."

"Annoying, isn't it? If I was your contact person that phone wouldn't ring at all."

This chick was up to something but I couldn't put my finger on it. Who gave a rat's ass how many times my phone rang? That's what voicemail was for. In an attempt to remain diplomatic, I smiled.

"I appreciate the offer but no thanks."

Emma's frown deepened. She rummaged through her bag again and handed me a business card. "I'll be in Glasgow for the rest of the week. If you change your mind or just want to chat, call me."

The light, floral scent of her perfume hung in the air long after she'd left. The horrible feeling of dread I'd had several times over the past week returned with a vengeance. Determined not to succumb to my habit of overanalyzing, I threw myself into my work. Rain drops slapped at the windows, their impact sounding more and more like those little plastic sheets of air bubbles I used to pop as a kid.

Once six o'clock rolled around, I grabbed my belongings and got out of the building as fast as my legs would carry me. I didn't see Paxton waiting, which saddened me because I didn't have an umbrella. The rain was still coming down in sheets, covering the sidewalk in its glossy sheen. Taking a deep breath, I exited the safety of the overhang to hail a cab. Out the corner of my eye I saw Stephanie ducking into the backseat of a black Bentley. I paused, watching Brent fold his tall frame into the car after her. A pang of regret swept through my drenched body.

I hope we could get past our fight. After all, she was my best friend and I'd love nothing more than to hash out all of today's happenings with her over a cheese pizza and some chardonnay.

"Amelia."

The sound of my name being called was almost drowned out by the downpour. Shivering, I turned back to the street and saw Alastair standing next to the gray Mercedes SUV.

"Get in the car, love."

Seeing him filled me alternately with anger and relief. Mostly relief, thank goodness. I jogged over and climbed into the back with him.

"Why on earth were you standing outside in this weather?" he asked, wrapping his arms around me. I snuggled into him, grateful for his warmth.

"Trying to hail a taxi."

"You'll have a better result if you actually face the traffic." His lips brushed against my temple.

I sat up straight. "I didn't know you were picking me up."

"Thought I'd surprise you."

The mere sight of his smile relaxed me in a way I desperately needed. Curling back into his side, I closed my eyes and reveled in the safety of his arms. Traffic was awful thanks to the bad weather so our commute home took longer than usual. I didn't mind. The delay gave me an excuse to stay entwined with him and focus on how insanely amazing it felt to be secured in his embrace.

The first thing I did when we arrived home was dart off to the bedroom to change. I was soaked right down to my underwear. The dampness chilled my bones in a way I hadn't experienced since growing up during the frigid winters in Connecticut. *Spoiled rotten by the Florida sunshine.*

I grabbed some leggings and Alastair's Oxford University sweatshirt. It was worn and old and I loved it. He'd kept it folded and buried under a pile of clothes on one of the bottom shelves. I found it while 'hunting for some closet space' after I moved here. Or that's what I'd told him.

"I keep meaning to bin that old thing," he said, walking into the living room.

"The shirt or me?"

"Cheeky." He kissed my forehead. "Hungry?"

I nodded, noticing how fatigued he looked. "You should change out of this suit and get more comfortable."

"I will. Later. Come with me." He tugged on my hand, leading me into the kitchen. "Are leftovers alright?"

"Sure."

I sat at the breakfast bar while he reheated some macaroni and cheese and set out the plates. As tired as he was, he kept shooting me flirtatious little smiles and even winked. I had no idea what had him in such a playful mood but I wasn't about to spoil it.

"Admiring my devilish good looks again?"

I laughed. "Who are you?"

"Just an average guy making an average dinner for my girl," he quipped, placing a heaping plate of mac and cheese in front of me. "Make sure you finish all of it."

"Aye, aye." I grinned, mock saluting him.

"If you're going to be my first mate, you'll have to work on that."

"The salute? Don't get used to it. We work better as co-captains."

He smiled, hovering his lips over mine. I shivered with anticipation, letting any lingering annoyance from my day slide away into oblivion. "I don't know about that, Meyers. I rather like telling you what to do," he said, planting a decadent kiss on me.

Butterflies commandeered my stomach, making it next to impossible to eat. Our intense connection sizzled, heightening all my senses. I studied his every feature, admiring the glow in his eyes and impish grin.

"If I didn't know any better, I'd say you won the lottery or had the best day ever."

He lifted a brow. "How so?"

"You look happy."

"That's an easy one. I get to come home to you at night."

"Alright," I said, putting down the fork, "what's going on. Why all the romance and sweet talk?"

"Suspicious little thing, aren't you?" He stood and caged me on the barstool. "You need to stop overanalyzing everything and enjoy the moment. I know you had a trying day and— Don't interrupt me. Tonight is about you and me. All that outside noise can wait. As for all the romance and sweet talk, well, I'm leaving in the morning and wanted to treat you to a special night."

His efforts to distract me from talking about Emma's visit to my office were working. I didn't want to spend the night arguing with him. Besides, he just looked so damn *cute* right now.

A shy smile curled my lips. "Okay, Mr. No-Relationships-Non-Dater. My apologies."

"Accepted." He left a trail of velvet kisses up and down my neck. "Finish your dinner so we can go somewhere a little more comfortable."

Making his way around the breakfast bar, he grabbed two glasses and a bottle of merlot.

"Trying to get me drunk?" I asked, watching him pour a generous serving. Without answering, he sat next to me. My heart rate kicked up seeing the controlling, sultry spark in his eyes. I had a feeling tonight was going to be one hell of an adventure.

We finished our food and, yes, I had more than one glass of wine. How could I not? It was delicious and, if nothing else, helped settle my frayed nerves from the afternoon. I curled up on the couch with a full tummy, happy and content. Any worries or annoyances that lingered in my subconscious were silent for now. I let my mind wander, imagining what our wedding would look like. I wanted something simple, something that complimented both our personalities. As beautiful as my sister's wedding had been, I didn't want a castle or an extravagant location. Although with Alastair, that's more than likely what I'd get. I mean really, his idea of a 'proper date' when we'd first met was an evening at the opera.

Not that I'm complaining. He made me feel special and cherished in ways that material items could never accomplish. Plus, the not-so-subtle way he had to have me at a moment's notice never failed to make me believe I was the most desirable creature on the planet in his eyes. I'd never been able to admit that to myself before but with him, it was a no-brainer.

"What are you smiling about?"

I opened my eyes, surprised to see him next to me on the couch. I hadn't heard him come in or felt the cushions move. Sitting up, I positioned myself so I faced him and laced my fingers with his. "Thank you."

"For what?"

"Being you."

His breath caught as disbelief ghosted behind his eyes. Leaning close, he kissed my forehead. "Is that the wine talking?"

I cupped his chin and smiled. "No."

"You're doing it again," he whispered.

"What?"

"Making me feel safe."

Love surged through me so powerfully I was certain he could see it bleeding from my pores. My skin tingled with a heightened awareness, as though our souls had entwined. He touched me with such reverence I shivered in delight.

"I want to try something with you."

"What?"

A slow, seductive grin spread across his face. "I'm not telling. Just trust me."

"Okay," I answered a bit more breathy than usual.

"Close your eyes."

I did without hesitating. His fingers on my chin were the first things I felt. He tugged my bottom lip down and kissed me. I sighed, welcoming the warmth and firmness of his mouth on mine. He held my face, deepening the kiss. His quiet moan intensified my already raging pulse.

"Keep your eyes closed, love," he whispered. I could hear the rustling of clothes, like he was undressing. My lids popped open.

"What did I say?" He smirked, unbuttoning his shirt. "Closed. Or I'll blindfold you."

"You wouldn't dare."

Lifting a brow, he fingered the silk tie laying on the coffee table. "Is that a challenge, Amelia Grace?"

"I can't keep my eyes closed knowing you're going to be naked. It's a fact of life."

His eyes darkened. "It's settled then. Stand up and turn around."

Excited and curious, I did as I was told. The soft material covered my eyes, turning the outside world dark. He secured it in a knot and then turned me so I faced him. At least, I think I was facing him. I couldn't see a damn thing. My other senses were now on high alert. I could hear him breathing and felt the heat radiating off his body.

"Feel okay?"

"Yes."

"Good."

I anticipated his next move, wondering if he'd kiss me. His fingers brushed against my chin again, tugging down my lip.

"Tonight, I want you to experience what it's like to have zero control over how you feel. You won't be able to see what I'm going to do, you'll only guess. I promise I won't do anything to make you uncomfortable but if I do, you have to tell me, alright?"

"I trust you, Alastair."

He let go of my chin and, for all intents and purposes, left me standing blind. I focused on listening to my surroundings. At first, all I heard was the tremendous beating of my heart. Footsteps padded along the carpeted floor. My stomach rustled with restless anticipation. I wanted his hands on me and I wanted it now.

"What are you doing, Holden?"

"Patience." His rich voice slid through my veins like honey. I hadn't expected him to be so close. Unhurried and methodical, he undressed me, touching every inch of my bare skin after each article of clothing was removed. His touch always drove me wild but this was different. This was far more intense. His fingers never left my skin. Their soft strokes traced my shoulders and arms, moving toward my lower back and down my legs. I shuddered from the euphoric sensation when he slid his fingers along my tailbone and then followed the curve of my backside. Standing up straight was becoming difficult.

The unmistakable scent of his body cloaked me. I bowed my head, halted by his chest. The hairs tickled my face as I kissed and nipped at his skin. I hooked my arms around his waist only to be restrained by his firm hold.

"No, Lia. I'm not finished with you yet."

"But I want—"

"I know what you want," he said, cupping my breast. "We're doing this my way right now. I need you to lie down."

He pulled me to the floor. The onslaught of sensuous touching continued, lighting a fire in the pit of my stomach. I had no idea where his hands would land next but I knew, without question, he kept avoiding the one place I wanted his touch the most. Every time he teased the skin along my pelvis, I shook. Not knowing when he'd give me what I wanted drove me crazy.

Parting my lips with his tongue, he groaned as he kissed me. At some point, he'd want me to touch him. He could never go long without needing to feel my hands on him. Kissing him with as much love, lust and passion as I could muster, I grabbed a handful of his hair and pulled.

My attempt to turn the tables was short-lived. My body quivered the second he outlined the sensitive skin around my clit. I gasped, arching my back.

"Don't stop. That feels so good." I clawed at the carpet.

And then it all came to a screeching halt. I trembled, unable to breathe. He wasn't finished, was he? He can't be. I wanted more. I wanted it all. "Alastair, please."

I felt him hovering over me. Something warm and hard slid along my thigh when he flexed his hips.

"Is it too much, kitten, what you're feeling?" He kept rubbing his erection against my raw, needy skin sending shockwaves through me. "Should I stop?"

"No," I panted. "Don't ever stop."

Pinning my arms to the floor, he pushed the full weight of his body into mine and traced the outer edge of my lips with his tongue, heightening my arousal. Every inch of my body screamed for him. I squirmed under his weight, wrapping my legs around his hips.

"I need you to stay still, Lia."

The heat of his body disappeared seconds before he helped me stand. My knees were so weak I was afraid I'd topple over.

"Hold on to this." He placed my hands on what felt like the back of the sofa. I dug my nails into the material to ensure I wouldn't lose my balance. Thank goodness I did. The second his fingers moved down my spine I practically convulsed. Swiping my hair to side, he kissed the crook of my neck.

"You are so sexy," he whispered, grasping my behind. "I want you like this." The damp warmth of his lips touched my shoulders as he starting kissing down my back. His hands followed the same path, pausing at my hips. He pulled them back toward him, urging my legs apart. I bent forward, pressing my fingers into the couch so hard I assumed they turned white.

Gathering my hair in his hand, he pulled it, forcing my head to tilt back. I knew what was coming next but was too spent and overstimulated to fully prepare myself.

I cried out his name in a breathless rush as he swiftly and unabashedly thrust into my body. I had no idea how I was able to stand as his pace increased in speed and intensity. Wrapping an arm around my waist, he surrounded me.

"Amelia," he moaned, kissing the shell of my ear.

I became more attuned to my deepest desires upon hearing the unfiltered yearning in his voice. He was possessing me in every way possible, dominating all my senses, and I welcomed it with ease.

Another deep groan escaped his lips, bringing me to the edge. His feverish movements and low, sexy sounds coupled with the unbelievable sensations coursing through my body triggered an intense orgasm. My legs locked in place as wave after wave consumed me. My hands slipped forward. Alastair grabbed my hips and pushed into me so deep and hard I orgasmed again with him. Shaking and gasping for breath, I let him turn me and sagged against him when he banded his arms around me.

Not saying a word, he removed the tie from my eyes. I squinted against the dim light until he came into focus. A tsunami of emotions washed over me as I looked into his clear, unveiled eyes.

"Are you okay?"

I nodded, still trying to catch my breath. He grinned, nuzzling into my neck. "Thought I'd give you a preview of what's to come for your birthday on Thursday."

"I'm going to need a week to recover if that was only a preview."

The frantic ringing of the doorbell drowned the sound of his gorgeous, throaty laugh. We looked at one another.

"Are you expecting anyone?" I asked.

Loud pounding on the door made us both stiffen. He let me go, putting on his pants. I scrambled for my own clothes, dressing quickly before following him to the front door. The bell rang again and again.

Alastair opened the door, revealing a soaked and crying Stephanie.

"Lia," she whimpered, rushing in and hugging me. "I didn't know where else to go. I'm sorry. I'm sorry."

I held my best friend as she quivered and sobbed. Alastair and I exchanged concerned glances.

"It's okay," I said. "What's wrong?"

She pulled away, heaving and unable to speak. Mascara ran down her cheeks in thick, black rivers.

"Come inside, Stephanie," Alastair said. "Let's get you dried off before you catch pneumonia."

"No," she yelled. "I can't. Lia." She looked at me, her eyes wide and terrified. "I'm pregnant."

# *CHAPTER FIFTEEN*

Stephanie's hand shook as she raised the mug and sipped tea. She was a mess, both physically and emotionally. At least she'd calmed down enough to change out of her soaking wet clothes into something dry.

"Your fiancé makes awesome tea."

"The perks of dating an Englishman."

"I'm an asshole," she said, raising her ice blue eyes to meet mine. "I shouldn't have said all that stuff last night."

I waved my hand. "We're like sisters. We say stupid shit to each other, fight, don't talk and then make up. It's all part of the deal."

"Yeah but—" she searched for the words "—I always go for the low blow. Sorry."

I reached across the table and patted her hand. As hurt as I still was, she didn't need me to be salty. She needed a supportive ear, not a grudge. "So, I'll pick you up at eight tomorrow morning. We'll go to the doctor, get the blood test and see what happens."

"Ugh. I hope the home pregnancy test was wrong." She looked guilty. "Was that mean to say? I'm so not ready for this."

I smiled. "Everything will work out. Either way, at least you'll know."

"Thanks, Meyers," she grumbled. "How were you so calm when you went through this with Nathan?"

I stiffened. The horrid memory of when I'd told him I thought I was pregnant washed through me. Stephanie's eyes widened.

"Are you okay? You're squeezing the life out of that napkin."

Looking down, I was surprised to see I had the cloth in a death grip. I dropped it. "I'm fine."

"That's a hefty serving of bullshit right there."

"It's old news, Steph."

"Okay. Fair enough." She sipped her tea. "I should get home."

As she stood up and approached for the conciliatory hug, I couldn't help but feel that our friendship was still fractured. I loved this girl to pieces and knew, deep down, that our bond was far stronger than any fight but this whole situation felt different. She'd been hiding a relationship from me. Not that she had to tell me every single detail of her life but this was unlike her. I knew about every date, good or bad, she ever went on when we lived in Orlando. I'd been in Glasgow for six weeks and had no clue she was dating Brent Garrison. No clue at all.

Alastair looked up from a file of documents he'd been sifting through on the couch when we walked into the living room. His hair had that disheveled look it gets from constantly running his hands through it in frustration.

"Feeling better?" he asked Stephanie.

"Yeah. Thanks. Sorry for interrupting your night."

"No worries, love," he said, standing up. "I'll have Paxton drive you back to your flat."

Stephanie turned to me and smiled before following him to the door. She really did have a gorgeous smile and it was great to see it make an appearance. I cleaned up the kitchen and went to the bedroom. It was after midnight and my body ached with exhaustion. The plush bedding felt so damn good as I sank into it with ease, closing my eyes.

"Stop lurking by the door and come in here, chief." I smiled. I always knew when he was near, even without seeing him.

The mattress shifted from his weight as he sat. "Quite the night, wouldn't you say?"

I gazed into his stunning emerald irises. "They always are."

"I have some more work to finish before coming to bed. Don't wait up for me."

"Try not to stay up too late. This bed is way too lonely without you."

The small, shy smile that melted my heart curled his mouth. I sat up and hugged him. He sighed into my embrace, nuzzling against my neck.

"What's this for?"

"No reason." I squeezed him tighter. "I just felt like it."

"Lucky me."

Resting my forehead to his, I couldn't shake a sense of trepidation. Stephanie had touched on something I hadn't allowed myself to think about in months.

"I've lost you to the depths of your mind again, haven't I?" Alastair's gentle question brought me back to the present.

"Do you ever wonder about us…having…" I paused, unable to control the tremor in my voice.

"I do," he answered, seeming to know what I'd meant. His touch was comforting but unease shrouded his expression. "One thing at a time, Lia. Right now, I'm focused on marrying you and having you all to myself for a bit."

I grinned. "You always have me all to yourself. In back offices, front hallways, kitchen tables, private planes, penthouse bedrooms, bubble baths, showers—"

Interrupted by his kiss, I wrapped my arms around him. I knew I should let him go work but I wanted him next to me. Selfish? Yep. But really, who cares? He wasn't too bothered by my efforts either.

"Take off your clothes," he whispered on my lips.

"Again? I thought you had to finish—"

"I can do it on the plane."

Who am I to argue with that?

*  *  *

An exorbitant amount of yelling came out of Julian's office as I walked by on my way to the micro kitchen. For a fleeting second I thought maybe the salacious text had come back and bitten him in the ass.

The door flew open, sucking in a gulp of air and rustling my skirt.

"Lia. In here. I need you." Julian shot me a pleading look, complete with a pout.

I rolled my eyes and walked in. Nobody else was in here which led me to believe he'd been shouting at random into the universe.

"My brother is on his way," he said, pacing the office. "Take him to lunch. Show him the newsroom. Keep him out of my hair."

"What?" I raised my eyebrows. "You have a brother?"

"Yes. And you have a sister. Now that we've bonded over siblings, will you keep him occupied?"

"I hate to break it you but I'm not your personal assistant."

"But you *are* my executive producer and I need you."

The wheels spun in my head. "Why me?"

"Sam is still salty about the non-penis event and Robbie has the personality of a diaper. You're friendly, pretty and can hold a conversation. My brother and I aren't what you would categorize as close but we're similar in personality. You handle me just fine, so you'll be able to handle him."

Fantastic.

"I don't have time to babysit your family, Julian."

Throwing his head back in frustration, he continued to pace the room. "Is it the goddam questions I asked Garrison last week? Is that it? Are you still holding that over my head?"

"No. But now that you mention it."

"Lia, come on. I'm a journalist. I wouldn't be doing my job if I didn't ask those questions. I admire your wanting to protect Holden but he's a big boy. He can take care of himself. Besides,

Holden World Media is about to make a huge announcement regarding the future of the company." He folded his arms. "As I'm sure you already know."

Mindful to keep a placid expression, I nodded. My head spun. I had no idea what he was talking about but didn't want to give him the satisfaction.

"I have to get back to work." I left before giving him a chance to answer and went to my office. The phone was ringing, as usual. I answered with as much enthusiasm as I could muster.

"Amelia Grace. Why is it that one week has passed and you haven't called me to tell me that you're engaged?"

"Mom." I sat with a thud. "I know, I'm sorry. Work has been busy and then…I meant to call you. I did."

"The ladies are all asking me about a wedding date. Do you know what it's like trying to bluff my way through that conversation? Not to mention the fact they've started whispering with each other that you're pregnant and this is some kind of shot gun wedding."

"Jesus Christ," I muttered.

"The language." The tone in her voice was brisk. "Are you?"

"Am I what?"

"Pregnant."

"Oh my God, Mom. No. I'm not. Why all the hysterics?"

"This is a big deal. He's a global celebrity. It's spreading all over social media and the internet like wildfire. A day doesn't go by when I don't see your face on someone's blog or that Facebook thing or whatever they're called."

"You're on Facebook?"

"No. Annette is so she can stay in touch with Gary since he's all the way in Seattle for college."

"Why don't you just set up a Google alert in my name so you can keep track that way?"

"There's no need to give me any lip, Amelia."

"Sorry." I rubbed my temples. "It's been a long week."

"Whatever Alastair said when he called to get our blessing dazzled your father to no end. He can't stop talking about him. We adore him, even though he dragged you to the other side of the planet to live with him."

Leaning back in my chair, I laughed. How I could I not? That's her way; cushion with flattery and then jab with a sword at the end. "Dayna gave me a list of things you'd say. So far, you're sticking to the same script you used when she moved to England for Andrew."

A long, blustery sigh came through the receiver. "Someday when you have kids, you'll understand."

"Thanks for the warning."

"In case I can't reach you tomorrow, happy birthday."

"Thanks, Mom."

"I love you."

"You too."

Now that I'd spoken to my family about the engagement I felt better. It felt more real. I also wanted to know what my charming Englishman said to my dad. I glanced at the clock on the computer monitor. It was almost one. I fished my cell phone out of my purse.

**12:57pm Thank you x**

**12:59pm What for?**

**1:02pm Tell you later**

**1:03pm No hints?**

**1:04pm Nope. Go back to work**

**1:06pm Minx**

**1:09pm You love it**

"Lia." Julian burst through the door. "Randy will be here in ten minutes. Fortunately for you, he can't stay long."

I zoned out while Julian continued to pepper me with compliments and praise. Keeping his brother occupied wasn't that big of a deal. From the way Julian made it sound, Randy was only stopping by for a quick hello on his way to the airport. I had no idea why I was involved in any of this but whatever.

As promised, Randy Archer arrived ten minutes later. Much like Julian, he was tall with dark hair and carried himself with an air of self-importance. One Archer was a handful but two? I thanked my lucky stars they didn't co-host the show.

"You are a stunner," Randy exclaimed, grasping my hands. "Those tabloid photos do you no justice. Gorgeous. Absolutely gorgeous."

His thick Scottish accent made each word sound more special than they actually were. Julian, for all his bluster about wanting to keep Randy out of his hair, stuck around while we toured the studio.

"I've seen this place a million times. My brother likes to show off where he informs the masses."

"Where are you flying off to now?" Julian asked.

"China."

I stood silently listening to the brothers wax poetic about their past visits to the Great Wall. Yet again, I was surprised at how little I knew about my news host's activities outside of work.

Julian turned to me. "My brother owns a software corporation that makes enterprise software to manage business operations and customer relations."

"That sounds exciting." I smiled, not having a clue what he meant.

"It's busy," Randy said. "I'm never in one place longer than three weeks. The world is my office." He glanced at his watch. "I'm off soon but before leaving I'd like to steal Jules for a few minutes. Thank you for humoring my brother about keeping me away from him and being so gracious."

"No problem." I turned on my heel and walked away but not before catching the scowl that crossed Julian's lips. *Sorry buddy. I tried.*

Now that this mindless task was finished I did have some work to finalize before having lunch. Plus, I wanted a cupcake. I'd been craving one all day.

A box wrapped in that familiar Tiffany blue sat on the corner of my desk, all dressed up with a white ribbon. I grabbed it, revealing a small card underneath. I read the message and felt my heart flutter in my throat.

WEAR THIS TOMORROW SO YOU'RE NOT LATE
FOR A NIGHT YOU'LL NEVER FORGET.
YOURS, ALASTAIR X

Dizzy with anticipation, I opened the box. Inside sat a stunning vintage platinum watch, encrusted with diamonds. The delicate band glittered under the lights in my office. I was blown away, yet again, by this man I loved. I slid the watch onto my wrist, admiring how it sparkled. My stomach interrupted the gawking by reminding me that although diamonds were beautiful, cupcakes were edible.

Grabbing my coat, I scurried to the elevator and out into the brisk autumn sunshine. For the first time in days it wasn't raining so more people were outside taking advantage of the nice weather.

The usual group of photographers lurked by the strip of cafes and restaurants near my building. I managed to slip inside one without being noticed and ordered a sandwich and yes, a cupcake. Excited about the prospect of food and confection, I bumped right into someone on the sidewalk when I left the cafe.

"Oh! I'm so—"

My voice caught. I looked up, coming eye to eye with Olivia

157

Garrison. Words failed me. She stood with a bright smile on her face, like it was natural to bump into me on the streets of Glasgow. Unflustered by my lack of a greeting, her frosted pink glossy lips remained pulled back in a grin.

"Lia. How lovely to see you."

Thank goodness my hands were occupied because I wanted nothing more than to strangle her. Or slap her. Or maybe just yank some hair from her perfect little pixie cut. "I don't have time for this." The uncivilized tone in my voice came as a shock to me. Olivia blinked, clearly stunned.

"I'm not going to start anything, Lia. After all, you did walk into me. I was just minding my own business."

"Right. Sorry. Now if you'll excuse me."

I sidestepped around her but didn't make it far. She called out after me, "I'd really like for us to talk."

I spun around. "About what?"

She pulled her cream peacoat tighter around her body. "There's been a misunderstanding over some things you think I said at my brother's party last week. I want to clear the air."

"Misunderstanding? I heard you, Olivia. I heard you say I'd never satisfy him and he'd get bored with me. I heard you say that you should be his fiancée. Nothing needs to be cleared up. Now if you don't mind, I have to get back to work."

Out the corner of my eye I noticed several photographers snapping away. Great. This was all I needed. A public cat fight documented for the world to see.

Pushing her shoulders back, her cobalt eyes hardened. "You don't get it. And that's why he'll break it off with you, like he does with everyone else. He can't let anyone in, Lia. He's incapable of it. You might think his guard is down but it's not. You might think he loves you but he doesn't. He just wants to feel close to someone until something better comes along. He'll never marry you."

"You are pathetic," I seethed. "I have no time or patience to deal with your brand of crazy. Go to your fiancé before I make sure he knows what you've been trying to do behind his back."

Olivia stiffened, glaring at me. "Sergio barely registers my existence half the time. I highly doubt he'd care what I do. All he wants is for me to look pretty and stand quietly by his side. You know all about what that's like, don't you? A politician's girlfriend always knows her place."

I balled my hands into fists, crushing the paper bag that held my lunch. Olivia casually sussed out where the photographers were standing and smirked. "We have an audience. I'm always at my best when cameras are around. Aren't you?"

"From what I've heard you love performing in front of the lens," I snapped.

Smiling with an air of confidence so powerful that it shook my nerves, she leaned close. "It takes two to make the performance unforgettable."

All the air rushed from my lungs so fast I almost passed out. The world darkened around me.

"Miss Garrison. Come with me."

Startled by the deep, male voice coming from behind me, I turned and saw Paxton. I'd never been so happy to see that guy. His imposing bodyguard frame practically filled the sidewalk, blocking out the sun. Nothing about his stance was welcoming. In fact, even I was a little rattled by his presence and he wasn't here for me.

"Miss Garrison. Now."

Olivia huffed, shooting me one last parting glance. "You'll see I'm right, Lia. But by then it'll be too late."

# CHAPTER SIXTEEN

The cell phone rang and rang from the pocket of my coat. I sat in the main lobby of my building, focusing on nothing but my breathing. Businessmen and women walked by with purpose, on their way to meetings or for drinks or maybe even home. The ruined remains of my lunch lay crumpled in the paper bag on my lap. I didn't have the brain capacity to work at the moment so I just sat here, staring at nothing.

"Miss Meyers."

I looked up at the sound of Paxton's voice.

"Here." He handed me his cell phone. I put it to my ear and sighed.

"Amelia." Alastair's worried tone wrecked me. "Are you okay? Why aren't you answering your phone?"

"I'm fine. I just didn't feel like talking to anyone."

He stayed silent for several seconds. "Take the rest of the day off. Paxton will bring you home. I'll deal with Archer."

I smiled. "That's not necessary. I'm going up to my office in a minute. I wanted to—"

"I don't want you there. I want you home, where I know you won't be bothered." The edgy, commanding pitch that now colored his words irked me.

"Relax, chief. It was just a run in on a sidewalk. Everybody's still in one piece."

I could tell by his muffled sigh that he was scrubbing his face with his hand. I looked up at Paxton, who waited patiently for me to make my next move.

"I want you to do as I say."

"Hey," I snapped. "Enough. I don't need you ordering me around."

"This isn't negotiable, Amelia. I want you back at the house. Now."

"You know what else isn't negotiable? This." I hung up and tossed the cell phone at Paxton. "If he calls looking for me, tell him I'll see him when he gets home from London."

For the second time today, I wanted to strangle someone. I loved Alastair to bits but his overprotective streak pissed me off to no end. I stalked to the elevators, leaving Paxton to deal with the ringing cell phone. Back in my office, I shut the door and silenced my own cell phone before throwing myself into show preparations. Barely an hour had passed before my desk phone started ringing non-stop. I shut off the ringer, watching the red message light blink furiously. I knew, without question, the photos from my curbside encounter with Olivia were now all over the internet.

The funny thing about it was I didn't care.

* * *

Light from the candles flickered off the walls, giving the enormous bathroom a cozier ambiance. Music floated from the portable iPod station I'd sat on counter. I sank deeper into the warm water, swallowed by almond scented bubbles.

The ride home from work had been interesting. Paxton was silent, which led me to believe Alastair had laid into him about the whole Olivia thing. Poor guy. I stretched my legs. This egg-shaped tub was so huge I couldn't touch the other end even if I wanted to.

Alastair hadn't arrived home yet. I'd hoped he wouldn't stay in London too late. Maybe it was for the best that he wasn't here though. I did hang up on him and refused to take any of his calls for the rest of the day. He aggravated me so much sometimes that I ended up resorting to those less than adult ways of dealing with him.

I sighed, sinking farther under the bubbles. I stayed in the bath until the water turned cold and I couldn't take it anymore. After toweling off, I dried my damp hair, threw it up in a bun and put on my pajamas. I sat on the edge of the bed not really knowing what to do next. It was almost nine but I wasn't tired.

My body itched with nervous anticipation, reminding me of the first time I set foot in this room. The memory was so vivid and sharp. I'd been pulled into his orbit, craving him. But there was always that wall. That damned veil he used to keep me at arm's length. What Olivia said about him not letting anyone in was true.

I shook the thought from my mind. Letting it run wild wasn't the smartest thing.

The vintage watch sparkled on the nightstand. Need and want surged through me, striking my heart and taking my breath away. I wanted him here. I wanted him next to me. I wanted to feel his mouth on my skin and breathe in his scent. I wanted to lose myself in his love and never find my way back.

Seconds and minutes ticked away into hours. I must have carved a path through the house as I paced from room to room. By midnight, I resigned myself to the fact that he wasn't coming home. I went over to the media cabinet and put on some music. Snow Patrol blared from the speakers, pleading with someone to open their eyes. A jolt of electricity shot down my spine. All the small hairs on my arms stood at attention.

"Lia."

I turned and was enveloped in the most glorious hug I could ever want. He felt amazing. He smelled amazing.

Releasing me after a couple minutes, Alastair leaned his forehead to mine and smiled. "Hello, love. Sorry I'm late."

Any trepidations or agitation I felt melted away. I combed my fingers through his hair. "You're forgiven this time, chief."

He held my face, kissing me soundly. "My Lia," he whispered, running the pad of his thumb over my lips. "My angel."

"Did everything go okay at your meeting?"

Shrugging, he nodded. "As well as can be expected. I don't want to talk about work. I want to feel you close. Dance with me."

"Here?"

He smirked. "Yes. You already have the music on so we shouldn't waste it."

"Whatever you say."

Banding his arms around me, he pulled me close. I didn't recognize the song that was playing but was haunted by the woman's voice. Rather than break the mood and ask who it was, I sighed into his arms and let him guide me.

"Remember the last time we danced like this?" he asked.

"At the Kraft Azalea Garden. There wasn't any music."

He laughed. "You thought it was quite romantic though, if memory serves."

"It was a redeeming moment in your cheesy repertoire."

"Wow." He squeezed my waist. "We're back to cheesy now?"

I looked up at him, enamored by his charm and the warm glow in his eyes. A mischievous grin perked up his lips a split second before he bent me backwards in an exaggerated dip. I squealed with pleasure and laughed.

"Afraid I might drop you?"

"Never."

"Good." He pulled me upright, lacing his fingers through mine and swaying his hips. "Are you looking forward to your birthday celebration?"

"I don't know. Am I allowed to ask what we're doing?"

"No, kitten, you're not."

"One of these days you're going to give in to my curiosity."

"Possibly. This is not that day." He grinned.

"Control freak."

He lifted my right arm over my head and twirled me. "Sexy girl."

"Charmer."

Gently holding my arms behind my back, he kissed me. "I know today wasn't easy for you. I didn't mean to make it worse." The muscles in his jaw twitched.

"Your heart was in the right place. We'll work on your overbearing nature some other time."

"She likes to play mind games, Lia. She'll say anything and make it sound so convincing you'll second guess what you know is true. I don't want her filling your head with doubts."

I swallowed. "It'll take more than her telling me you don't let people in to fill my head with any doubts. I trust what you feel for me and I will never doubt that." To drive my point home, I grabbed his tie and yanked him close, planting a brazen kiss squarely on his mouth. I think it surprised him. He moaned softly, holding the back of my head.

"Tomorrow," he whispered as his lips brushed mine, "will be a day you'll never forget. I can't wait to spoil you. Now, come to bed."

* * *

The magnificent aroma of pancakes wafted into the bedroom. I stretched under the blankets and squinted at the digital clock on the nightstand. Six in the morning? I groaned. I could get away with at least another half hour of sleep before having to be up.

My attempt to roll over and snuggle under the comforter was thwarted by some kind of lump. *What the...?*

I sat up and turned on the light, waiting for my eyes to adjust. A sizable box took up a good chunk of the bed next to me. The wrapping paper was a decadent red topped with a snowy white ribbon. A little card with the words 'open me' rested on the box.

Grinning, I picked it up and shook it. Nothing rattled inside and the box was much too light for its size. Curious, I did what the card said and opened it.

Mounds of tissue paper filled the box. I dug through it, tossing some on the floor. The more I emptied the box, the more confused I became. Nothing was in there. I removed the last bit of tissue paper and saw a postcard at the bottom. A picture of a birthday cake was on it. I flipped it over.

IF YOU CAN FIND ME, YOU CAN EAT ME.

"For crying out loud," I muttered with a smile. Someone was trying to be clever. I was never one to make a huge deal about my birthday. Sure, I loved the cake and the presents but I didn't treat the occasion like it was a national holiday or anything. It was just another day. I should have known that would all change once Alastair Holden entered my life.

I tip-toed into the kitchen to catch a glimpse of my fiancé. He was already showered and dressed for work. I cannot articulate how hot it was watching a guy in a designer three-piece suit cook me breakfast. He even had a kitchen towel draped over his shoulder in case any of the batter missed the pan. I wanted to undress him with my teeth.

"You're not supposed to be in here, kitten."

"I can smell it from the bedroom."

He turned, flashing his megawatt smile and making me go all melty on the inside. "Get back in bed. Or else."

Good thing I did as I was told. He treated me to the most scrumptious breakfast in bed on the planet. Not only were the pancakes amazing, he'd garnished them with chocolate shavings and a dollop of whipped cream.

"We can use the rest of the chocolate and whipped cream later," he said with a gleam in his eyes. "If you want that."

"Works for me," I replied.

"This is your day, Lia. Whatever you want, you'll get it. Just ask."

I sipped my tea and smiled. "I want you."

His reaction bordered on bashful, which made me laugh. There wasn't a shy bone in his body.

"I love the sound of your laugh." He grinned. "Finish your breakfast."

I picked up the postcard and held it next to my face. "Do I get to have any guesses?"

"As many as you want. But I'm not telling."

"Fine." I sighed in dramatic fashion.

He wouldn't let go of my hand on the drive to work. Plus, his lips were permanently ticked up in a devilish grin as he scrolled through his cell phone checking emails. No matter how hard I tried, he wouldn't budge about telling me what he had planned.

"I'm keeping you on a tight schedule today. Don't be late for any of the times I've listed out for you. Understand?" His slightly raised eyebrow made me laugh.

"Whatever you say, chief."

"Good girl." He leaned close. "Happy birthday, my love. I'll see you in a few short hours."

I left a hefty amount of gloss on his mouth when I kissed him. I laughed, wiping it off with my thumb. "Plum isn't really your color."

"Probably not." The left corner of his mouth perked up. "But I like having a reminder of you on my lips."

I'm pretty sure all my bones liquefied as he ran his tongue over his bottom lip.

"You're a dangerous flirt," I breathed.

"You have no idea, kitten. Go to work."

For the umpteenth time since moving here, I walked into my office on shaky knees with a racing pulse and fired up libido.

* * *

166

The closer the clock ticked toward eleven, the more fidgety I became. The first 'surprise' of the day was supposed to take place in minutes so I made sure to be at my desk as instructed. I read through scripts to pass the time, making adjustments when necessary. The ringing desk phone made me jump.

"Jesus," I muttered before answering.

"Happy birthday, Lia."

"Sydney?" I exclaimed.

"The one and only. You're not busy are you?"

I was so happy to hear from my former co-worker in Orlando that I didn't realize I was bouncing in my chair. "No, I'm just reading scripts. How are you? What are you doing up so early?"

"Violet has a class trip to Cape Canaveral today and is beyond excited. She woke up before the sun. I figured since I was up, I'd call my favorite cube mate. I miss you. How's life in Scotland? How's that gorgeous British boyfriend of yours? And congratulations on your engagement."

"Life is good. Really good, actually."

"I keep seeing you on the Sentinel website. You look amazing. The cold weather must be agreeing with you."

I laughed. "Don't be fooled. It's hard to have a good hair day over here with all the rain. No different than Orlando with all the humidity, I guess."

A little girl's voice sounded through the receiver. I heard Sydney shush her.

"Sorry. That was Violet announcing that you need to come visit her immediately. She misses you like crazy." She paused. "So do the rest of us. Wes and Tyler were asking about you the other day at work."

The pang of sadness I always get when thinking of home struck. "I'd like to come visit before the end of the year. Maybe before Christmas. Alastair's been so busy with work. I'm sure he'd appreciate some time off. We'll see."

"If you get a chance to come in December we'll all have to go to Disney for our festive Christmas fix. Fake snow and all."

"That sounds amazing."

"Hopefully Stephanie can come, too."

Another pang of sadness hit with a vengeance. "Hopefully."

"Alright, well, I just wanted to call and wish you a happy birthday. Have a fantastic day, Lia. We miss you."

I hadn't expected to become so damn emotional from a phone call. I hung up feeling a bit empty on the inside. I missed my friends. Life had always been a series of new roads and experiences but I wished there could be a way for all the important roads to intersect.

Meredith interrupted my pity party for one with a knock at the door.

"This just arrived for you." She smiled and placed a small box on my desk. "Happy birthday."

"Thanks."

I held the box in my hand for a second before opening it. Inside was a silver chain with a key dangling from it. I had no idea what it unlocked or where I was supposed to use it. The accompanying note wasn't any help either.

**FIND THE LOCK AND WHAT LIES BEHIND IT WILL BE FOREVER YOURS.**

# CHAPTER SEVENTEEN

The next birthday deadline rolled around much faster than I anticipated. The early afternoon had been filled with production meetings so by the time I made it back to my desk another neatly wrapped package was already waiting for me. This one had a single white rose accompanying it.

I inhaled the beautiful scent while tearing off the wrapping paper. Inside were my ruby red sparkly heels and the crystal encrusted ones he'd given me over the summer. Now I was confused. *Why is he giving me my own shoes as a gift?*

Maybe the card held another clue.

WEAR US UNDER THE NIGHT'S SKY.

I ran my finger along one of the heels. Where were we going?

**2:11pm You're killing me, chief**

**2:15pm Patience, love**

The desk phone buzzed. "Miss Meyers? You have a guest in reception."

Assuming it had more to do with my birthday surprise, I went out to see.

"Hi, Lia."

Nope. Not what I wanted for my birthday. Emma Whelan stood smiling in my direction, eyes alight with determination.

"I hope I haven't caught you at a bad time. Do you have a few minutes?"

"Sure. Why not. Come to my office."

The sooner I listened to whatever it was she wanted, the sooner she'd be on a plane back to London and out of my life.

"Nice shoes," she remarked, noticing the open box. "Alastair always had great taste."

I lifted an eyebrow and scowled.

"I'm assuming he gave you those as a gift. He has a thing for high heels."

"What do you want?" I snapped, closing the box and putting it under my desk.

She frowned. "I'm not here to make trouble for you, Lia. I'm not. You have enough to deal with thanks to Olivia Garrison. I'm one of the good guys, even though it might not look that way to you." She paused, gauging my reaction. I sat stoically. "You're a strong woman but you've been thrust into this world of intense scrutiny and suffocating attention. I understand it more than you realize. I'm not asking for us to be best friends. I'm only asking that you trust me enough to help guide you through the rough patches."

"Why you?"

Emma shifted in the chair. "It's what Alastair wants."

"And he always gets what he wants, right?" I huffed.

"Lia," she said softly, "this is my job. Alastair is one of my oldest friends. I—"

"Friend? You made it clear you were the closest thing to a girlfriend he's ever had. Why should I trust you?"

"Because I know what Olivia did to him. I know he is nothing more than a prize to be won for some women. All they see is the money and the lifestyle. I don't want to see him get hurt." Her eyes hardened. "I also know how easy it is to fall in love with him and I know how impossible it is for him to love anyone back."

My head pounded. "So you are in love with him."

"No." She flicked her wrist. "I'm quite fond of him but he could never give me what I needed. And he never saw me as anything more than what I was; a friend with benefits. I earned his trust by not pushing him and not wanting anything more than he was willing to give. After university, he helped me start my own public relations firm. He was my benefactor and my first client. Once people found out I represented him, I couldn't stop the phone from ringing." A self-satisfied grin crossed her lips.

"So you used him for your business?"

"Used is a bad word. He helped me financially so I repaid him by keeping his private life under lock and key. Win, win."

This impromptu heart to heart was grating on my nerves. My hostility toward Emma dissipated some but I would be so much happier if she'd just go away.

"Does Alastair know you're here?"

"No. I came on my own so if we could keep this between us, I'd appreciate it. But I think Paxton saw me so I'm sure I'll get an earful when I leave."

I nodded, folding my arms. "Be grateful he hasn't come up here to escort you out."

Emma smiled. There was genuine warmth behind it. "I'm not a threat. Alastair won't give him the seek and destroy command."

I couldn't help myself and laughed. So did Emma. We laughed for a good minute, filling my office with a relaxed aura I wouldn't have expected in a million years.

"You know," she said. "Under different circumstances I think you and I would have gotten on quite well."

"Maybe." A smile still danced on my lips. "Thanks for looking out for his best interests. I don't mean me. Just…in general."

"It's my job, darling." She stood up, adjusting her Burberry coat. "I'll get out of your hair now so you can enjoy the rest of your birthday."

My eyebrows shot up. "How do you know it's my birthday?"

"It's my job, darling," she said again with a wink. "And no, I haven't a clue what he has planned for you."

* * *

When the clock hit six I scampered down to the lobby and out to the waiting Mercedes. Paxton nodded his greeting as he opened the rear passenger door.

"Where are we going?" I had nothing to lose by asking, even though silence was the only answer I knew I'd get. Paxton glanced at me through the rearview mirror and grinned.

"Not far."

We pulled into traffic as I settled into the soft leather seat. A bag holding my shoes and the keychain sat at my feet. The only other parcel that arrived was another single rose, only this one was red, not white. I held them both in my hand. For someone who didn't 'do' relationships, Alastair was certainly excelling at the task.

I'd been so preoccupied by the mystery surrounding my birthday surprise I didn't notice that I hadn't heard from Stephanie at all until now. No texts, no phone call, nothing. After the emotional wreck she'd been the other night I would have thought I'd at least hear about the results of her pregnancy test. Not receiving a birthday greeting from her stung. I thought maybe we'd moved past the fight but I guess I was wrong.

The car slowed. I glanced out the window and saw we were at the airport. *Oh, Alastair.*

He stood by the hanger with his hands clasped behind his back. He'd changed out of his suit and looked absolutely edible in dark jeans, black t-shirt and a black coat. I clutched the roses and the bag as I walked toward him.

The plane's engines whined with impatience. I shivered with

172

anticipation.

"Amelia." My name rolled of his tongue with such desire I almost dropped all my belongings. The corner of his mouth ticked up in a slight grin. "Fancy celebrating your birthday with me tonight?"

"Yes," I answered in a raspy whisper.

He motioned to the plane. "After you."

"Where are we going?"

"That's up to you. You have all the pieces to the puzzle in hand."

My mind raced. He'd given me a postcard with a picture of a cake, my own shoes and a keychain. Oh, and two roses.

"Not really following you, chief."

He smiled, illuminating the night. "Red or white?"

"What?"

"The roses. Do you prefer red or white?"

"Red, I guess."

"Are you sure?"

"Yep."

"Red it is then." He motioned to the pilot and pointed to the red rose. Turning back to me, he offered his hand. "Let's go."

"So was that some kind of code? The rose thing?" I asked, after we'd boarded the plane. A bowl of chocolate truffles sat on the small table near our seats. I also noticed my seat had a red satin sleep mask on it. "What's this for?"

"My curious kitten is full of questions."

"No shit, Sherlock."

He laughed, planting a kiss on my cheek. Once we were airborne, he reached across me and lowered the window shades.

"What are you doing?"

"Keeping you in the dark." He fingered the satin sleep mask. "This might not be enough."

"Are you planning to blindfold me again?"

"Yes." He brushed his thumb over my mouth, unleashing an intense wave of pleasure through my body. A low growl vibrated in the back of his throat. "There's my look."

If I hadn't appreciated the joy of flying on a private jet before, I did now. I couldn't stop kissing him. Not even the turbulence bothered me, if that shaking sensation even *was* turbulence. It could very well have been every cell in my body vibrating as I savored him.

"You're spoiling me, Holden," I said, resting my head on his shoulder. "I'll never be able to fly commercial again."

"You don't have to. This plane is as much yours as it is mine."

Snuggling against him, I sighed. "Emma came to my office this afternoon."

*Thank you, mouth. Thank you, brain. Thank you for being so moronic and ruining this moment.*

His chest lifted on a deep intake. "I know."

"She seems okay."

He unfastened my seatbelt and pulled me onto his lap. I did a quick sweep of the cabin as I straddled him. The one flight attendant on board was nowhere to be seen. Cradling my jaw, he smiled. "You're beautiful."

"Is that why you're marrying me?" I teased.

"You know it, baby," he responded in an American accent.

"Ah, there you go again." I squeezed his shoulders. "You have the most gorgeous English accent. Don't try to sound like every other guy I've ever dated."

He arched an eyebrow. "Other guys? Don't make me jealous."

"Jealous type, are we?" I slid my hands down his chest, pausing at the waistband of his jeans. His body stilled. The fact that my touch had such power over him amazed me.

"Mine," he whispered, fisting his hand in my hair. The rest of the flight passed by in a heady, lust-fueled blur but we didn't recreate our mile high adventure like we'd done on the way to New York City. We did, however, feed each other the truffles, which enhanced my enjoyment of making out with him. The chocolate tasted so good on his lips. Beneath that flavor was the one I craved even more; the distinct taste that was him. I couldn't get enough of it.

"We've begun our descent. Please make sure your seatbelts are fastened." The pilot's announcement sliced through my brain in the most unwelcome way.

"You heard the man. Buckle up." Alastair planted one last luscious kiss on me.

I returned to my seat in a daze, running a finger over my swollen, well-used lips. We hadn't even officially arrived at our destination and I already wanted time to slow down to a crawl. After the plane touched down, Alastair picked up the satin mask.

"Put this on."

"Can't I just close my eyes?"

His hearty laugh made me smile. "No. You'll peek and I can't have that."

"How am I going to get off the plane if I can't see where I'm going?"

He leaned close, sliding the mask over my eyes. "Trust me."

Never in my life had I instilled such trust in a person. I knew he'd never let anything happen to me but still. Walking down a flight of stairs blindfolded wasn't my idea of fun. Alastair's vice-like grip around my waist helped. A chilly wind swept over me, invigorating me with its crisp urgency. Alastair kept his fingers firmly laced through mine as he led me across the tarmac. He helped me into a car and settled in next to me.

"Red, please," was all he said.

That rose held more answers than I'd realized.

I strained to listen for any clues that would tip me off as to where we were. I heard the distinct sounds of a city but almost every city sounded the same so that wasn't any help.

"You have the most adorable look on your face when you concentrate really hard." Alastair was close to me. Too close. His breath tickled my temple and made me clench my legs together. I heard him exhale in a soft laugh. The sounds he made drove me insane on a normal day when I could see him. But now? Unbelievable.

His scent surrounded me, filling my lungs with every breath I took. I closed my eyes behind the mask, darkening my world even further. The feel of his hand on my arm made me gasp. I was hyperaware and hypersensitive. The combination was an aphrodisiac.

"Where are we?" I whispered.

"Almost there." He tucked me under his arm, enveloping me in his warmth. "Feeling alright?"

"Yes."

I felt his breath on my mouth the second he tilted my chin up. The reckless pounding of my heart drowned out all other sounds. I wet my lips, losing my mind when he moaned. The car rolled to a gentle stop. I heard the click of a door opening and felt a rush of cold air. The heat from Alastair's body left me.

"This way."

He grasped my hand and helped me out. I paused briefly, sliding my foot to see if there was a gap between the road and a sidewalk. Once I was convinced it was all level, I climbed out. He led me a few steps and paused. I heard him thank the driver before we walked into a building. I had no idea if this was a restaurant or a hotel or a house. I just knew we were indoors. The distinct chime of an elevator eliminated the possibility of being in a house or a restaurant.

Alastair remained silent as we rode up. He kept my hand secured in his, pulling me gently when the elevator doors opened. We walked a fairly good distance before stopping.

"Ready?"

I nodded. The mask loosened, its soft satin sliding up over my head to reveal a dimly lit hallway. I blinked, waiting for my eyes to adjust. We stood in front of a cream colored door at the end of a long hallway. No other doors were visible which led me to believe this was either a penthouse suite or an expensive apartment complex.

Alastair stayed quiet, standing to my left. He held my belongings and the roses. "Open the door, Lia."

"But I don't have a…" I paused. "Do I need that key for this?"

He smiled. "No. It's unlocked."

"Okay." I sucked in a breath and twisted the knob. "Oh my God."

The apartment's entry was all in white with polished marble floors. A dark wood table sat against one of the walls, displaying the largest, most elaborate bouquet of long stemmed red roses I'd ever seen. There must be at least three dozen of them in the crystal vase. The delicate perfumed aroma filled my lungs. I looked past the flowers and saw the entry way opened into a stunning living room. It was also all in white with luxurious, dark brown furniture. Enormous French doors opened to a balcony. A soft breeze rustled the floor length drapes, making them billow out like a ball gown. But more amazing than the room and the decorations were the countless lit candles that circled the entire space. They flickered from end tables and shelves, bathing everything in a soft, golden glow.

With every step I took, I noticed more long stemmed red roses. They weren't in vases. They were laying on a dining table and on chairs and pillows. There was so much to take in I became overwhelmed.

And then I walked out onto the balcony. The candles weren't the only source of golden light that bathed this apartment. Twinkling so close that I could almost reach out and touch it was the Eiffel Tower.

# CHAPTER EIGHTEEN

"Paris," I said as tears welled in my eyes. "He brought me to Paris."

"Do you like it?"

I turned, bursting with love for the man standing in the doorway. "I love it."

Tilting his head to the right, he motioned for me to look in that direction. Sitting on a table set for two was a bottle of champagne and a slice of birthday cake. I laughed.

"You brought me to Paris for a piece of cake?"

"Among other things."

"I don't know what to say. I'm…this is…" I blinked back the tears. "I don't know what to say."

Bowing his head, Alastair grinned. "Speechless, huh? That doesn't happen very often with you."

"Come here and kiss me before I go insane."

More than happy to oblige, he approached in less than three strides and kissed me with more love and affection than I expected him to succumb to. A shudder streaked through his body, shaking me to the core.

"I love you," I breathed, holding him tight. "Always."

His smile was heartbreakingly gorgeous. For real.

"Don't move." He opened the champagne and poured it. Accepting the glass he offered, I stood next to him.

"A toast—" he raised his flute "—to the most amazing, enchanting, intelligent, beautiful woman I've ever known. Every day with you is a gift. I can't wait to call you my wife and spend the rest of my days making that smile appear."

"You're one hell of a romantic for a guy who doesn't do relationships," I said as a tear made a slow trail down my cheek.

In a rare moment of pure unguarded candor he said, "It's easy with you. Everything is easy with you. I don't have to make any effort to love you and that's why it can be so scary for me. It's just there and for someone like me—" he caught himself, stopping. Clearing his throat, he regained his trademark cool-as-ice demeanor. "Happy birthday, Amelia Grace."

I kissed the corner of his mouth before clinking my glass with him. "Charmer."

"We'll see how charming you think I am in a bit," he said with a hint of danger. "Have a seat, kitten."

"Why?"

His eyes widened. "Because I said so."

"Hmm." I smirked. "Bossy on my birthday? I don't know about this." I sat facing the Eiffel Tower. Unreal. We were so close to it. Seriously. It was across the street. Larger than life, the famous landmark was more beautiful than any photo I'd ever seen. And here I thought the most elaborate thing he'd do would be to rent out an entire restaurant and take me for a quiet dinner somewhere in Glasgow. Silly me.

"Don't pretend you don't like it when I'm bossy." He was so close his lips brushed against my ear. "Your body betrays you."

I exhaled, losing control of basic motor skills while he swiped his finger through the buttercream frosting. "Birthday girl gets the first bite." He wagged his frosting coated finger in front of me. "Unless you'd like to defer."

"Not a chance, Holden." I grabbed his wrist and pulled him closer, taking my time as I sucked the sweet confection from his finger. "Not bad," I said, rubbing my lips together. The dark stare he leveled at me made it difficult to concentrate. I reached forward, swiping my own finger through the frosting. Grinning, I looked up at him.

"I get the second bite, too." Tracing his mouth with the frosting gave me a rush. His body stilled but his eyes sparked with lust. I licked the remaining frosting off my finger and leaned forward. "Mine," I murmured, running my tongue over his lips, reveling in the sugary sweetness of the frosting and the delectable flavor that was one Alastair Holden.

A soft moan filled the space between us as he took control, his tongue darting past my lips. I felt him trying to curb his own restless desire as he kissed me. I wasn't sure why he would do that. Breaking his mouth away, he stared at me beneath heavy lids and commanded softly, "Do that again."

I took my time tracing his mouth with the frosting, spurred on by his raspy breaths. I could tell he was itching to take me and do as he pleased. I wanted that, too, but couldn't deny how fun it was to have him at my mercy. To be honest, his ability to control his ravenous desire was impressive. I'd never known him to play the submissive. Even the times I thought I was running the show in the bedroom, he always had a way of letting me know he was still in charge.

I teased him, sucking on his bottom lip and then tracing over it with my tongue. A low moan vibrated in his throat.

"We'll finish the cake later," he growled, claiming my mouth in a deep, lusty kiss. The way he tasted and savored me with the long, slow strokes of his tongue dissolved my mind. I was only aware of two things; how he felt and how he sounded.

Holding both my hands, he led me into the bedroom and methodically undressed me as I stood under the amber glow of the tower's lights. My skin tingled when he traced along the lace edge of my bra before unhooking it and letting it fall to the floor. Gathering my hair, he swept it over my left shoulder and kissed down my neck to the swell of my breasts. A heady rush consumed me, making me sway. Closing my eyes, I anticipated his next move.

"Look at me," he ordered. My lids fluttered open and I was caught in his fervid gaze. I wanted him and that enticing stare. I wanted to possess him and claim him over and over.

An alluring grin pulled at his lips. "Do you know how beautiful you look right now? How perfect you are?" He slid his hand along my pelvis and between my legs, hooking his fingers under the edge of my panties. "Am I dominating your thoughts, love?"

Unable to speak, I nodded.

"Good. I want every inch of you tonight." His lips brushed against my skin as he spoke. "Not just your body. I want you to feel me in your soul and breathe me into your lungs."

I trembled, as he slid his fingers inside me.

"My Lia." He curled them, sending a shudder through my body. "What you do to me."

He kissed me almost savagely, sucking my tongue into his mouth and making my bones melt. My back hit the mattress with a quiet thud. His parted lips forged a path from my neck to the curves of my breasts and down my stomach slowly, slowly, slowly until he reached my inner thighs. Slinking my hands through his hair, I held him there as he worked my body with finesse until I was achy, breathless and clinging to him.

"Do you have any idea how good you are at this?" I groaned, surrendering to the rush of ecstasy.

Hovering over me, his mouth covered mine. Locked in his kiss, the taste of myself blended with him on my lips. I gasped at the surge of desire that streaked through me. Nudging my legs open wider with his knee, he flexed his hips into mine, teasing my needy skin to the point where it was almost torture. I was throbbing and raw and close to the breaking point.

"Alastair," I moaned, writhing beneath him. "Please."

Pressing my arms into the mattress over my head, he kissed me again and whispered something unintelligible on my neck.

Cocooning his body around me, he entered me swiftly and

with conviction. I couldn't feel or see anything but him. I didn't want to. I was exactly where I was destined to be, losing myself in the only person who mattered. I was his. He was mine. We possessed one another over and over, proclaiming to the world that we belonged to each other for eternity.

* * *

Alastair pulled the dark red plush throw blanket around us tighter as I snuggled into him. We'd moved back out to the balcony and were cuddled up on one of the chaise lounges. The Eiffel Tower winked at me, seeming to know that another couple had fallen under its spell.

"Can we come back here someday and stay longer?" I asked.

"We can go anywhere in the world you want. You know that."

I lifted my head so I could see his face. Looking at him always took my breath away, especially now. I'd never seen him so at peace. I loved spending this private time with him. I loved seeing him let go and relax. There weren't any interruptions for the first time ever in our relationship. No phone calls, no texts, no ghosts from our pasts: just bliss.

"I can see the wheels turning in that pretty head of yours." He smiled, dragging his fingers through my hair.

"Just thinking about you."

"Good girl," he teased, kissing my forehead.

"Muppet."

That got a good laugh out of him. "Ah, Lia. I do love it when you try to sound all British in your cute little American way."

I squeezed his waist, making him jump. "Who's being cheeky now?"

Securing me in his arms, he dropped a sweet kiss on my nose. I sighed into his chest, content to listen to the beating of his heart and feel the softness of his skin. Our bodies fit so well together in this post-coital embrace.

His sigh gave me pause. I linked my fingers with his. "You okay, chief?"

"Never better."

I smiled against his skin. "Wanna skip work tomorrow and fly somewhere far, far away?"

"Let me guess. Fiji?"

I snapped my head up and blinked. "You remember that?"

"I remember a lot of things, kitten. You were quite perplexed about my lack of adventure with flying to random places around the world for fun. Fiji is now on my list and you're coming with me."

"Hmm." I raised my eyebrows. "I like the sound of that. You could use a long vacation. All these board meetings and flights back and forth to London are wearing on you."

"Think so?"

"Alastair, you're half asleep right now. It kills me to see you work so hard and be so stressed out. I worry."

"I'm half asleep right now because I just had the most amazing sex with the most gorgeous woman in the world."

"Lucky her."

He hugged me tighter. "Lucky me. No more talk about work. I'm staring down another long day tomorrow and an even longer week starting Monday. All I want to do now is stay wrapped in your delicious body."

Can't really argue with that, can I? Our conversation drifted along several different topics. None of them were earth shattering. He teased me about being a cheerleader in high school and I refused to believe he'd never played a video game in his life. Every kid did, even me. When talk started to revolve around family, I felt his body stiffen slightly but he never retreated behind the safety of his wall. By this point, I think I he felt safe enough to trust me with matters involving his childhood and the accident. At least I hoped so.

"Can I ask you something?" I asked, running my fingers down

his bare chest.

"You can ask me anything."

"Do you ever go visit them? Your parents and sister?"

Air rushed out of his lungs so fast that I sat up straight. He paled, avoiding my gaze. "No."

"Have you considered it?"

"No."

I brushed back a few pieces of his thick, disheveled hair. "I'll go with you when you're ready. I mean, I'll go if you want me to."

Tightening his jaw, he looked at me. A myriad of emotions swirled behind those astute eyes. The silence stretched on for so long I was afraid he'd never say another word for the rest of the night. Talking about his mom, dad and sister was always a delicate dance.

"You would do that for me?" he finally said.

"Of course. I'd do anything for you. You know that."

Unsure of himself, he opened his mouth to say something then reconsidered. I made sure to keep touching him, whether it was playing with his hair or resting a hand on his skin. I knew how much his touch soothed me and could only imagine mine having the same effect on him.

Bright emerald irises met mine. "You would really do that for me?"

"Yes." I snuggled against his chest again, holding him close. "Say the word, chief, and we'll go."

"I'm not making any promises, Lia. I'll think about it. That's all I'll do for now."

"Fair enough."

We remained quiet for a long while, only communicating through soft touches and sweet caresses. I kissed along his collarbone, whispering my thanks on his skin. Fisting his hand in my hair, he pulled, forcing my head back. Love and desire burned in his eyes.

"What's on your mind, kitten?"

"What did you say to my dad when you called to tell him you were proposing?"

Both eyebrows lifted in amusement. "A good businessman never reveals his secrets in the art of negotiations."

"Oh my God," I snickered. "Well, you must have said something out of this world because my mom said he hasn't stopped talking about how great you are."

Folding his arms behind his head, Alastair grinned. "I am pretty great, aren't I?"

Laughing, I jumped on his lap and tickled him. Not for long though. He had my hands pinned behind my back within seconds.

"Feisty little thing aren't you?" His unfiltered joy not only lit up his words, it illuminated his eyes.

"You know you love it."

"Fair point." He placed his hands on my waist. "Fancy staying out here longer or would you rather go inside?"

I glanced over at the picture perfect view of Paris we'd been enjoying all evening. An idea hit me, making me smile.

"Let's stay out here." I leaned down to kiss him. "I'll be right back."

I slid off the chaise lounge and scurried to the bedroom. The box with my sparkly heels sat in a corner. I grabbed the ruby red ones and slipped them on, then put on a black silk baby doll nightie. After a quick glance in the mirror, I went back outside. Alastair leaned against the wrought iron railing with the blanket wrapped around his waist, covering up my favorite cotton pajama bottoms. I couldn't see his expression but hoped it was still serene.

"Hey, English," I said, unable to stop a huge, goofy grin from spreading.

Alastair turned, shaking his head. The smile curling his mouth left me giddy with joy. "Hey, Yankee."

"Wow. A quick comeback. Impressive."

His languid gaze traced every inch of my body before he responded. "I don't know what to do first; kiss you or shag you."

"Both options are acceptable and encouraged."

"You chose the red ones." He grinned, looking at my feet. The shoes glittered in the light.

"Well, I figured I'd keep with the theme." I chewed on my lip for a second. "Where would you have taken me if I'd chosen the white rose?"

"I guess that'll remain a mystery."

"Seriously? You're not going to tell me?"

He looked at me in that way he had, with dominance and yearning and desire. Nothing fired me up more.

"Patience, Lia. I'm not through with you yet."

I swallowed. Hard. "There's more?"

Dropping the blanket, he approached with purpose, dominating my line of sight and all but making the Eiffel Tower look pedestrian next to his magnificent physique. My already wobbly thighs and shaky knees from our round of love making failed me. I placed my hands on his chest to steady myself.

"Your touch," he whispered, leaning his forehead to mine, "is my weakness and my strength."

The warmth of his hands on my skin quickened my pulse.

"Dance with me."

My shy laugh surprised me. "There's no music."

"Then it's perfect." He held me close and we swayed to the sounds of Paris of night, sheltered by the lights of the Eiffel Tower. I never wanted this night to end. I never wanted him to let me go. If this is what he was capable of for my birthday I could only imagine what he had in store for our wedding. I couldn't wait.

"When did you become such a romantic?" I asked.

He chuckled. "I had no idea I was one. I just wanted to make you happy."

I looked up at him, at his handsome face, mesmerizing eyes and shy smile. This was one of those moments where I needed to be pinched to make sure it was real. I held him tighter, resting my head on his chest and losing myself in him with every breath I took.

"Alastair?"

"Yes, my love."

"I never did find that lock to go with the key you gave me."

His cheek brushed mine as he smiled. "Yes you did."

# CHAPTER NINETEEN

Lively conversation and raucous laughter filled every corner of the pub as I sat at my table, sipping sparkling wine. Post-show food and beverages were exactly what the doctor ordered for this Friday night after a long day at work. Also, I was finally getting to see Stephanie. She'd been radio silent since appearing at my front door on Tuesday, drenched and crying. In true Stephanie fashion, she'd glossed over missing my birthday by blaming it on 'the twenty-four hour flu' and apologizing left and right. Oh, and she also nonchalantly let me know that she was not, in fact, pregnant.

I had no idea what was going on inside my best friend's head.

"Paris," she said with a dreamy look in her eye. "I'm so jealous. Where is he anyway? Why aren't you guys attached at the hip?"

"He's at a client dinner with some of his staff. I'd rather hang out with you." I smiled, ignoring her last comment.

"He doesn't care that you're not with him?"

"It's a business dinner. I'd be bored out of my skull."

She shrugged, glancing at the menu. Something about her demeanor wasn't right. She appeared almost…offended? My suspicions about her budding friendship, or whatever the hell *that* was, with Olivia grew. Steph had a good head on her shoulders but she was also gullible and loved to take other people's words as gospel. She'd done it over the summer when her boss, Cassie, filled her head with negative gossip about Alastair.

"Why does it matter to you that I'm not with him?" I asked, unable to curb my annoyance.

She rolled her eyes. "It doesn't. I just figured he'd want you with him. Guys like that usually want their pretty significant others at their side. You know, like Nathan did."

"Whoa," I said, holding up my hands. "I'm not an ornament for him to show off and he's nothing like those guys, especially that asshole. You know that. What's gotten into you?"

She shrugged again. "I don't know. A lot's been going on with me and Brent and everything and I just don't…I don't know. Sorry."

"Is someone filling your head with this crap? Because you've never said these things to me before." I clenched my fists. "Is it Olivia?"

Stephanie sighed and bowed her head. "Like I said. A lot's been going on with all that. I don't really want to talk about it right now."

"You would tell me if she said something, right?"

"Of course." Her smiled appeared forced. "There's just a bunch of crap I need to sort out in my own head."

"Are you still going to the shower tomorrow?" I asked and then took a healthy sip of wine.

"I suppose." Her shoulders slumped as she tilted her head to the side. "I wish you'd come."

"I love you like a sister—" I put my hand on my heart "—but I am not voluntarily going anywhere near that girl. She's nuts."

"The whole…*thing* that happened with her and you the other day was a—" she struggled to find the words "—a…she won't do that again."

"What are you, a double agent?" I laughed. "How do you know?"

"She feels bad."

"She got caught and was escorted away. She doesn't feel bad. Her ego was wounded." I downed the rest of my wine and reached for my purse. "I'm getting a refill. Want one?"

"Sure."

Something was up with my best friend and if I had to pry it out of her using sparkling wine, I would. I scrolled through my phone while waiting for the bartender. I had a text waiting for me from Alastair.

**8:02pm How's girl's night?**

**8:25pm OK**

**8:26pm You sure?**

**8:27 Yep**

**8:28pm Hurry up and come home so I can get you naked**

I laughed, putting the phone back in my purse.
"Hi, Lia."
I looked up, shocked to see Emma standing in front on me.
"Emma. I thought you'd be back in London by now."
"So did I. Found out a friend of mine is performing later tonight at one of the clubs downtown so I thought I'd stick around and check out his show." She waved the bartender over. "What are you having?"
"Oh, you don't have to. I'm here with a friend and—"
"It's not a bother. We got off on the wrong foot this week and I want to make it up to you. My treat. What would you like?"
"I don't think—"
"Look. If we're going to be working together we should at least be civil to one another." The way she looked at me gave me pause. She seemed genuine but I could see distrust hovering behind those smoky violet eyes. In the bizarro world that had now become my life, I let her buy us the drinks.
She ordered and followed me back to the table. Stephanie looked as surprised as I felt when she saw us.

"Steph, Emma. Emma, Steph," I said, taking my seat.

I could not for the life of me wrap my brain around the fact that I was hanging out with Emma Whelan when only minutes before I'd been brushing off my best friend's attempts at trying to convince me that Olivia Garrison wasn't the spawn of Satan. The other wacky thing? The three of us were actually enjoying ourselves. Blame it on the alcohol but after a couple of rounds, Stephanie loosened up and Emma had us both in stitches with some of her work stories. She never mentioned any specific names but some of her more famous clients were quite the handful.

"So, he was fired from the series and left the business completely," Emma said. "I think he owns a pet shop now or something."

"All because he posted pictures of his bare ass online?" Stephanie asked.

"Bare ass and full frontal. He was trying to impress a girl." Emma lowered her voice, putting her index finger and thumb close together. "Not very impressive."

Our table erupted into laughter. I finished my glass of sparkling wine, enjoying the fuzzy warmth that was spreading through me. The server walked over, dropping off a round of shots.

"Courtesy of that table over there," she said.

All three of us looked in the direction she pointed and saw a group of college aged guys watching us with eager anticipation.

"Ooh, frat boys," Stephanie mused.

We waved in thanks and went back to our conversation.

"Ladies. Having a good time tonight?" one of the guys asked in a slight southern drawl. We hadn't noticed him approach us. "Where y'all from?"

Emma answered first. "London. Thanks for the drinks." She picked up a shot glass and handed it to me, then passed one to Stephanie.

"All three of you are from London?" The blondish frat boy grinned, motioning for his friends to join.

Stephanie downed her shot. "Nope. Florida here—" she pointed to herself "—and—" she pointed to me "—there."

I lifted my shot glass in a greeting before drinking it. What the hell did they send us? Gasoline? The strong liquid burned going down my throat. I made a little noise, thankful the sounds of the pub drowned it out.

"North Carolina here. We're studying abroad for the semester."

"Exciting." Stephanie widened her eyes. I knew she was over-exaggerating with the flirting. She got a kick out of younger guys and these boys couldn't be any older than twenty.

Frat boy took her 'interest' as an invitation to stick around. Emma and I exchanged glances.

"We've actually got to be going," Emma said, standing up.

"Where to? Hot girls like you must know of a few places in this city." Frat boy looked expectantly at her.

"A concert. Gotta run." She motioned for Stephanie and me to follow her and we left the college guys in the dust. "Do you two want to come with me?" she asked when we walked outside.

"Who's playing?"

"A friend of mine fronts a band called Before Day. They're in town for the weekend. Do either of you like Keane or Coldplay or anyone like that? Their style is similar."

Stephanie scrunched up her nose. "Not really."

"I'm okay with it." I shrugged.

"It's up to you two. I'd be more than happy to have some company and I'm sure the boys would appreciate more people in the crowd."

* * *

There wasn't enough room in this place for an amoeba to move, let alone the three of us. I don't know why Emma made it sound like this band needed a bigger audience. The place was packed, sweaty and louder than anything I'd experienced in a long time.

The band was already into their set on a small stage bathed in lavender lighting. Emma guided us through the crowd toward the left side of the stage. We stood against the wall as it vibrated from the bass and drums.

These guys weren't bad at all. The lead singer had that smoldering magnetism that could propel them to worldwide fame. His voice was low and smooth, with a hint of a rasp when he hit certain notes. Clad in jeans, t-shirt and black leather jacket, he owned the stage. Even Stephanie looked a little smitten with the dark haired singer. She had that familiar glint in her eye when she's bowled over.

*I guess things with Brent aren't so shiny and fabulous.*

"Is that your friend?" she asked Emma, raising her voice to be heard above the music.

Emma nodded. "His name is Colin. Fantastic vocalist."

When the next song started, some of the women in front of the stage cheered and waved their arms in an effort to get Colin to notice them. This song was slower. Not quite a ballad but not as raucous as the last one. In true rock star fashion, Colin serenaded the ladies in the front, coming down on one knee to sing directly to them. When he stood, his piercing blue eyes swept through the crowd. The venue was small so it's possible he was able to see most of the people. Striding toward the side of the stage we were standing closest to, he made eye contact with me, then Emma, then Stephanie. He winked in Emma's direction and carried on with the song.

Stephanie grabbed my arm and mouthed, "He's so hot."

I gave her a look.

"We'll talk," she mouthed.

After the concert ended, Emma led us behind the building where the band was hanging out by a tour bus. Again, I was surprised at how nonchalant Emma had been about their success. Scantily clad girls hovered by the fence, recording every move the band made with their smart phones and screaming their names in the hopes of being plucked out of the crowd.

"Emma." Colin wrapped her a hug. "Thanks for postponing your trip home." He slung an arm over her shoulders and smiled at Stephanie and me. "Introduce me to your friends?" The way his English accent hugged every syllable was mesmerizing.

"This is Lia," she gestured in my direction, "and her friend Stephanie. I sort of gatecrashed their night and dragged them here with me."

"Did she feed you the line that we needed a bigger audience?"

I laughed. "As a matter of fact, she did."

Colin shook his head with a grin. "She loves throwing herself into her work."

"Is she your publicist?"

"Unofficially. We've been trying to build a decent fan base so we can get signed. I can't tell you how many labels have passed on us."

One of the other band members sauntered over and introduced himself as Paul. He also offered us each a beer.

"So what are two Americans doing living here in Glasgow?" Colin asked, looking pointedly at Stephanie. She seamlessly adjusted her stance, cocking her left hip provocatively and running a finger up the beer bottle's neck. I knew this pose. She was going in for the kill.

"Lia is engaged to Alastair Holden," Emma interjected. "Stephanie works for Sarah at Finley's."

I stiffened at Emma's choice to introduce me as his fiancée first, without mentioning that I also had a moderately important job in the city. It made me feel like the arm candy the papers described me as being.

"Holden, huh? Haven't had the pleasure of meeting him but our manager has tried to get us signed to their label. No luck yet."

Emma looked at me expectantly. I started to feel uncomfortable and wondered if she only brought me here to act as a back door for getting her friend a record deal. She knew Alastair. Why didn't she just hit him up for a favor?

"These beautiful ladies don't want to talk business," he said, winking at Stephanie. "Come back to our hotel for some post-gig drinks and a little something to eat."

I thought Stephanie's fingers were going to puncture through my skin she was grasping me so hard.

"I have an early flight, I can't. Sorry." Emma frowned turning to us. "I do have to be going. Do you want to share a taxi? I'm only staying in the West End."

I was about to answer when Stephanie clamped down harder on my arm. I knew she wanted to go to the after party. "I think we're going to stick around a little bit longer."

Emma looked at my best friend and grinned. "Have fun."

Without much fanfare, she kissed Colin goodbye, thanked Stephanie and I for hanging out with her and disappeared into the night. I really wanted to go home but Stephanie kept making eyes at Colin in between giving me her pouty look.

"We'll go for a little while," she pleaded with me while winking at the singer. "It's Friday. It's not like we have to be up early tomorrow."

"What about Brent," I whispered. "You were all hot and heavy with him a week ago. That visual is burned in my memory for life. Is he taking a backseat suddenly because some singer made googly eyes at you?"

Her grip pinched my arm as she dragged me closer to the building. "I'm not seeing him anymore. After the whole pregnancy scare I reevaluated my relationship status and decided it was best to move on. I'm not looking for something long term right now."

Typical.

"So why are you still going tomorrow?"

She pushed out a sigh. "I don't know. I feel bad for her. She's, like, this mousy little thing who—"

"Stop talking," I interrupted. "Just stop. If you want to bang the band guy, do it. I'm not letting you go to some seedy hotel by yourself though."

"I'm not a child, Lia. For crying out loud, you ran off with

Alastair to that remote cottage when you were shitfaced. You'd known him for what, ten seconds? And how do you think I felt after you passed out cold and stayed here an extra day? Do you think I liked leaving you behind in a foreign country? He could have been a serial killer."

"Okay. Alright." I put my hands up in retreat. "You've made your point."

She grunted in frustration. "I hate that we've been at each other's throats all the time. I miss our stupid little fun moments together. Being here has turned everything upside down."

"And blue eyes over there is going to make it all better?" I teased, catching Colin staring hard at my friend.

"He's so fucking hot," she breathed. Snapping herself out of the hormone induced moment, she grabbed me and hugged me. "I'll get his number. I'll call him and maybe meet for drinks or something this weekend." Pulling back, she searched me for a reaction. "I miss my best friend."

"I'm right here, Steph. I haven't gone anywhere."

Having a heart to heart with her in this environment felt so weird. Screaming girls still crowded by the fence, clamoring for a one night stand.

"Let me go get his number and then we'll find a cab and get the hell out of here. Sound good?"

"Sure."

While she flirted with Colin I dug my phone out of my purse. I had several missed calls and texts from Alastair.


**11:58pm On my way home now. Sorry. Was at a concert and couldn't hear the phone**


**11:59pm You had me worried. Where are you? I'll send Paxton**


**12:00am Some club downtown. I'm with Steph. We'll get a cab.**

**12:01am I'd feel better if Paxton picked you up**

**12:03am Stop worrying, chief**

**12:06am Text me when you're in the taxi**

Stephanie bounded over with a huge smile on her face as I shoved the phone in my purse. "All set. We're going out tomorrow night." The trademark Stephanie Tempe grin lit up her face. "Score one for me, zero for those desperate chicks behind the fence."

We linked arms and walked out to the main road. Scores of people leaving various pubs filled the sidewalk. Weaving our way through, we chatted like old times. I chalked up all of her moodiness and strange behavior to stress over work and more than a little bit of homesickness.

A car whizzed by, blaring its horn just as we were about to cross the street.

"Slow down, ass clown," Stephanie shouted from the crosswalk. "Jeez. They drive worse than New Yorkers."

I laughed. "Because you've been to New York so often."

"You do know a good chunk of the people who live in Central Florida are from the northeast. You included. As far as I'm concerned, you're all bad drivers."

At the next corner we stopped to hail a cab. Stephanie lived closer to the West End so we told the driver to drop her off first. I sent Alastair a quick text to let him know we were on the way. After Stephanie hopped out and we said our goodbyes, I settled into the seat. What a strange night this has been. I couldn't wait to get home and snuggle under the blankets with my future husband.

The cab slowed at the red light, coming to a stop. Glasgow, in my opinion, was at its most beautiful at night. I leaned my head against the window, gazing up at the city lights. I felt bad that Steph was having a hard time adjusting to life here. She'd always been hesitant about leaving Orlando. Dayna once told me it takes about six months to really become acclimated to a new city after moving to it. Stephanie had only been here since the end of July. Maybe she'd grow to love it if she gave it more of a chance.

My phone beeped so I reached into my bag to grab it. The cab pulled forward as I read Alastair's text.

**12:36am Hurry home, love. The bed is too empty without you.**

A flash of light blinded me followed by the sickening sound of metal crushing metal.

# CHAPTER TWENTY

Searing pain filled my head, making it difficult to move. I touched my temple, confused by the stickiness. When I opened my eyes, I noticed I wasn't sitting in the same spot I'd been in a few seconds ago. I heard shouting from outside the car. The cab driver was yelling at someone. I opened the door and climbed out.

"Miss, miss! Are you okay?"

"I'm fine," I said, feeling woozy.

"You're bleeding. Here. Sit down." He led me to the curb and handed me a handkerchief. I pressed it to the side of my head and got a good look at what happened. Apparently, we were broadsided. The other driver had run the red light and slammed right into the back of the cab where I'd been sitting.

*That explains the massive headache.*

Adrenaline kicked in, pushing me to my feet. I needed to find my phone and call Alastair. He was expecting me and if I didn't show up he'd go ballistic. His little quirk about always needing to know that I'm safe wasn't something to take lightly. I climbed into the backseat, feeling along the floor. My fingers hit something small and hard. Bingo. I grabbed the phone and went back to the sidewalk. My hands shook more than I wanted them to as I dialed.

"Missing me?" he answered after half a ring.

"Always. Um, something—"

"What's wrong?"

"I'm okay. There's been an accident. Can—"

"Are you hurt? Where are you?" The panic in his voice gave it a raspy whine I'd never heard before.

"Um," I looked for a street sign. "Gibson Street near the university, I think."

"I'm on my way. Don't move."

An old church wasn't too far from where I was standing. I glanced back at the cab driver and the guy who hit us before sitting on the steps in front of the church. The impact sounded worse than it actually was. The taxi had a sizable dent just behind the driver side door and the other car was banged up but for all intents and purposes, it was a minor collision.

I shivered, closing my eyes and leaning my aching head on the iron railing. The adrenaline faded, leaving me tired and wanting nothing more than to curl up in bed. A chilly breeze swept through, making the stone steps I was sitting on feel even colder. I pulled my coat tighter, hoping Alastair would get here soon.

Opening my eyes briefly, I saw the cabbie and the other driver each talking on their cell phones. I leaned my head against the railing again and closed my eyes.

"Amelia."

The same panicked whine he'd had on the phone echoed through the night. I looked up seconds before Alastair engulfed me in his arms.

"Christ, you're bleeding," he growled, holding my face in his hands. Anger flashed through his eyes. "I'm going to take care of this. That bastard will lose his license when I'm finished with him. Have you given your statement to the police yet?"

"No. Are they here?"

"Yes. Come with me."

He kept a protective arm wrapped around my waist as I recounted what happened to the officer on scene. When they were satisfied with my version of events, they told me it was okay to leave. Alastair hugged me again, not letting go for the longest time. When he finally did pull away, he kissed me with desperation. The way he looked at me tore me to pieces.

"Stare at me any harder and you'll drill a hole in my head, chief."

"I want you home and safe. Let's go."

The ride back to the house was silent and tense. I couldn't get a definitive read on what was going through Alastair's head. I knew, without question, this triggered his deep seated guilt over the death of his family. He blamed himself for causing that accident and I wouldn't be surprised if he blamed himself for this one. His grip on the steering wheel turned his knuckles white. I wanted to comfort him, let him know that I was fine.

He ushered me into the house, leading me straight to the bedroom. Disappearing into the bathroom, he returned with a damp facecloth and cleaned the dried blood from my head.

"Does it hurt?" he asked.

"There's a dull ache. I could use an Advil or something."

"I'll get you one. It looked worse than it is. There's just a small scratch but you'll have a nasty bruise in the morning."

I changed into some pajamas while he fetched me a drink and the pain killers. Crawling into bed felt so damn good. I sighed into the mattress, snuggling into Alastair's embrace.

"Are you sure you're alright?" he asked.

"Yes. It was just a little fender bender." I felt his body seize with tension. His grip on me tightened. "Don't break me, chief," I said, nuzzling into his neck.

"I can't stand the way this feels," he murmured. "I can't. It's too much."

I was afraid he'd disappear to the dark place in his mind. His fear of loss was more consuming than I realized.

Stroking his hair, I held him close. "I'm right here, Alastair. Tomorrow we'll wake up and you can make me your famous cheesy omelet with toast. Then we can take a long, lazy bubble bath together and climb back into bed and stay here all day."

Rolling on top of me, he sealed our mouths together. I loved his kisses but this one was laced with too much anxiety.

"Hey," I whispered, nipping at his bottom lip. "Look at me."

Raising his eyes to meet mine, I lost myself in their green depths. He was so beautiful and so scared for me it made my heart hurt. Blowing out a shaky sigh he wrapped himself around me.

"I want you safe, Lia. Always."

* * *

I woke up in an empty bed a couple hours later. My head rumbled when I sat up, making its case for me to stay horizontal. Ignoring the discomfort, I got up and went to Alastair's office. As expected, he was seated at the desk typing intently on the computer. I stood in the doorway, unsure if I should bother him. Flicking his eyes to me, he closed the laptop and gestured for me to sit. I felt the way I did the first time I walked into this office after waking up in a daze. The feeling was unsettling.

Alastair watched me, never softening the intensity of his stare. I went to him and straddled his lap.

"Come back to bed," I urged, touching his cheek. "I want you next to me."

Apprehension wracked my body. He was shutting down in front of me and there wasn't a damn thing I could do to stop it.

"I need you, chief." I kissed the soft skin at the crook of his neck, sucking on a small patch. His fingers pressed into my lower back but the rest of his body remained still. I kept touching him, hoping to calm his fears.

Feeling his arms band around me quieted my pounding heart. We held each other like this for the longest time.

"Go to bed, love."

The absolute deadness in his voice destroyed me. I looked at him, searching for a way to break through this wall. There was

202

no way. He was unreachable, lost to the depths of thoughts only he could see.

I lifted his hand and placed it over my heart. Parting his lips, he moaned. "Lia. Don't."

"Feel me." I pulled his hand down my chest. "Touch me."

"Please don't," he whispered hoarsely.

I refused to let him succumb to the emotionless black hole he'd disappeared into for far too long.

"I want you. I love you." My lips brushed his cheek. "Tell me you love me, Alastair. I need to hear you say it."

He gripped my arms so tight, I gasped. Clenching his jaw, he shook his head. "You have no idea what you're doing to me right now. Please don't."

As rigid as his body had become, mine was lax in his arms. I bowed my head, grasping for ways to break through to him.

"This wasn't your fault, Alastair. There wasn't anything you could have done to—"

"I should have insisted that Paxton pick you up," he yelled. "I should have sent him with you in the first place. You had no business being at that concert without protection. That *will not* happen again."

I stared at him, horrified at how hysterical he sounded. "You can't control everything."

"Yes I can," he snapped. "I have been my entire life."

I wriggled free and stood up. That was the root of the problem right there. He kept a tight leash on every aspect of his life so he wouldn't be thrust into chaos. I paced his office like a caged animal, stopping in front of the cluster of photos hanging on the wall. The sad little boy throwing leaves in the air still lived in him. I thought after everything we'd been through, he'd finally left that boy where he belonged; in the past.

Turning to face him, I saw the man I'd met in April. Stoic and unreadable with eyes as hard as stone, he stared into nothing. The transformation was flawless and complete. I longed for the man who'd taken me to Paris only forty-eight hours ago. I longed to see him playful and happy and open. Tears stung the corners of my eyes.

"I feel like I'm losing you, Alastair. I'm losing you and it's effortless."

He didn't look at me. He didn't even flinch.

* * *

Work was my oasis. I was actually happy to be sitting in the weekly editorial meeting listening to Sam, Robbie and Julian bicker back and forth. The weekend had passed like a bad dream that I was still living. Alastair had stayed holed up in his office preparing for a conference call with a production house in Los Angeles. At least that's what he told me. We barely spoke after what happened Friday night.

Stephanie went to Olivia's shower and texted me every two seconds to tell me how bored she was and how good Brent looked. Then she went out with Colin on Saturday night and forgot Brent ever existed. I don't know what she was looking for in her relationship quest but when she found it, or if, I hope it lived up to her expectations.

By lunchtime I was twitchy and on edge. More so than I'd been all weekend. Julian was out with a field producer on assignment and Sam was stuck in meetings for the rest of the afternoon with some corporate bigwigs from our parent company. I tapped a pen on my desk, staring at the framed photo of me and Alastair. It was from my first weekend here. We'd gone to his cottage and spent more time in bed than out. I'd wanted to take an impromptu couple picture so I'd grabbed his camera. The photo was candid and sweet. I'd timed it just as he was kissing my cheek.

My chest tightened. I don't know how many more of his Grand Canyon sized mood swings I could survive. This one had to be the worst. His distance killed me. I figured giving him some space and time to process what happened would be best but my patience was wearing thin.

I don't know what possessed me to pick up the phone.

"Mom?" I said when she answered.

"Lia. This is a nice surprise."

"Well, you know, just thought I'd say hi."

"What's wrong?"

"Nothing. I'm…I had a shitty weekend."

I heard shuffling noises in the background and knew my mother was pushing aside some magazines or whatever she'd been reading to give me her full attention. "What happened?"

I recounted the accident, complete with having to confirm every three seconds that I was, in fact, physically fine. I don't really know what advice I was seeking from her. I just figured she'd help give me some clarity.

"He had a rough start to life, Lia. He lost the people he loved the most and now you're the person he loves the most. What happened Friday night probably shook him and he feels like he almost lost you. The accident might have been minor to you but to him it's astronomical. I'm not going to pretend I know what's going on inside his head but I will say that after seeing the two of you together I have no doubts that you'll be able to work through this."

"I just wish he wouldn't push me away like this. I wish he'd let me be there for him."

"Men compartmentalize. You know that."

I sighed. "Yeah but with him it's survival mode. I really thought we'd made a huge breakthrough the other night in Paris. He was so open and…I don't know."

My mom's soft chuckle filled the gap in conversation. "Paris. I thought men like him didn't exist in real life."

"Mom."

"Don't let this consume you. I've told you this before but it bears repeating. The heart is vocal in situations like this. Listen to it. Don't be afraid of what it tells you."

"I know that. It's Alastair who needs convincing."

"Give him time. This is a bump in a very long road the two of you are traveling down. Be there for him even when it feels like that's the last thing he wants."

Talking to her made me feel a little better. I promised to call again before the end of the week and hung up. The words in the script I was staring at blurred. My level of concentration was nonexistent. Since anybody who was of importance was either on a shoot or in a meeting, I decided to call it a day at four-thirty. I told Meredith if anything major happened to call me on my cell phone. Grabbing my coat, I went down to the lobby. I stood there for a long time, staring at the traffic outside. As I turned, I bumped into Paxton.

*Of course he's here.*

"Is everything alright, Miss Meyers? Are you heading home?"

"Will you take me to him?"

"Of course."

The ride to the financial district felt like an eternity. I don't know why I was so nervous. When Paxton parked in front of the modern glass building I stared out the window. The name Holden World Media hung proudly in large brushed steel letters over the main entrance. I took a deep breath and went up to the top floor.

Simone greeted me with her trademark look of disinterest. I couldn't for the life of me understand why he'd hired such an unpleasant person to be the first human contact people had when they came here. She'd be rather pretty if she cracked a smile.

By the time I reached her desk, she had the phone in hand. "Miss Meyers is here for you," she said. "Right away." She put the receiver down and motioned for me to go in his office.

Alastair stood with his back to me in front of one of the large windows. I highly doubted he was admiring the breathtaking view of Glasgow. His office was as pristine and well put together as he looked. More smoke and mirrors for the general public and business associates so they wouldn't see the damaged man behind the mask.

His suit jacket was draped over the back of his chair. I liked it when he wore three-piece suits. I dragged my eyes over his charcoal gray pants and vest. His arms were folded in front of him but I knew a silver tie rested on his crisp white shirt. I wanted to slide my hands through his dark red hair, tangling my fingers in its thickness.

Turning his head to the right, he looked down and spoke. "I'm glad you're here, kitten." He swiveled his body to face me. As always, he took my breath away, even though his eyes were cold as ice.

"Are you?" I asked with a bit more uncertainty than I wanted.

Wincing against unseen pain, he nodded. "I have a video conference call in fifteen minutes but you can stay as long as you want."

The rich, velvet sound of his accent lulled me into believing we'd be able to work through our problems. I wanted that with every fiber of my being. He walked around to the front of his desk and sat on the edge. I still hadn't moved from the center of the floor.

"Come to me," he commanded quietly.

I did, surprised when he wedged me between his thighs. I thought I felt a tremor but dismissed it. Brushing back my hair, he traced a finger over the bruise on my temple. He didn't have to say anything for me to know it bothered him to see me injured. As impassive as his expression remained, I knew every twitch of his jaw muscles signaled what he felt deep down.

Overcome by my love for him, I leaned in to kiss him. My heart shattered when he restrained me and turned his head.

"Don't," he breathed. "It's too much."

"Stop fighting it. You haven't let me touch you or kiss you all weekend. It's driving me crazy."

"You and me both."

"Then why are you being this way? Why are you making me feel this way?"

"I told you. I don't know any other way to be."

"That's bullshit," I snapped. "I refuse to let you wither away and lock yourself behind that fucking wall."

The sun escaped from behind a cloud and blazed through the window, reflecting off my diamond and shooting fractured, fiery shards of light on Alastair's clothes and the floor.

His bitter laugh clashed with the gentle way he held me. "It's the only place I'm safe, Lia."

"Are you *serious* right now?"

"I can't control myself or the way that I feel when you're near me," he said through clenched teeth. "I'm like a loose cannon. I've lost my grip on that goddam cliff and now I'm scrambling. Don't you understand?"

"I understand that you're being selfish right now and using your family's death as a crutch and a way to destroy any happiness you might have. You're shutting me out. What I don't understand is why you just can't let yourself love me."

The stinging echo of my words filled every corner of his office. I shook, defeated as he let go of my arms. *I'm such an asshole.* Something shifted in the air between us. A rift had opened, puncturing the love that bound our souls.

Running a hand through his hair, he squared his shoulders. "I'm going to be in London for the rest of the week. Paxton will be here if you need him."

"Alastair I'm—"

"You've said all there is to say, Amelia."

"I'm sorry."

"So am I." The love and affection that gave his eyes the glow I adored was gone. He stared at me dispassionately.

"Mr. Holden, your call with Los Angeles is starting soon." Simone's detached voice floated through the intercom on the desk phone. Alastair turned and held down the talk button.

"Thank you. Have them start reviewing the specs. I'll join them in a few minutes."

I backed away, shocked at how tightly he'd held me between his thighs. I shouldn't have come here. I made everything worse. My presence was hurting him. I could see it even though he was shrouded by the protective shield.

"When do leave for London?"

"Tomorrow morning."

"Please don't work late tonight."

A small tremor streaked through his body. It was subtle but it was there. "I have to start this call now."

Swallowing down the acerbic taste of regret, I showed myself to the door. Glancing over my shoulder, I noticed he remained sitting on the edge of the desk with his hands folded. He never did come home that night.

# CHAPTER TWENTY-ONE

"It'll be just like old times. Only in a way better condo." Stephanie squeezed my shoulder and carried my overnight bag upstairs. I'd decided to stay with her on Tuesday night mostly because I couldn't stand being in that house by myself. The townhouse she shared with Darren with beautiful. Since she moved here, she added a more feminine touch to the space with her love of scented candles, bright pops of color and quirky artwork. Much like their friendship, everything gelled together with ease.

"I've been ordered to make you some tea, young lady," Darren said with a wink. "Just honey, right?"

I smiled. "You got it."

Settling onto the oversized couch, I let out a huge sigh. Work had been a challenge today so relaxing with good friends was just what the doctor ordered. Stephanie bounded down the stairs and flopped on the couch next to me.

"I don't think you've been here since, like, the weekend after you arrived."

"Has it been that long?"

"Yep. We went on that picnic in the freezing cold, remember?" She shivered for emphasis.

"Come on, Steph. It was twelve Celsius out. That's a luxury for us this time of year." Darren placed the mug of tea on the table in front of me. "Wait until the winter really gets going. You'll wish you were basking on Cocoa Beach."

"I already do," she grumbled. "I didn't think I'd miss that damn city this much." She turned to face me. "Do you miss Orlando at all?"

"Sometimes," I shrugged. "I miss Sydney and the guys at the station more than the actual city. Although, running at Cranes Roost Park would be heaven right about now."

"You should play tennis with me," Darren exclaimed. "That one doesn't want to break a sweat so it's hard for me to get into the game."

"Why don't you just double up with that girl you keep staring at every time we're on the court. I'm sure she'd be a much better partner for you."

"Could be." Darren looked thoughtful. "But then I'd miss out on all this quality time with you." He ruffled Stephanie's hair, much to her immense displeasure. If I hadn't known them as well as I did, I'd be a huge advocate for the two of them hooking up. But they were friends, great friends. Nothing more.

"Do you see what I have to put up with daily?" she squealed.

I sipped my tea, half listening to their faux brother-sister bickering. Darren continued to tease her, forcing her to exclaim -on more than one occasion- that she's an only child for a reason.

"Alright, Meyers. No pouty face," Stephanie said, throwing an arm over my shoulders. "Every time you pout I'm going to make Darren sing *Total Eclipse of the Heart*. Believe me, you don't want that to happen."

"Watch it now," he said. "I have a great voice."

"For dogs, yes. For humans, not so much."

Amused, I frowned on purpose. "But what if I want to hear him sing?"

"Oh no," she groaned. "Now you've asked for it."

Darren stood in the center of the room, bowing to an audience of two before clearing his throat.

"Those judges on X-Factor don't know what they're missing." He smiled and launched into the most tone deaf, horrible version of that song I'd ever heard. The hilarious part was how passionate he was as he sang. At one point, he spread his arms wide and looked to the heavens while out-of-tune notes and the occasional incorrect lyric saturated the room.

"*Your love is like a shadow on me all of the time,*" he screeched.

I laughed and clapped, encouraging him to do more. His enthusiasm was contagious. I hopped off the couch to join him and launched into a so-so rendition of *Don't Stop Believin'*, because, why not.

"You're both going to make me go deaf and I'm only thirty. Stop." Stephanie covered her ears and smiled. Satisfied that we'd performed the greatest concert ever in the history of living room concerts, Darren and I rejoined Stephanie on the couch. For the rest of the night they did their absolute best to keep my mind off of a particular redhead who'd disappeared to London.

We had wine and beer. We laughed. We even made a pizza. I was fortunate to have a strong support system here and I hugged them both fiercely before we retired for the night.

I sat on the bed in Stephanie's room, pulling at the comforter. It was all I could do stop myself from looking at my cell phone to see if any texts were waiting. My best friend climbed into bed and snuggled under the covers. The last time we slept in the same bed was during a weekend in Daytona. We spent the entire night up talking about the most random life stuff and then ditched the hotel room for the beach to watch the sunrise.

"So, how are you feeling? I mean, your head is okay from the accident?"

"Oh yeah, I'm fine. The bruise is fading which is nice. I still can't believe that guy ran the light."

"Bad drivers are everywhere my friend." She looked at me. "I'm going out with Colin again tomorrow night. The band has a few days off."

"Wow. Another date. Sounds serious."

"We had a good time on Saturday. I'm really excited to see him again."

"No more Brent, then?" I asked, shifting to face her.

She frowned. "Nope. He's a great guy but I'm not cut out for that lifestyle. No offense."

"None taken."

"I mean, he treated me like a queen but I always felt like I owed him something. I don't know what to do with myself with all the fancy dinners and nice cars and expensive houses and…it's just so not me. Don't get me wrong. The sex was amazing. I'll miss that."

"But you have Band Guy now. I'm sure he fills the void."

"I don't know." She lifted her shoulders and scrunched her nose. "We didn't sleep together."

"Really? The way you were talking about the date I assumed you guys had."

"Nope. We sat up all night talking." She gave me a look. "I know. Who am I, right?"

"There's nothing wrong with that," I laughed. "It means you might actually like him as more than just a conquest."

A dreamy look took hold of her pretty face, making her eyes sparkle. "He's smart and talented and makes me laugh like nothing you've ever seen. And he's a gentleman with a wicked bad boy streak."

"Ah. So he's the perfect man for you." I grinned.

She pushed herself up and hugged me. This was a big hug. The apology hug. I squeezed her tight and smiled. No matter the fight, no matter the circumstance, we'd always pull through.

"I was such a bitch about the whole Olivia bridal shower thing," she said, breaking the embrace. "I have no excuse, really. I just thought maybe…if things could be smoothed over with her—"

"It's okay. Your intentions were misguided though. I'm not going to sugarcoat that. She's not what you think. She's manipulative."

Stephanie's shoulders slumped as she nodded. "Brent worries

about her. He's not so much pissed at Alastair as he is at how everything was handled."

I swallowed. "Did he tell you?"

"Yeah. It's shitty, Lia. It's really shitty. But Alastair had his back against the wall and had no choice I guess. Don't worry. I'll never breathe a word of this to him. I love you too much to make you guys feel uncomfortable about this. You trust me, right?"

A week ago I wouldn't have known how to answer that question. "I do."

Relief swept through her, visibly relaxing her body. She engulfed me in another hug. "When can we start planning your wedding?"

I stiffened, swallowing down a bitter lump. Stephanie looked at me with concern.

"You guys are getting married. I have zero doubt about that. He's just being…I don't know…he's being a douche but he loves you. The accident must have scared the shit out of him. That's the only thing I can come up with."

"I know," I said quietly. "He's so frustrating sometimes, you know? And then I say stupid crap to make it worse and it's a dumb, annoying cycle that we go through."

"The level of passion between you two is out of this world. You argue as hard as you love. But at the end of the day, he's your guy and you're his girl and nothing will ever change that."

I chuckled. "When did you become so poetic, Tempe?"

"I'm dating a musician. Everything he says is always so poetic and cool. It must have rubbed off on me."

"You went on one date."

"Oh, Lia. It so much more than a date. Did I tell you how hard his abs are?"

I threw a pillow at her as we laughed and settled under the covers. We talked late into the night, like we'd always done when having a sleepover. Before drifting off to sleep, I heard her mumble, "Good night my unofficial-little-sister-official-best-friend. I can't wait to watch you walk down the aisle."

The next day at lunch I decided to do a little impromptu retail therapy. Meredith was with me, so it was a nice chance for me and her to bond a bit more. She had tons of questions about the news business and I happily answered them to the best of my ability.

"Do you think I'll make a good producer someday?" she asked.

"Absolutely."

"You're just saying that."

"No, I'm not. You have a good head on your shoulders and you're smart. Plus, you're a hard worker." I paused. "Julian thinks you're great and you know how he is."

"He does?" Her eyes widened.

"Yep. He told me this morning after you pitched that story idea about the independence referendum."

"Wow." She stopped walking. "I'm speechless."

I laughed. "See? The only thing holding you back is your own self-doubt."

"Do you think we'll be able to stay in touch once my internship ends? I'd love to have you on my side after graduating next spring."

"Of course."

We strolled through the bath and body department. I grabbed more of my favorite almond scented bubble bath and lotion. I'd be using them tonight for a long bubble bath after indulging in some heavy carb laden meal. I walked to the cashier to pay for my items and bumped right in to Olivia fucking Garrison.

"Really?" I said, putting the lotion down.

"Lia." She smiled. "What a coincidence."

"There are no coincidences with you," I muttered.

"And who's this?" she asked, sizing up my intern.

"Meredith Sanders. I work for The Archer Hour with Lia." She offered her hand and Olivia made a half-hearted effort to shake it. Turning her attention back to me, she grinned.

"I adore that scent. So does Alastair, I imagine."

My blood boiled. I turned my back on her and paid the sales-woman, who was listening and watching us intently. I lifted a brow in her direction and started for the exit. Olivia followed me out like a little eager dog nipping at my heels. Thank goodness the sidewalk was crowded. It left no room to stop and talk.

"Lia," she called after me. "This isn't going to end."

Okay, that made me stop. I whipped around. Meredith stared at me with huge eyes. The last thing I wanted was to have this out in front of her. "Go back to the newsroom and tell Robbie I'll be a little late for our afternoon meeting."

She nodded and scurried off. I glared at Olivia.

"This isn't going to end because you keep inserting yourself into my life. Jesus Christ. You're getting married in a month. Go pick out flowers or music or something. Focus on your own life and leave Alastair alone."

Her eyes glazed with a distant look. "The way he looks at you and talks about you…he was never like that with me."

"I don't know what you want me to say."

"You reached him. I don't know how but you did it." She set her jaw. "He really did say he would marry me, you know. He'll never admit it to you but he did. We were in love, Lia."

"I'm really all set with your shit," I lashed out. Keeping a handle on my emotions wasn't easy. We were so different, her and I, in every way. And not just physically. She just didn't know when to let something go.

"He knows he didn't treat me well," she continued. "He knows we could have had something special. I only did what I had to do when he discarded me like an old pair of shoes."

"You blackmailed his family and threatened to expose his most private moments with you. You broke whatever trust he might have had in you. That makes you a bitch and not worthy of his love."

Sidling closer, a cunning smile curved her mouth. "Has he ever gone down on you at the beach under the moonlight? Fucked you in a hot tub overlooking the Alps? Made love to you on a balcony in Greece?"

By the grace of some higher power, my urge to slap her dissipated the second I saw the dozens of photographers surround us. This would make for one hell of a show, wouldn't it? I kept my expression as placid as possible while my insides raged.

"Olivia."

I turned and saw Brent standing next to a black Bentley.

"We have to go. Sergio is expecting you."

She looked at her brother and turned into a completely different person. Sugary sweet and all smiles, she hugged me goodbye. I cringed.

Brent walked over after she climbed into the car. "I'm sorry about this, Lia. I am. She's not— I'm sorry."

"Keep her away from me."

He nodded, setting his jaw in determination. "I know you're frustrated but she's my sister. This hasn't been easy for her."

I tightened my hold on the bag, keenly aware of the photographers nearby. "I get it, Brent, I do. But you and I both know this can't go on anymore. I know everything that happened and I know it sucked but it can't be changed. At some point, she has to own what she did and accept the consequence. And you have to help her get to that point."

Turning back to glance at the car briefly he sighed. "I've been trying." He looked at me. "It's all such a mess." A small smile pulled at his mouth as he took in all the paparazzi. "Thank you for being so graceful about this in public."

"Well, like you said to me once before, regardless of your history with Alastair, I'd never do anything to embarrass either one of you in the press."

Nodding, he returned to the car. I let out a long sigh and went back to work.

* * *

The doorbell rang around nine that night, startling me. I shuffled to the hallway, zipping up my hoodie. I figured it couldn't be anybody threatening since Paxton was stationed in front of the house while Alastair was away. My heart seized just thinking about him and the awful things I'd said. I still hadn't heard from him but Paxton reassured me that he was working in London and he was fine.

Shaking it off, I opened the door.

"I hope I'm not bothering you. I tried calling but your mobile went straight to voice mail."

*Two of them in one day*? I blinked at Emma as she stood holding a bottle of merlot. This girl couldn't have picked a worse time to show up on my doorstep.

"What are you doing here?"

"Can I come in?"

"Why?"

"I have to talk you and I'd rather not do it standing on the front steps."

"Fine. Whatever," I said.

She followed me into the living room and put the wine bottle on the coffee table. As far as I knew, she'd never set foot in this house before due to Alastair's former 'rule' about not bringing women over. Then again, she knew where he lived so, there's that.

"I'm going to get right to it," she declared, sitting down. "I've spent the last two nights talking Alastair off a ledge. He's an absolute mess. What did you do to him?"

Her violet eyes blazed with anger. I overcame my shock quickly and held her formidable stare.

"That's not any of your business."

"It is my business when he shows up at my flat, drunk off his ass and ranting about how he fucked it up again."

I was too stunned to say anything. *Why is he running to her*? A horrible realization dawned on me. He always goes back to her. That's what she'd told me.

Emma shook her head in disgust. "This isn't the first time he's come to me because of something you did. I gave you the benefit of the doubt after what happened in June but I warned him about letting his guard down. I told him to stick to what he knew and that you'd only end up breaking his heart. I fucking hate what you're doing to him."

My head spun. Who does this girl think she is? "I'm not doing anything to him. We're—"

"Not doing anything to him?" she blurted. "He's broken, Lia. And because of you he doesn't know which way is up anymore. You think you know him so well? You don't. If you really love him, you'll break off this engagement and let him be."

"Get out."

She laughed. "I'm not going anywhere."

"What makes you such an expert on my relationship? You have no idea what we've been through."

"Oh no? I'm the only constant in his life, Lia. I know exactly what you've put him through."

A dull ache throbbed in my head. "Then you also know how he feels about me."

"He doesn't know what he feels," she grumbled. "He never has. We bonded over our similar backgrounds as kids. I was abandoned by my birth mother and grew up in foster homes until I was adopted when I was nine. I don't trust a soul. When I met Alastair, he lashed out at everyone. We clicked because neither one of us feels safe enough to let anybody else in. He fears loss and I fear abandonment. I helped him channel his fears so he'd be able to control his emotions. When it came to relationships, we agreed it was best to get what we wanted without having to deal with all the emotional baggage that comes with love and sex and fucking feelings. It worked for us."

I balled my hands into fists. I couldn't believe what I was hearing.

"His life was great until last spring," she continued, "when he told me not to meet him at that cocktail party because he had a date with some American girl." She glared at me. "I went anyway just to see what the fuss was all about. I disliked you the minute I saw you. You kept staring at him, like every other woman does, with those fuck me eyes. Only you wanted more than a one night stand with him. You saw a future and it gave him hope. It gave him something he's been longing for all his life. I warned him that night to stay away from you."

"You sound jealous," I gloated. "He chose me over you."

"He said you were different," she raised her voice. "He claimed to see purity and honesty in your eyes. He was in love with you the second he met you and it freaked him out. But he kept saying he had to have you. I told him to forget about you, that you'd cause him nothing but trouble."

I smirked. "Good to know he didn't listen to your advice."

"Don't be flippant. You've caused him more pain in the last six months than I cared to witness."

A cold shiver streaked down my spine. As annoyed as I was with her, my jealousy over her intimate knowledge of what made him tick clawed at me.

"He's not the same person he was when you met him," I said much more evenly than anticipated. "He's learned to trust his emotions. He has a long way to go but he trusts what he feels for me and he trusts that I love him just as much, if not more."

A ruthless grin curved her glossy lips. "You don't get it, do you?"

I stiffened, hearing the lilt of Olivia's voice saying those exact same words to me a week ago. "Get what?"

"He always comes back to *me*. I'm his safe place. I have his trust, Lia. Not you. Leave him the fuck alone."

Without saying another word, she stood up and left. Anxiety shook me to the core. I grabbed the bottle of wine she'd brought, walked out the front door and threw it into the street, shattering it under the moonlight. Paxton got out of the car and approached while talking into his cell phone.

"She's upset," he said. "Do you want me to take— Understood."

He hung up and escorted me back to the house. I covered my mouth and held in a sob. Alastair knew she was here. He knew and he let that happen. He didn't want to talk to me. He only wanted to know what was going on.

I sat on the bed, staring at my engagement ring. The diamond and halo of emeralds shimmered. I loved him with everything that I am but his damaged, broken soul still had so much healing to do. Whether or not I was the person he'd allow to join him on that journey remained a mystery. Maybe I had to let him discover the person he wanted to be on his own. I slipped off the ring and laid it on the nightstand before crawling under the covers.

# CHAPTER TWENTY-TWO

Music?

I woke with a start. The room was dark and the bed was empty so I thought maybe I'd been dreaming.

No. There it was again.

Panicked, I climbed out of bed and edged into the hallway. The music was coming from the living room. My heart fluttered. *He's back?*

I padded down the hall, stopping just shy of the entry. Alastair stood by the media cabinet, holding a photo in his hand and singing along quietly with The Script's *For the First Time*. His voice was low and raspy. Never in a million years did I expect this.

"This song makes me think of you," he said, not looking in my direction but clearly aware I was there. "It's so fitting, especially now."

I walked into the room and stood by one of the couches. I wanted so desperately to hold him.

Putting the photo down, he faced me. A good amount of reddish-brown scruff covered his face from lack of shaving. He appeared softer, less guarded than he was at his office. Unable to control myself, I ran to him, touching his cheek just to make sure he was in front of me for real.

"I'm here, love. I'm here." His scent engulfed me as he banded his arms around my body. I clawed at him, pulling him closer, refusing to let this be a dream. The song swelled, filling the room. Blending together with the smooth vocals of the lead singer was Alastair's voice. I felt his warm breath on my skin as he sang about times being hard and not giving up. I held him tighter, mesmerized by this moment.

"Lia," he whispered. "My Lia."

The tremendous pounding of my heart flooded my ears. As hurt and upset as I was over his leaving, and as emotionally exhausted as I was over my run-ins with Olivia and Emma, I wanted to make things right. I held his face in my hands. "I'm so sorry I said all those horrible things to you."

Cupping the nape of my neck he leveled an intense stare at me. "Don't be. You were right. I am selfish and afraid and hide behind my guilt to avoid happiness. But I don't want to be that way with you. Be patient with me. Please, Lia. Be patient."

"I always have been."

"I know." He slid his hand under my shirt. The feel of his skin on mine was electric, reawakening me after days of uncertainty and stress. "That accident…I know it was minor but I lost my mind. I couldn't think straight. All I saw…all I felt…was how my life would be if you were taken from me. It was worse than any nightmare I've had." He paused, wetting his lips. "I was so angry with you and with myself for letting that happen. My first instinct is always to—"

He clutched his stomach, noticing the diamond ring wasn't on my finger. I swallowed down a sob.

"My first instinct was wrong. I should have held you. Comforted you. Kept you safe. These feelings are too consuming for me at times. It's a shit excuse but it's all I have."

"Emma said—"

"Emma was wrong to say anything and I'll deal with her soon enough. If I'd known she took it upon herself to fly here and—" His eyes flashed. "She knew me at a time in my life when I hated myself. She doesn't understand what I feel for you."

"But you ran to her. You left me and you ran to her."

Lacing his fingers through mine, he led me to the bedroom. Sitting on the mattress, he leaned against the headboard and pulled me onto his lap to straddle him. This position was always comforting for both of us.

Brushing his thumb along my lower lip, he continued. "I thought she would help give me clarity. All she did was try to talk me out of being with you. At first, I figured it was her way of protecting me like she always had. But this time…this time was different. She's never gotten past being abandoned. She's never allowed herself to fully trust another person. Until I met you, neither had I." His body stilled. "You look so gorgeous right now. All I want to do is kiss you and lose myself inside you."

Lowering his head, he kissed my breast through the cotton tank top I was wearing. "I don't think—" I gasped, cut off by the sensation of him sucking on my nipple. "Alastair," I moaned. "Sex can't always be the answer to our fights."

My protests didn't do much to convince me, let alone him. He felt so amazing. I leaned into his mouth, surrendering. His fingers sunk into the soft flesh on my thighs.

"Let me." He looked at me with such hunger, such yearning. It was enough to leave me breathless. Instead it incited a riot of emotions.

"I hate that you shut me out," I blurted, feeling the surge of hurt and anger build like a growing storm. "I hate that you chose Emma over me and told her everything that was bothering you. I'm supposed to be that person for you, Alastair. I'm supposed to be the one you trust with everything." My lower lip quivered making his expression falter. "I'm supposed to be your safe place, not her."

"You're more than my safe place, kitten. You're my lifeline."

"Then please stop shutting me out when you're thrust into emotional chaos."

Closing his eyes, he took a deep breath. I could tell this weighed heavily on him even though he tried to mask it, like he always did. I leaned forward, resting my forehead on his. We communicated in the one way we both knew worked; through touch. For me, feeling his hands on my skin quieted the chorus of doubts and insecurities that plagued my mind.

"I missed waking up with you," he said after a few minutes. "I like hearing you first thing in the morning and feeling your body close. My day isn't right if it doesn't start that way. You have no idea how overwhelmed I am by you."

I ran my fingers along his jaw and through the stubble. "I think I do, chief. I think you might need a safe word."

That got a smile out of him. "We'll see about that." He tucked a strand of hair behind my ear and fixed a bright green stare on me. "You're so beautiful."

Goosebumps commandeered every inch of my skin, rippling across my body. Bowing his head, he frowned. "Why aren't you wearing your ring?"

I glanced at the glittering diamond on the nightstand and reached for it. He watched me, remaining still and quiet.

"I thought." I paused, shaking my head. *I was being an idiot, as usual.* "I don't know what I thought. I was overanalyzing again."

Arching an eyebrow, he took the ring and slipped it back on my finger. The dominant spark returned to his eyes. "Don't take it off again, kitten."

"Do you promise not to shut me out anymore?" I challenged.

"Only if you promise to stay patient with me."

"Always negotiating, Holden."

"Always feisty, Meyers."

I hugged him, relieved to feel his body relax and meld with mine. "I'm so glad you're home."

Breaking our embrace, he cupped my jaw and regarded me with great interest. Determination sparked behind his eyes. "Brent called me this afternoon," he said, playing with my hair. "He told me what happened. I'm going to take care of the whole Olivia situation once and for all."

"So you actually talked to him?"

"About a few things, yeah. He's worried about her and right-fully so. I can't change what she did or pretend it didn't happen but all of this needs to stop."

"What are you going to do?"

"That's for me to worry about." He grinned. "You look exhausted. Get some sleep."

"Only if you never leave me alone in this bed again. If I have to sleep in here all by myself one more night I'll go nuts."

"That gives me an idea."

"Oh really?"

His fingertips glided along my lower back, scattering more goosebumps in their wake. "A brilliant idea in fact."

"And what's this brilliant idea you have, English?"

The left corner of his mouth ticked up in a grin. "We stay in bed until the sun comes up."

I pouted. "That's not much longer. It's already four in the morning."

He leaned in and nibbled on my neck. "You didn't let me finish. When the sun comes up on Friday."

"That means— Wait. Skip work? You? That's unheard of."

"Someone once told me I was due for some time off and since I'm the boss—" he smirked "—I approve the request."

"Convenient," I snickered. "There's one problem though. You're not *my* boss, so I have to go to work."

"Interesting thing about that. You have the rest of the week off."

"Alastair," I exclaimed. "I can't—"

"It's done. I've already cleared it with Sam, so you have nothing to worry about."

I folded my arms and gave him a look. "When did you do that?"

His nonchalant shrug irked me.

"I have a show to produce. Just because you're a crazy control freak doesn't mean you can dictate—"

He kissed me quiet, owning me with every tongue stroke.

"I can and I did," he said with a knowing smile. "You'll thank me later."

"Arrogant bastard. You know what that tone of voice does to me."

"The same thing your defiant little pose does to me when you cross your arms and challenge me with those eyes."

"You're a lot of work, Holden. I'm exhausted just thinking about what it's going to be like married to you."

He squeezed my waist, making me jump. "Not as exhausted as you'll be after I take you in every position, on every surface, piece of furniture, shower, bathtub, car, airplane—"

"Holy fuck," I gasped.

"Exactly."

With one arm, he tossed me onto my back, yanked down my sweats and proceeded to have his way with me on the bed until the sun rose.

* * *

Ringing bells echoed in my head. Cloudy with sleep, I grunted. The bells rang again, louder and more persistent this time. *Go away.* Tangled in Alastair's embrace, I managed to squint toward the nightstand to see what time it was. Noon? I haven't slept in this late since college. The doorbell sounded a third time. Alastair stirred next to me.

"Are you expecting someone?" I asked, thinking about another surprise visit from Emma, or worse.

"Yep." He sat up and yawned, ruffling his hair back and forth. Anyone who claimed to not be a morning person clearly never woke up next to a naked Alastair Holden. Even groggy with sleep he was hot. Standing up, he stretched. I was now eye level with his bare backside so I took the opportunity that was presented and grabbed a handful.

"Hey," he said, turning after I pinched him. "Save it for later." With a wink and grin, he slipped on his jeans and left the room. A few seconds later I heard his voice along with another man's. I leapt out of bed and threw on the first clothes I could find. It sounded like they were heading toward his home office. Curious, I went after them and hovered just outside the door.

"Everything's in order, mate. I just need the signatures." The guy with Alastair handed him a folder. He was dressed professionally, unlike my scruffy fiancé who was shirtless and had barely completed the button-fly requirements on his jeans. "Jason sure is chuffed about the whole thing."

"He should be. He's been wanting this for years. Pain in my ass."

The other guy laughed. "Good to see you two are close as ever."

Alastair stilled and turned in my direction. Not only was I now under the watchful gaze of his emerald eyes but his associate's blue ones as well.

"Hi." I almost didn't recognize my own voice; it sounded so shy.

"This must be Amelia." He looked from me to Alastair. "You didn't tell me she was this much of a knockout in person."

If looks could kill, this guy would be dead after the one Alastair threw in his direction.

"Gerard Wilson," he said, extending his hand. "I have the unfortunate pleasure of being his attorney."

I shook Gerard's hand and stood next to Alastair, who couldn't get his arm around my waist fast enough. Gerard looked strangely familiar to me but I couldn't put my finger on it. He wasn't as tall as Alastair but he was muscular. Stocky, even. *Built like a bulldog*, my dad would say.

"I can change your fortune, if you'd prefer," Alastair said, arching an eyebrow in Gerard's direction.

"Where's the fun in that? My other clients are boring and wouldn't dare greet me half naked at the front door."

"My other attorneys are seen and not heard unless they have

something useful to tell me."

I was fascinated listening to the two of them spar with each other good-naturedly. I'd only seen Alastair interact with Darren in a friendly manner. His history with Brent had been less than cordial and, well, he expressed his dislike for Nathan with a closed fist more than once.

"So when's the wedding? I trust my invitation is in the mail." Gerard shoved his hands in his pockets and smiled at me.

"We haven't set a date yet."

"No?" He looked at Alastair. "For fuck's sake what are you waiting for, Holden? If you don't hurry up and marry her a line will start forming down the street. Gorgeous women like this don't linger on the market long."

"Anything else you wanted?" Alastair's grip tightened on my waist as he shot Gerard another deadly look.

"Stand down, soldier." He winked. "Save it for the rugby pitch."

Rugby? That's it! This was the guy who'd shouted in Alastair's direction that day I ran into him at the field. I should have known this was the same guy. The look he'd given Gerard back then was identical to this one.

"You wouldn't be saying that if we played on different sides, G."

"Bollocks. You're not that good." Gerard looked at me. "Do you see what I have to put up with? I hope he knows what a saint you are. I wouldn't marry him if he was the last man on earth."

"He's a handful but I think I have it covered," I smiled.

"Probably more than you realize. The ice man melts for no one. Imagine my surprise when he said he proposed. I lost a bet."

I glanced up at Alastair. "So I really am the only one who didn't know that everyone else knew about our engagement."

He just shrugged and kissed my forehead.

"The man is a master," Gerard said. "Not to be an old bore but if you could sign those I'll send them off to the London office for tomorrow morning."

While Alastair scrutinized the legal documents, Gerard

continued chatting with me. I could tell he was being more flirty than was necessary just to get a rise out of my overprotective boyfriend. I didn't feel threatened by it at all. Truth be told, it amused me. I liked him. His easygoing demeanor and kind face offset his intimidating build.

"We're done here, then," Alastair said, slapping the folder against Gerard's chest. "Thanks for stopping by."

"The pleasure was all mine." He turned to me and shook my hand. "Absolutely stunning. If you ever get sick of him, I know a great divorce attorney."

"I'll keep that in mind," I said, laughing at his parting shot to my somewhat amused and more than likely annoyed fiancé.

"Let me escort you out," Alastair muttered. "And you," he looked at me with a hint of danger, "stay here."

I mock saluted him and perched on the edge of his desk. Several more files were spread out on the surface. Nosey thing that I am, I propped my feet up on his chair and peeked at one. Nothing exciting from what I could see. A lot of legal mumbo jumbo with 'Holden World Media' and 'The Company' interspersed.

I felt his presence before I saw him. Boy, did the sight of him rev up my engine. He'd shoved his hands in his pockets, making the jeans hang a little lower, exposing his bare hips. Barefoot, shirtless, disheveled hair and unshaven. *Yum*. I'd never seen anything more sexy. And that look in his eyes. So help me…

"Should I expect any more work interruptions today?" I asked as he approached.

"No. Should I expect any more flirting with other men?"

"Aw. Are you jealous?"

He leaned into me, hooking my legs around his hips. "Very."

I smiled. "Perfect."

"You're too bloody sexy for your own good, you know. Next time wear something less flattering."

I knotted my fingers in his hair. "I thought your boxers and my tank top were a pretty unsexy pairing."

"There is nothing unsexy about your wearing my clothes." He closed his eyes briefly and wet his lips. "I don't know whether to throw you against the wall and fuck you senseless or do it right here on my desk."

The wall won. So did the desk.

# CHAPTER TWENTY-THREE

I slumped on the couch, pretending to watch TV while Alastair prepared some dinner for us. I had some mindless movie on because my brain no longer existed. It had been screwed out of me somewhere between his desk and an extra-long shower. My thighs were so tingly and sore I made the executive decision never to walk again for the rest of my life. I don't know what had gotten into him but he'd been a beast all afternoon. Not that I'm complaining.

He sauntered into the living room carrying two plates of shepherd's pie, looking so unbelievably gorgeous I wanted to climb him like a tree. If I could move.

"Looks delicious," I said as he placed the food on the table.

"Yes, you do."

"Stop it. You destroyed me. I'm on a sex hiatus and won't be able to do anything for at least a week, maybe two."

"I doubt that."

"I can't even move to eat."

"I'll feed you," he said with a wicked grin. "Come here."

It was a struggle to sit up. My bones were liquid and my muscles rioted against having to work. Only my sheer force of hunger enabled me to grab a fork and dig in.

"Atta girl. You need the energy."

"Jackass."

He laughed. "Not quite what you were calling me earlier. I like 'sex god' better. 'Sensational lover' is also high on the list."

"I was under the influence."

"You were under me."

"Case in point."

"Of all the little pet names you call me," he said, leaning close, "'mine' is my favorite."

"Well, you are."

"Without question."

"Right answer."

His cell phone rang, interrupting our refueling session. He gave my knee a quick squeeze before answering with a gruff, "Holden."

For someone who was supposedly on a day off, his phone never stopped. Lucky for me, he ignored it most of the day, only interrupting our sex marathon once for a call. I wondered why he didn't take tomorrow off as well. I had no idea what I was supposed to do here all by myself. Recuperate probably. My body ached with great pleasure, no doubt, but man his stamina was inhuman.

"Why the fuck is that in here." Alastair's agitated shout echoed through the house. I put down my fork and stood up gingerly, tiptoeing toward his office. That tone of voice was never a good sign. I was almost to the door when another angry outburst sounded. "I'll destroy that deal so fast you won't know what hit you. I can. I own fifty-one percent. It's mine unless you have the means to buy me out and we both know that's not the case."

I had no idea who he was yelling at. Emma? She did mention he supported her business financially to get it up and running. I don't think he owned it though. Then again, maybe he did. Who knows.

"Nobody is signing it. I didn't even know Gerard brought it with him. I'll be in the office tomorrow to deal with this."

This had something to do with his company. Was it Jason on the receiving end of his tirade? Probably. I went back to the living room before he ended the call. Alastair stalked in a few minutes later, heated from the conversation.

"You okay, chief?"

His fiery gaze halted my efforts to eat. "I'm fine. Don't worry about it."

I didn't believe a word coming out of his mouth but chose not to press him on the matter. We'd had a shitty enough week as it was. Exhaling slowly, he sat on the couch.

"You're too far away," I said, spreading my arms. To my immense pleasure, he curled up with me. I could tell he was restless though. I turned his head so he looked at me. "What can I do to help?"

"Exactly what you're doing right now."

* * *

Alastair's nightmare woke me up with a start. He clutched the sheets, twisting and pulling. Letting out a sharp cry, he rolled toward me, clamping his arms around my waist and yanking me into his chest.

"Don't leave me," he whined.

Even though his grip was suffocating, I didn't try to free myself. I whispered to him, letting him know I was close. Waking up, his eyes popped open as he drew in a sharp breath. I brushed my knuckles down his cheek.

"Hello, love," I said.

"Did I hurt you?" he asked, shaking off the remnants of his dream.

"No."

"You would tell me if I did?"

"You didn't hurt me, Alastair. You just hugged me, like you always do."

He blew out a sigh, nodding. "Okay."

"Want to tell me about it?"

Grimacing, he remained silent. I kissed his forehead and stroked his hair until his breathing became heavy and even and deep with sleep.

*　*　*

The bed was empty when the first rays of daylight streamed through the windows. I rubbed my eyes, yawning. I hated waking up without him. Dragging myself out of bed I went to his office. Much to my surprise, he wasn't in there. I shuffled toward the living room and found him sprawled out on the couch, fast asleep. *My tragic angel.*

He stirred and moaned softly as I knelt on the floor in front of him, brushing pieces of messy red hair off his forehead.

"Amelia," he mumbled. I loved how his voice sounded when he first woke. So deep and rough and sexy.

"Good morning, handsome. Felt like camping out on the couch?"

"Mmm." He stretched. "I didn't want to wake you up again. Come here."

I obliged, snuggling against his warm body. He rested his cheek to mine, sighing.

"I don't mind being woken up by your bad dreams. I'd rather have you next to me then have to search for you in the morning."

He held me tighter. "Fair enough."

"Do you have to go to work today?"

His drowsy smile turned me on in a way I didn't expect. "Yes. Come for lunch after your morning at the spa."

"The spa? I'm not going to the spa."

"Yes you are. I made an appointment for you. You deserve to be pampered on your day off."

"When were you planning to tell me about this?"

"Right now." He kissed me. "I get less back talk when you're still half asleep."

"Ass." I knew he was right though. "I thought you liked my

smart mouth."

"I like the things you do with that mouth more."

I nuzzled his neck, kissing just under his ear. I got the reaction I wanted when a low groan vibrated in his throat. "What time is my appointment?" I asked before sucking gently on his earlobe.

"Ten. Paxton will take you and pick you up." He exhaled in a rush. "Christ, Lia, that feels good."

I'd slid my hand between his legs and started running my fingernails along his inner thigh. He couldn't control how his body reacted to my touch. Such a turn on.

"Glad you like it."

"I thought you said I destroyed you yesterday."

I laughed. "You did. I'm still on the sex hiatus so rein in your insatiable advances. I need some recovery time."

His pout was so seductive. "How long?"

"I'll let you know." I grinned, sitting back on my heels. He covered his face with his hands briefly before sitting up and sighing. Something was bothering him. He seemed distracted and distant. Looking at me with tired eyes, he cupped my jaw. The feeling of dread that had been hanging around returned with a vengeance, making me antsy.

Alastair kissed me softly before getting up to shower. I watched him dress for work in the bedroom, admiring his athletic physique as I always did. Clean shaven and freshly washed, the last remnants of my scruffy, unbridled lover morphed into a controlled, powerful businessman. The tailor made three piece suit molded to his body perfectly. I'd take him either way, just so long as I could have him.

"So I'll see you after your spa appointment?" he asked, adjusting the cufflinks I'd given to him over the summer.

"If you're not too busy."

He leveled me with those intense emerald eyes. "I'm never too busy for you, kitten. You know that."

I smiled as a rare bout of shyness swept through me. He made me feel so special, like I truly was the most important thing in his life. Tilting my chin up, he gazed at me with such gentleness and affection it brought me back to our night in Paris. My heart ached with love.

* * *

For the second time in as many days I couldn't move. I'd been wrapped, scrubbed, massaged and pampered all morning. The luxurious scents of jasmine, sandalwood and rose lingered on my skin, adding an extra layer of serenity. Stephanie and I would go to spas at the fancy hotels in Orlando on occasion but we'd never treated ourselves to this level of indulgence. This was decadent and borderline excessive. I smiled, sipping on some cucumber water in the lounge. My future husband knew how to score brownie points.

A couple of other women were in here too and they had the same dreamy, peaceful expressions on their faces as I did. It was a struggle to leave this oasis but the promise of seeing Alastair for lunch spurred me on. I grabbed my black leggings, t-shirt and hoodie and redressed, remaining make-up free and throwing my hair up in a ponytail. Not the most glamorous look but it totally fit the vibe of this day so far. Besides, Alastair thought it was cute when I dressed super casual.

As I was walking toward the reception area, a tall brunette stared at me hard and frowned.

"It is you," she muttered. "I see you've made yourself quite comfortable with the Holden lifestyle."

Her salty tone got my hackles up. I had no intention of spoiling my day so I just looked at her coolly, smiled and went to the waiting Mercedes. A sizable group of photographers and reporters waited with cameras at the ready. Somebody from inside the spa must have tipped off the press. They descended on me, taking pictures and shouting questions.

"Have you recovered from the accident?"

"When is the wedding?"

"Are you pregnant?"

"Is it true Holden World Media is dissolving its music division due to bad finances and rumors of embezzlement?"

I stopped short, staring at the bearded guy who asked that question. The look on my face must have answered it for him. I had no idea what he was talking about.

"Miss Meyers. Come with me." Paxton muscled through the crush of media, placing a secure grip on my arm. The reporters shouted after me while the photographers stuck their lenses as close as they could, snapping away with every move I made.

Once inside the safety of the SUV, I watched them grow smaller and smaller when Paxton drove off. I twisted the engagement ring around my finger. Embezzlement? Dissolving part of the company? Maybe that was the reason for Alastair's angry phone call last night. I always tried to respect his wishes and not bring up work matters when we were home but this was huge. He must have known I'd catch wind of it sooner or later. After all, I was the executive producer for a news magazine show. *Which I'm not at today, for what it's worth.*

I stared out the window at the city as it flew by. Was this why he didn't want me at work yesterday or today? Julian had mentioned a big announcement regarding the future of the company was coming.

When we arrived at the HWM building I hopped out of the car and breezed through the lobby. The security guard nodded a greeting to me as I went to the elevators. For the most part, my body and mind were still drunk with relaxation so I wasn't anxious about seeing him. If anything, I just wanted to be in his arms.

Simone wasn't at her desk when I arrived at the top floor. I did a little happy dance on the inside. Not seeing her oh so unpleasant face was a gift.

I turned the knob and opened the door to Alastair's office. My heart dropped right out of my body. Olivia stood in front of him with her hands on his chest. Her lips were parted and she was gazing up at him like a lovesick puppy. I clutched my stomach.

"What the fuck?"

"Amelia." He turned to me, sounding so calm and unflustered.

I glared at him. "Why is she here?" I asked, failing to keep a civil tone. Any remnants of my glorious morning at the spa dissipated. He was now standing in front of me but I turned my attention to the blonde leaning against his desk. She appeared flushed and out of breath.

"Stop," he ordered softly. "Look at me."

I did, against my better judgment. "Start talking, Holden."

"It's not what you think." He gripped my ponytail, pulling on it slowly. If these were normal circumstance I'd be turned on by the tugging. But they weren't and I wasn't.

"Not the best way to start this conversation."

His next tug was harder and more intense, wreaking havoc on my determination stay angry. "Don't," he growled. "I told you I was going to put a stop to everything. Let me take care of this."

I wanted to tear that suit off him, sprawl him out on the floor and have my way with him to show her just who he belonged to and how nobody would ever come between us. This surging jealousy filled every inch of my being. I never pegged myself to be the jealous type but this girl brought out the absolute worst in me.

Leaning close, Alastair brushed his cheek to mine. "Careful with that look, Lia," he whispered. "Go wait out in reception. I promise this won't take long."

"I'm not leaving you in here with her."

"You don't trust me?" he asked, his eyes widening.

"I trust you with my life, chief. It's her I don't trust."

"You have nothing to worry about." The second his lips touched mine I wrapped my arms around him, kissing him with more desperation than I wanted. "My Lia," he smiled. "Your enthusiasm is appreciated."

I grabbed his tie, keeping his body close to me.

"You're mine."

"Ditto, love." He kissed me again. "Now go do as I say."

It took all of my strength not to latch myself onto him when he walked back to her. I could see how much she wanted him. I could feel it emanating from her body. Simone stared at me in horror when I walked out and closed the door.

"When did you get here?" she asked, sounding like she had a serious head cold.

"In time to see what was behind door number one."

She paled. "I'm sorry."

Surprised, I folded my arms. "You are?"

"He'll probably fire me."

"Why?"

"I was supposed to call Paxton and tell him to stall you. But I have this damn flu thing and I needed more tissues so I went to the loo to grab some. I didn't do what he wanted and now he's going to fire me."

In all of my interactions with her, this was the most she'd ever said to me. And to top it all off, she no longer had that disinterested look on her face. Now she was just worried about her employment status.

"I doubt he'll fire you," I muttered. "You've been his assistant for ages. Nobody else probably has the patience to put up with him."

She laughed. She actually laughed. "My girlfriend says the same thing."

The desk phone started ringing so I let Simone get back to work. I paced around the luxurious waiting area, running my hand along the leather sofa. The feeling I'd had when I left the spa seemed to be a million miles away now. Nothing ever came easy for us, did it? If it wasn't Nathan, it was Olivia or Emma or the press or something. I sighed, staring blankly out the window at downtown Glasgow. I don't even know how long I stood like this. Half an hour maybe? My anxiety grew with each minute that ticked away. The sound of a door opening broke through my reverie.

Olivia came out, looking just as flushed as she had been when I was in there. A sickening, crushing sensation seized my chest. She caught my eye and lifted her chin; a defiant move signaling she wasn't going away without a fight. We stared at one another; one man's past and future locked in an age old battle. She was about to say something when Alastair appeared.

"Paxton is waiting downstairs, Olivia," he said. "He'll take you home."

"Thank you." She turned to him, a demure smile curving her mouth. "For everything."

My one saving grace was that he didn't escort her all the way to the elevators, just to the end of the hall. I couldn't stomach seeing them together. I didn't like the familiarity between them as they walked side by side. It felt like I was watching them as they used to be when they dated.

I inhaled, allowing the cleansing breath to calm me. Alastair waited a beat after the elevator doors closed before coming back to me. The hesitation toyed with my emotions. Extending his hand, he asked, "Are you coming?"

I nodded, letting his fingers entwine with mine as I followed him back inside his office. The atmosphere felt heavy, like something monumental had just occurred and I wasn't privy to the results.

"You," he said cupping my jaw, "are glowing. I take it they treated you well at the spa?"

"It was amazing, thank you."

"You deserve to be treated to the best this world has to offer. I'll send you anytime you'd like. Just say the word."

I searched his guarded expression, disheartened by his distance. "What di—"

Cut off by his kiss, I snaked my fingers through his hair, holding on as tight as I could. I had that sinking feeling again that if I let him go he'd disappear.

"Hey." The smile that I loved crossed his lips. "How about we go off the grid for the weekend? I'll fly you somewhere beautiful and spend every minute of every hour focused on nothing but you."

I couldn't help myself and grinned. "Where?"

"That's for me to know. Meet me at the airport tonight at eight?"

"You're serious."

"I've never been more serious about anything. Will you come with me?"

I hesitated, not knowing how to answer. "You're trying to deflect what just happened in here."

He shrugged, playing with my ponytail. "I'm trying to spend a weekend alone with my future wife."

"But what about Olivia? I'm…she's still in love with you and I—"

"We have an understanding, Lia," he interrupted. "She knows the consequences if she pushes too hard."

"I don't trust her."

"I know."

"Brian Kenner is on line one for you, Mr. Holden." Simone's voice floated from his desk phone. "He's in New York."

Alastair scowled before going to his desk. "Tell him I'll be with him in a minute." Flicking his eyes up at me he sighed. "I have to take this. I'm sorry."

"Don't apologize. You're at work. I'll go home."

His expression altered. "Come here."

Driven by his gentle command I circled around the desk. He sat on the edge and wedged me between his thighs like he'd done the last time I was here. Being so close to him accelerated my pulse. I played with his tie, gazing up at his perfect face. Lowering his head, he sealed our mouths together in a lush, passionate kiss.

"Stay with me," he murmured, fitting a wireless earpiece onto his right ear. Reaching back, he pushed the talk button. "Holden."

Placing his finger to my lips, he slid his other hand between my legs. I inhaled on a sharp intake. While he was on a business call?

"I've read the entire proposal and while I appreciate your ideas, this isn't quite what we're looking for. Jason has been rather specific with what he wants."

Down went my leggings.

"No. We want a complete user experience. Streaming the media online will stay the main focus."

The sound of tearing cotton signaled the demise of my underwear.

"Because it's what works, Brian. We're not going to screw around with what we know is successful."

My nails sank into his shoulders when he outlined the sensitive flesh near my clit before sliding his fingers inside me. I closed my eyes and gasped. *He's really doing this.*

"We'll start in the U.S. market first, then roll out in Canada and the United Kingdom within a year. Yes. Ask him if you want but that's the timetable."

Not much else from the conversation registered when his other hand grasped my backside. I was at his mercy. I buried my face in his neck to muffle my moans when he stroked along my tailbone. The more I made noise, the deeper he pushed his fingers inside. Oh God, he curled them. My legs shook. Lifting my head to see him, I was amazed at how his eyes shimmered with desire but his expression remained all business.

*Cool as ice.*

I was hot as the sun.

"It's a brilliant concept," he said, his voice sounding a little strained. "We're not changing it."

Unable to control myself thanks to the intensity of how his fingers slid in and out, I lunged forward, kissing and sucking on his neck. I felt his pulse speed up when I grabbed a handful of his hair. His body went taut. I knew he was having a hard time keeping a handle on his urges.

"You're a bad boy, Alastair Reid Holden," I whispered in his ear. "I like it."

He shoved a third finger in me, making my body quake. I bit down on his shoulder in an effort to stay quiet.

"Revise the proposal and send it to me Monday. Talk to you then." He yanked the earpiece out and tossed it on the desk. Eyeing me with a hunger so palpable I could feel it, he picked me up and nearly threw me down in his chair. In seconds he was on his knees with my legs tossed over his shoulders. My God. Seeing him in this position, dressed in his urbane suit and tie, and being so carnal and raw was too much. I shoved both hands in his hair, pulling hard. He sealed his mouth against my now throbbing clit and finished me off, leaving me shaky and spent.

"I'm supposed to be on hiatus," I panted, sliding down in the chair.

Alastair smiled in his crazy-sexy way and leaned close. "I told you I wanted you to come for lunch."

*Lethal.*

# CHAPTER TWENTY-FOUR

"I'm not keeping you from anything monumentally important, am I?" I asked, watching Alastair read through a file. I was still sitting in his desk chair and he was on one of the couches in the middle of his office.

He looked up and grinned. "No. I don't have anything scheduled for another half hour."

I leaned forward, resting my chin in my hands. The picture of me in that ridiculously large sunhat sat on his desk next to the computer monitor. Hard to believe it was taken only one year ago. My life had changed so much in that time. I gazed at my future husband as he studied a document. He appeared relaxed with an arm draped along the back of the couch. Intelligence and professionalism reflected in his eyes and serious expression.

"Are you working late tonight?"

"Not planning on it."

"Really?"

"You sound surprised."

"I don't know, Mr. CEO. You're a big, important guy and you've already played hooky once this week. The boss won't like you slacking off again."

"I thought you were the boss."

I leaned back in the chair and laughed. "Finally. It took you long enough."

"Don't tell anyone," he said, marking up the page with his pen. I still wanted to ask about what that reporter said to me earlier but didn't quite know how to bring it up. I'm sure I'd be covering whatever the story was at work next week. I'd rather walk into the storm somewhat prepared.

Alastair regarded me curiously. "What's going on in that pretty head of yours?"

There really was no delicate way to bring this up. "A bunch of reporters were at the spa when I left. One of them said something about you dissolving the music division and that there's a rumor about embezzlement."

His brows furrowed in frustration. "They asked you about that?"

I nodded. "Is it true?"

He stared at me impassively. *Great.* "One of the lower level executives in the music division was caught stealing from the royalties department. He's since been fired but it wasn't a major blow to the finances. And no, I'm not dissolving the label."

"Oh. Okay." I paused. "So what was that stuff you signed yesterday?"

He smirked. "Trying to get an exclusive for Julian?"

"No," I said, horrified he would think that.

"I'm teasing you."

"Not cool, Holden."

He put the documents down and leaned forward. "You look good behind that desk."

"Oh no, no, no. You're not seducing me into silence."

"I'm not trying to." He came over and perched on the edge of his desk. "We're moving forward with the plans for a production company in Los Angeles. I've made Jason the president of that division since it's what he's wanted for ages. The call I was on before—" he grinned "—had to do with our on-demand subscription service that we're launching online for people to stream movies and television programs. The formal announcement for both won't be made until next week."

"So you *are* taking over the world one media outlet at a time."

Kneeling in front of me for the second time in less than an hour, he held my hands. "I've told you before. I'm not interested in taking over the whole world. Just yours."

"Charmer." I smiled, looking away. "You're making me blush and you know how I don't like to do that."

He stood up, pulling me to my feet. "I like it," he whispered, leaning his cheek to mine.

"Can I ask you one more thing?"

I felt his chest rise and fall.

"Yes, kitten, you can."

"Why were you so angry with your uncle on the phone last night?"

He looked at me, confused. "Jason? I wasn't on the phone with him."

"But I thought— I heard you yelling at someone about signing something and—"

"Lia," he said, holding my face. "That wasn't my uncle." He shook his head and chuckled. "Always the investigative reporter, aren't you?"

"Well, you sounded really pissed off. I just assumed."

"I know my relationship with him is strained and we've had our share of blowouts but—" He caught himself, swallowing hard. "I'm trying to do what you suggested. I'm trying to let them in. It's slow going at the moment but it's something."

My heart swelled with pride. He traced his fingers over the diamond encrusted 'A' on the necklace he'd given me.

"I like that you wear this all the time," he said.

"It's my favorite."

Disbelief ghosted through his eyes like smoke. "You never cease to amaze me, Amelia Meyers."

"And you never cease to be the best boyfriend on the planet."

A flash of white appeared when his brilliant smile lit up the office. "Head home. I'll finish up here and be with you no later than six."

"Do you feel like doing something tonight? I might want to treat you to a date to say thank you for the spa treatment."

"I thought I was flying you somewhere far away."

"Another time." I squeezed his hand. "I want to do this for you."

"What did you have in mind?"

A huge smile bloomed on my lips. "I'm not telling."

"Wow." He laughed. "The smart mouth returns."

"It never left," I said dryly. "Now do you want to have a date with me tonight or not?"

"Not sure."

I folded my arms and gave him a look. "What do you want?"

He grinned. "I'll agree to your date night proposal *if* you let me take care of dessert."

"Okay. You have control over dessert but I decide on where we eat it."

"If it's on you, I'm in."

I shoved him. "Stop it. I'm still on hiatus."

"That won't last, love." His smoldering eyes burned a deep, forest green.

"Alastair," I said with a pout. "Don't hijack my date night."

Brushing his thumb on my lip, he smiled. "Fair enough. I promise I won't do it intentionally."

"I suppose that'll have to do."

"My Lia." He draped an arm over my shoulder and escorted me to the door. "I'm sure whatever you have planned will be lovely."

Simone was on her feet the second Alastair and I walked out of his office. "Your two o'clock just arrived downstairs. I've got the conference room almost all set up." She grabbed a stack of files and went down the hall.

"She thinks you're going to fire her," I said while Alastair pushed the elevator call button.

"Why?"

"Because she didn't tell Paxton to stall me."

Smoothing down his tie, he moved closer to me. "Don't tell her but that's not quite a fireable offense. Annoying, but not fireable."

A tone sounded signaling the elevator's arrival. Alastair walked in far enough to trigger the sensors so the doors wouldn't close right away. "Date night, then?"

"Yes." I smiled.

"Do I have a shot at getting lucky at the end of the night?"

"You don't ever stop do you?"

"No. And I generally don't hear any complaints out of you about it."

"I'm not complaining. I'm trying to take command of the situation, which you like, by the way."

My knees almost buckled when he ran his finger along his mouth. I wanted to bite him.

"Challenge accepted, kitten."

"Good. If you behave, I might revisit your request to get lucky."

"Looking forward to your final decision." He laughed, backing out. I kept my eyes glued to his handsome, happy face until the doors closed.

* * *

I spread all the ingredients out on the counter and set to work. Alastair should be home in less than an hour and I wanted this dinner to be perfect. My plan was to cook for him and then take a nighttime drive along the coast. I know it was cold outside but I missed spending time by the ocean and figured we could just park somewhere scenic and stay in the car. Whatever dessert he had in mind would have to be mobile. Or we could just save it for when we returned home.

I'd turned on some music and had my own little concert in the kitchen while preparing the food. I wasn't as polished in the kitchen as my sister was but I knew how to make a few dishes and tonight's was something I'd been craving so badly that I could almost taste it; steak with garlic mashed potatoes and asparagus.

An old Spice Girls song came on and I fully threw myself into the singing and dancing. It was a production for the ages enjoyed only by the stove and refrigerator.

"I'd no idea I was marrying a pop star."

Startled, I spun around with the spoon poised in front of my mouth like a microphone.

"You're home early."

Alastair smiled and leaned against the counter with his arms behind his back. "Don't let me stop you."

I eyed him curiously while placing the spoon down. He'd changed his clothes, which meant he'd been lurking. I narrowed my eyes. "When did you get home?"

"Just in time." He swiped some of the mashed potatoes on his finger. "Tastes good," he said after licking it off. "What else do you have?"

"Don't put your fingers in the food," I scolded. "God knows where they've been."

He raised both eyebrows and gave me a look.

"Don't say it," I laughed, turning my attention to the asparagus. I seasoned them and placed them in the oven. When I faced Alastair again, he'd seated himself at the breakfast bar with a long-stemmed white rose in hand.

"Flowers?"

"Well, this is a date and I'm a gentleman, so yes."

I scooted around the counter and hugged him. "Thanks, chief." I put the rose down and finished preparing our meal. Alastair proved helpful by pouring us both some wine. I shooed him off to sit at the table so I could put the finishing garnishes on the steaks when they were done. I presented our meal on a pretty silver tray that I'd found in one of the cupboards. It looked like it had never been used before so I figured why not.

Alastair kissed my hand when I walked by to take my seat.

"What else do you have planned for our date tonight?" he asked between mouthfuls. He was clearly enjoying the food and hadn't uttered a word until now. I had to pat myself on the back. These steaks were phenomenal.

"I thought we could take a ride to the coast and park somewhere. Maybe look at the stars."

"The stars, huh?" A smile played on his lips. "I think I can make that happen. Are you driving?"

"Um, no."

"Why not? You did such a good job with my sexy little car that time I gave you lessons."

"Right. But that was during the day on an empty road. This is, you know, night and highways."

He laughed. "You'll be used to driving on the wrong side of the road in no time. Trust me."

I sipped the wine and watched him finish his dinner. All the drama that we'd trudged through this week felt miles away all because of the glow that now lit up his eyes and the smile on his lips. This was *my* Alastair and I would stop at nothing to keep him this way for the rest of my life.

"You have that look again," he said. "I'm beginning to think all your talk of being on a hiatus was just for show."

"Well, when you look this hot and this happy I can't control my facial expressions."

Locking me in a sultry, flirtatious stare he leaned forward. "Maybe we should take the SUV so there's more room for us to play in the backseat."

I dropped my fork in the mashed potatoes. He had me right where he wanted me and he knew it.

"Then again, my car is much cozier."

I swallowed, regaining some of my composure. "You still need a warning label."

"So do you."

He helped me clear the table and clean the kitchen even though

I protested and told him to go relax on the couch, mostly because his unrelenting flirting was clouding my brain. Every time I passed by him he'd reach out and tickle me or stop me for a kiss. I don't know how long this phase of domestic bliss would last once we were old and married but I planned to enjoy it for as long as I could.

"Are you going to put this in water?" he asked, holding up the rose.

"Sure." I reached for it and noticed a white ribbon tied to the stem. COME FLY WITH ME was written on it. I looked at Alastair. "What does this mean?"

"It means what it says."

"Fly with you where?" My heart started pounding.

"Follow the rose and you'll find out."

"You're hijacking my date night, Holden," I said with a grin. "I wanted to sit under the stars with you by the ocean."

"Then that's what we'll do. You call the shots, kitten."

"Good. I'm going to grab a sweater and then we'll go to the beach." Throwing a suspicious look in his direction, I went to the bedroom and opened the closet. He was up to something, as usual, and was using my insatiable curiosity against me. The last time I 'followed the rose' I ended up in Paris. I wrapped a gray cardigan around myself and went back out to find my scheming fiancé. The rose was now in a vase, staring at me from the kitchen counter.

I unraveled the ribbon and read it again. He did say he wanted to fly me somewhere beautiful for the weekend.

Flipping through a magazine without a care in the world, he glanced at me when I walked into the living room carrying the flower. "Ready?"

"Where are we going?"

"To look at the stars." He held out his hand. I drank in his very essence, astounded by how relaxed and at peace he appeared. Not one trace of his wall remained. I took his outstretched hand, absorbing the jolt of electricity from his touch.

"I love you," I whispered, standing close to him. The unrelenting force that fused us together felt stronger.

"I love you, too," he said, staring at me with fervor.

My soul soared. "This—" I held up the rose "—is where I want to go."

# CHAPTER TWENTY-FIVE

The flight was relatively short, wherever it was that we'd landed. I looked out the window and saw nothing but an onyx sky dotted with stars. There wasn't a mask or anything to prevent me seeing where we'd gone. I didn't have a clue anyway. It was so dark outside he could have flown us to the North Pole for all I knew.

I followed Alastair off the plane to a waiting horse and carriage. I stopped short. *What the...?*

"Did we go through a time portal or something?" I asked.

"No, love. This is the only way to get around here."

Alastair extended his hand and helped me onto the carriage. The driver nodded and tipped his hat in my direction. I honestly felt like I'd been transported back to the 1800s.

"And where exactly is *here*?"

The horse neighed and started walking. I snuggled closer to Alastair when he tucked me under his arm.

"Just enjoy the ride and the view," he requested, kissing the top of my head.

Excited by the prospect of the unknown for the first time in my life, I rested my head on his shoulder and listened to the slow rhythm of the horse's footsteps on loose gravel. Not too far from where we were, I could hear the ocean pounding against the shore. I smiled, burrowing closer into Alastair's side. If not for the cold air and horse-drawn carriage I'd have thought we'd flown back to Orlando and were sitting on the beach.

A velvet kiss stirred me from my thoughts. I looked up and was greeted by Alastair's beautiful face.

"Come with me."

What those three words did to me. I stepped off the carriage onto the soft earth. A gorgeous two-story stone house sat in front of us. Mesmerized by its old world charm I stared for a few seconds.

"Alastair, where are we?"

Smiling, he tucked my hair behind my ears. "We are at the place where it all begins."

Spurred on by a healthy dose of curiosity I followed him into the house. The cozy interior gave me the same at home feeling as his cottage. A bottle of champagne and a bouquet of white roses sat on a small end table by the couch.

"Did you fly me here for more cake?" I joked.

He tipped up my chin and gazed at me with the purest love I'd ever seen. "If that's what you want."

"I can hear the ocean," I said, touching his cheek. "Can we go outside and look at the stars now?"

"Yes, of course." He kissed me. "You should go up and change first. It's a bit chilly outside." He brushed his fingers down my arm. "And then meet me out in the backyard."

"Change? I'm already in a sweater and—"

"Just do it." He grinned, tilting his head to the side. "You'll thank me later."

Watching him stroll out of the room rustled a few butterflies in my stomach.

I trotted up the stairs, amused and puzzled about what this night had in store for me now. A trail of white rose petals led toward what I assumed was the master bedroom. *When did he have time to do all this?* I walked into the room and inhaled sharply. Hanging from an armoire was an ivory silk cocktail length dress. The sleeveless, v-neck bodice was intricately woven with lace and shimmered in the light. My crystal encrusted Louboutin shoes sat beneath it on the floor.

"Oh my God," I whispered, touching the material and admiring its mix of simple and sexy. "A wedding dress?"

Tears pricked the corners of my eyes as I went to the window and peered out into the yard. I couldn't see anything. Turning back, I noticed a vanity filled with makeup and hair accessories. I sat in front of the mirror trying to calm the ferocious beating of my heart. I surveyed the array of products and took a deep breath.

"Here we go," I muttered, applying some lip gloss and blush. My skin was still sun kissed from all the Florida sunshine so I didn't need to add much.

I left my hair down in loose waves, just the way Alastair liked it. Taking another deep breath, I turned toward the armoire. Fixing my hair and putting on make-up was one thing. A wedding dress was something completely different. I stood up and focused on it, memorizing every last detail.

My hands shook as I took the dress off its hanger. So many emotions swirled through me as I slipped it on. The elegant silk hemline skimmed my knees. I stared at myself in the mirror, disbelieving what was about to happen.

Dozens of thoughts rushed through my brain. *Am I ready? Is he ready? Are we rushing into this?*

The girl staring back at me glowed. Her eyes were alight with joy, not self-doubt or any doubt for that matter. *I am ready.* Composing myself, I slipped on my shoes and went downstairs.

"Hey, kiddo."

I stopped short, stunned to see my father. "Dad," I exclaimed, breathless. I ran over and wrapped my arms around him. "What are you— How is—"

"Your fiancé takes all the credit. I was just told to be on a plane." He smiled, his eyes shining with pride. "You look beautiful. Shall we?"

I nodded as he looped my arm though his and led me out the

back door. My knees went weak.

Alastair waited for me in the center of the yard. He'd changed into a dark gray suit, sans tie, leaving the collar of his white shirt unbuttoned. My heart raced a little faster when he smiled. That was my smile, the one he saved only for me.

A muffled sob tore my attention away from him. It was my mother. She stood in the yard next to my sister Dayna. My heart beat faster and faster as I took in my surroundings. Andrew was also there, along with Darren. Tears welled in my eyes when I looked to my right and saw Katherine, Jason and Samuel. *He wanted his family here, too.*

Darren motioned for someone and then I saw Stephanie. My best friend smiled, put her hand on her heart and then blew me a kiss. This was absolutely, undeniably the most astonishing moment of my life. I squeezed my dad's arm just to make sure I wasn't dreaming.

He patted my hand and smiled. "Surprised?"

I think I nodded. Out the corner of my eye I saw Paxton standing near Alastair. He winked at me and grinned.

"Everyone's here," I whispered.

"There she is," an unfamiliar voice announced. "Shall we?"

Next thing I knew, my dad walked me toward a justice of the peace.

At exactly midnight, surrounded by all the people who meant the most to me, I married Alastair Reid Holden under a sky full of stars. Even the Milky Way joined us, spreading from one corner of the glossy black horizon to the other and putting on one hell of a celestial show. The serenity and happiness I felt as we exchanged simple vows overwhelmed me. When Stephanie walked over and handed me a stunning platinum band to slide onto Alastair's finger I couldn't stop smiling. The guy who once claimed he didn't 'do' relationships had thought of everything. I didn't think it was possible to love him even more than I already did.

When the justice said those magic words about pronouncing

us husband and wife, everyone clapped.

"I told you we were going to see the stars," Alastair said before locking me in a kiss far too passionate for anyone else to witness. I heard Darren and Andrew both whistle and cheer.

Breaking the kiss, he lifted me and hugged me soundly. I couldn't believe this actually happened.

"You're married," Stephanie yelled, throwing her arms around me when Alastair let me go. "I hope you realize you are the only person I'd stand outside for in the freezing cold at midnight."

"The sacrifices you Floridians make," I laughed, hugging her for an eternity before my mother's pleas forced us apart. In true Lillian Meyers fashion, she nearly suffocated me with excitement. Her make-up was immaculate except for the black smudges under her eyes where the tears landed.

"Two weddings in one year," she said. "I can't believe it."

"You're going to squash her, mom. I want in on that," Dayna said sandwiching me in a hug with our mother. A flash went off next to us, blinding me.

"Sorry," I heard Andrew say. "It's not every day all the Meyers women are in one place."

I laughed, finally free from their embrace. "If there's no photo, it didn't happen, right?"

Darren was next for the parade of hugging. He lifted me up and spun me around, making me squeal with delight. "You're a gorgeous bride, lass."

My family and friends continued to chitchat next to me as my attention turned to my new husband, who was surrounded by his own family. His aunt had him in a secure embrace. His back was to me so I couldn't see what, if any, expression was present. Much to my surprise, he held her just as tight. Samuel patted him on the back and then pulled him in for a quick hug. Now I could see his face. He caught my eye and grinned.

When Jason went over to him, I stilled. His body seemed to stiffen as Jason offered his hand to shake. I wanted so much for them to have this moment without any tension. After a few seconds, Alastair shook his uncle's hand and nodded. Their interaction wasn't overflowing with warmth but it was a start.

Tilting his head, he waved me over so I could be embraced by the Holden family. Katherine beamed as she engulfed me in her arms. "I am so happy for you." She pulled back and held my jaw. "Thank you."

I knew what she meant. Looking into all of their eyes, I also knew that she spoke for the entire family. I smiled and gave a little shrug. Alastair was hovering close by and slid an arm around my waist. He wouldn't let me go as our families mingled, talking and laughing like they'd known each other for years. I overheard Katherine inviting my parents to the house while they were here. *Where is here, by the way?*

Grabbing Alastair's hand, I led him over to where Steph, Darren, Andrew and Dayna were chatting.

"Lia," Stephanie squealed. "Isn't this amazing? Were you surprised?"

Her eyes widened as I let the question sink in.

"You knew?" I asked.

"Yep. We all knew. Do you know how hard it was to keep your mother quiet about this whole thing?"

I looked up at my new husband who, on cue, employed an impassive expression. "Sneaky," I said, shoving his shoulder. "How long have you had this planned?"

"I'll never tell." His little smart ass grin made me laugh.

"Unreal."

"Paxton," Stephanie called. "Can you come here for a second?"

He appeared in front of us, ready for whatever Stephanie wanted.

"Would you mind taking a picture of us all?"

"No problem."

Andrew handed him the camera and we all stood in a group, with me and Alastair in the middle. He held me so tight it made me a little nervous but one look at his content face quieted my worries.

"I love you guys to death but I'm an ice cube," Stephanie said through chattering teeth. "We're all meeting for brunch in the morning at the hotel. Inside. Where it's warm."

"Toughen up, lass," Darren teased. "Winter isn't here yet. This is nothing."

One by one, we said goodnight to our wedding guests and escorted them to the front of the house where three horse drawn carriages waited. I still couldn't get over the fact that this was how people got around here. *Here...?*

I hugged Paxton as well before he left.

"You've made him very happy, Miss Meyers," he said, pausing. "My apologies. I mean, Mrs. Holden. Congratulations and enjoy your weekend."

Paxton was a man of few words so for him to say that to me meant the world.

"Mrs. Holden?" Alastair's low tone sent shivers down my spine. "Have I exceeded your expectations?"

I drank in every inch of him as we stood beneath the expansive beauty of the universe and reached for his hands.

"You amaze me," I whispered, resting my forehead to his. "I love you so much."

The most joyful, dazzling smile curved his mouth. "So this wasn't cheesy?"

"No. This was perfect."

We remained enclosed in our private bubble, gently touching one another and reveling in the stillness of the night. My stunning diamond ring twinkled in unison with the stars when I ran my hand through his hair. As far as I was concerned, anything that wasn't in my immediate surroundings didn't exist.

"Do you own this house?"

"No. But I'll buy it if you want it."

The shy laugh that escaped my lips sounded foreign to me.

He'd cast such a spell on me tonight.

"Where are we? Because right now all I can think is that we're in paradise."

"This is the Isle of Sark," he answered. "Although anywhere with you is paradise."

"Are we still in the United Kingdom?"

"We're very close to France in the southern English Channel."

I looked up, dazzled once more by the glowing Milky Way. "How did you ever find this place? I've never seen the sky so—"

Alastair cut me off with a gentle kiss, which made my knees buckle. "Dance with me?" he asked.

"There's no music." I smiled.

He led me to the backyard and we danced to the intense quiet of the night under a gorgeous sky I could only have imagined in my dreams. I heard Alastair's breathing grow labored, as though he was struggling for air. I held him tighter, aware that this was his way of telling me how he felt.

Pulling back, he kissed me again before focusing a powerful, heated gaze on me. I lost myself in his emerald eyes as they glittered in the moonlight.

"You make me feel alive," he said, his voice strong and filled with passion.

I grabbed his hand and placed it over my heart. A tremor shook his body for the briefest of moments.

"Ditto, love," I whispered.

Tracing his thumb over my lips, he leaned in. "I love you, Amelia Grace."

He wrapped me in his arms again and we kept dancing under the glorious canopy of stars long into the night. If I had my way, this would never end. Looking up, I touched his cheek and smiled when his hand covered mine.

"We have a decision to make," he said.

"Oh? And what's that?"

"I know how much you love to look at the stars, so I was

thinking we could grab a blanket and lay out here for awhile. Or," he paused, adopting a more sultry tone, "we could enjoy one another in a long, hot bubble bath."

"Can we do both?" I blurted.

His throaty laugh echoed on the breeze. "As you wish, m'lady."

The bubble bath won out as the place to start. I went upstairs and filled the tub, which by the way was the size of a jacuzzi, while Alastair poured the champagne. I caught him staring at me from the mirror and grinned.

"Like what you see, chief?"

"I will once you get out of that dress."

Turning around to face him, I placed my hands on my hips. "You're awfully frisky."

"You don't say?" He slipped off the suit jacket and unbuttoned his shirt. I got that awesome weak in the knees feeling watching him undress. Moving in slow, calculated strides he crossed the bathroom, stalking me like a lion. Every muscle in his toned, athletic torso moved with fluid beauty. My mouth watered. Staring into his hooded eyes wiped my mind clean of any thoughts, even the great ones about how freaking hot he was.

Reaching around me, he shut off the water. *Jesus, he smells good.*

"Do you want to finish undressing me?" How he managed to make that question sound illegal in a hundred countries I'll never know. Not having to be asked twice, I ran my hands down his bare chest and traced along the edge of his waistband. My plan to seduce him with slow and deliberate actions flew out the window the second he wet his lips and moaned softly. I may or may not have torn the button off his pants when I wrenched them open.

Amused by my lack of control, he shook his head and backed away. "There's no rush." He removed the rest of his clothes and fixed a dark stare on me that ignited a fire in the pit of my stomach. Skimming his fingers over the swell of my breasts and down to my hips, he kissed me and gradually unzipped the dress. Goosebumps scattered along my skin as the soft silk material glided down my body. It hit the floor with a sigh, pooling at my feet.

"Leave the shoes on," he said, unhooking my bra and removing it with ease. Taking a step back, he devoured me with dark, molten eyes. "You are exquisite." Mischief lit up his face. "You're coming with me."

In one fluid motion, he picked me up and tossed me over his shoulder. I squealed, not knowing what was happening. I heard my shoes fall to the floor with a thud. Next thing I knew, he was walking at a fast clip down the stairs and out the back door.

"Alastair," I yelped. "I'm naked and it's freezing. What are you doing? We can't be outside like this."

My feet hit the cool grass and I nearly bolted back to the house.

"Not so fast," he said, draping a robe over my shoulders. "Feel better?"

I hugged the plush robe around me and gave him a dirty look. He just grinned and proceeded to spread a blanket out on the ground, all the while still remaining stark naked. I looked around and realized that we were, for all intents and purposes, alone. I couldn't see another house or even any street lights.

"Are you going to keep me warm or stare into the unknown all night?"

Smiling up at me, he'd already put on his own robe and made himself comfortable on the blanket. I knelt down next to him and sat back on my heels. He mimicked my stance and pushed the robe off my shoulders. I shivered, both from the cold and from nerves.

"Nobody is here, Lia. This house is secluded."

"What abo—"

He cut me off with a searing kiss, letting his hands roam freely over my body. Every caress warmed and calmed me. Pulling me down next to him, we curled up together, snuggled under the warmth of our robes. I felt so small staring up at the sky. The stars and Milky Way seemed to stretch for an eternity, their distant beauty so vivid I wanted to reach up and touch them.

Alastair leaned his head so it rested on mine as I splayed my hand on his stomach. If anyone had told me a year ago that I'd be lying on a blanket —naked— outside in the middle of the night on an island I had no idea existed, I would have laughed in their face.

"What are you thinking about?"

I lifted my head and gazed down at my gorgeous husband. "You."

He smiled, brushing my hair back over my shoulder. Bowing his head, he swallowed hard. "Tell me what you want."

I tilted his chin up so I could look into his eyes. "I already have it."

* * *

Alastair and I strolled lazily along a dusty path that wound its way up a cliff overlooking the English Channel. A cottony layer of clouds blended into the cobalt sky while a soft breeze tickled my shoulders. I couldn't help but notice how the rocky coastline seemed to frill the island like a cupcake wrapper. Waves pounded against the cliffs as seagulls circled overhead. Smiling, I still felt like this was paradise.

Draping his arm over my shoulder, Alastair stood quietly with me as we gazed out toward the horizon. It stretched endlessly, beckoning us with the promise of a clear, bright future. I knew the journey would be far from perfect but it was *our* journey and we'd already survived so much.

"Are you hungry?" he asked.

"A little."

We'd spent the majority of the morning lounging in bed before finally taking that warm bubble bath we'd abandoned last night. Needless to say, we also missed brunch with my family.

"We can go into town and grab some lunch if you'd like."

"Maybe later."

He glanced at me out the corner of his eye. "You're turning down food? Stop the presses."

"Hey." I punched him lightly in the arm. "I'm not turning it down, you muppet. I just said 'later.'"

The sound of his throaty laugh drifted on the chilly breeze. I stood in front of him so I could hook my arms around his waist. The early afternoon sunlight reflected off his rich, dark red hair accentuating the chocolate flecks. *Stunning as always, Holden,* I thought with a smile.

The corners of his eyes crinkled as he returned my smile. "What's got you so happy?"

"Some guy."

"'Some guy,' huh?" He smirked and I knew that meant I was in trouble. Fast as lightning, he grabbed my waist and tickled me hard. My shrieks and peals of laughter bounced through the quiet air as loud as cymbals. I managed to break away from him and ran several yards down the gravel path, still laughing. He caught me in no time and held me close.

"Amelia Grace Holden." The way my name rolled of his tongue with such ease thrilled me. "No matter where you run, I will always catch you."

"Lucky for you, then. I want to be caught."

# *EPILOGUE*

I felt her before I saw her.

"Everyone's waiting for you, birthday boy."

Lia grinned and leaned against the wall in the penthouse office. Her chestnut hair hung in tousled waves at her shoulders. A short burgundy sundress hugged her hourglass figure, accentuating her curves. The sight of her did what it always does to me. One year later and I still had zero control over how she made me feel.

"Are those legal documents really that exciting?" she teased.

Her light, melodic voice slinked its way through my bloodstream. It had a slight raspy edge to it, which became more prominent when she was moaning my name. I leaned back in my chair, letting my legs fall open.

"No rest for the wicked, love."

"Whatever, Holden." She pushed herself away from the wall and walked towards me. The tantalizing sway of her hips came as naturally to her as breathing. It was one of my favorite things about her. She had no idea how mesmerizing her walk could be and that made it even more desirable. I'd seen it turn more than a few heads when we were out. People have been staring and leering at me my whole life but it was different when they did it to my wife.

Hitching up her dress, she straddled me. I swallowed down a moan, feeling the pressure tighten in my throat and in my pants.

"You're not allowed to work *at all* today, chief. That includes during your own party," she said, slinging her arms over my shoulders. I grasped her hips as a way to center myself. Her scent and body were overwhelming my senses.

"I'm not working. I just needed to make sure these were in order for tomorrow."

"Look at them in the car on your ride to the office."

Fiery amber eyes locked onto me with determination, boring into my soul. No other person could see me so clearly or so completely. From the first moment she looked at me through the car window I knew she was different and I knew I was in trouble. If I'd had half a brain I would have gone ahead with my original plan and told Paxton to get me the hell out of there. That benefit hadn't been one of my mandatory social engagements last spring but I'd been advised by my grandfather to show my face.

And then Lia happened. Catching her when she tripped wasn't part of the plan either. Holding her in my arms and allowing those bright eyes to peer into my soul a second time had caught me off guard.

I had to have her.

I should have walked away.

"You're distracting me, kitten."

"Am I?" She leaned close. Too close. I fisted my hand in her hair and pulled. A small intake of breath lifted her chest, making her breasts swell. Her skin flushed and her lips parted. This look would drive me bloody insane for the rest of my life.

"I'm not used to celebrating my birthday. You know that."

The sharp, stinging pain of guilt over my family's death commandeered my body. I don't care how many goddam years have passed. It would remain with me forever. Lia did help make it more bearable. Her touch, her patience, her mere presence made existing more bearable.

"I know," she said, stroking my cheek. "But there's cake involved."

A laugh escaped me before I knew it. That was the effect she had on me. Disarmed and enchanted, I loosened my grip on her hair and held her closer. Her body was so soft and delicate next to mine. I wanted her. I needed her. My urges to claim her endlessly were relentless. And I wasn't alone. She'd managed to surprise me on more than one occasion with her own insatiable desires.

"Reckon I can't say no to cake then, can I?" *Or you.* Saying no to her wasn't in my nature. I mean, Christ, look at her. Lia could bring me to my knees at a moment's notice. She owned me with those eyes and could tame me with one touch.

"What's going on inside that head of yours, English?"

I hovered my lips over hers in an effort to slow my racing heart. If I didn't, I'd lose all control and fuck her senseless where we sat. Not that she'd mind.

The second I felt her hands in my hair I took her mouth. She tasted of champagne. Beneath that was the sweeter, unique flavor that was hers alone. The nonstop pulling of my hair as I kissed her drove me to the edge. I groaned, sliding my hand under her dress and up her leg, running my fingers along the soft skin I craved. Nothing felt better.

"Frisky." Her full, just-been-kissed-lips pulled into a smile. "Come on. Let's go."

No.

Standing up, she smoothed down the dress and held out her hand. I took it because I wouldn't have been able to stand otherwise. Framed by the panoramic backdrop of New York City, she glowed. And I unraveled. I sat on the edge of the desk and wedged her between my thighs to steady the quaking in my knees. *What this girl does to me.*

Rubbing her thumb over my mouth to remove the gloss, she grinned. "Not a bad color on you."

"Think so?" I rested my forehead to hers in an effort to delay the inevitable. I didn't mind spending my birthday with our friends but I didn't want the extra attention. Staying holed up in the bedroom or this office or anywhere with my wife seemed a more perfect option.

The softness of her lips brushed mine, inciting the riot of emotions I'd spent most of my life suppressing. With every gentle stroke of her tongue, she calmed me. I never believed a kiss could be so powerful until I met her. My world had finally come into focus when she entered my life.

"We're in this together, Alastair," she said. "Always."

I smiled on the inside, relaxing in her embrace. My walls would always be there. I needed them for protection. Not from her though.

"We'll mingle for a bit." I smirked. "Then I want to have my way with you in a secluded corner."

The challenge of my proposition sparked in her eyes. Her brows lifted but I knew I had her where I wanted her.

"We'll see about that, chief."

Lacing her fingers through mine, she led me up to the roof deck. We'd been in New York for the past month while I finished some work on our revamped record label. I knew Lia loved being in this city, especially now that her sister and Andrew had moved back at Christmas after finding out they were expecting. Family has always been important to my wife. My own relationship with my family was improving but had a long way to go.

I could now stomach being in the same space as my uncle without feeling as though he blamed me for his brother's death. We could hold a conversation without being at each other's throats. It doesn't erase the fact that I'd been a prick to him while growing up, constantly reminding him that he wasn't my father. We'd probably never be close but at least we had an understanding.

The closer we got to the top of the stairs, the more I itched to turn around. Lia sensed it and squeezed my hand.

"Focus on the cake, Holden."

"I'd rather focus on licking the frosting off your body."

She leveled me with her eyes. "You're lethal."

"You love it."

Her musical laugh made my insides melt. With her by my side,

I felt invincible.